Advance Praise for *The W*

C000115168

"Cheryl A. Ossola delivers an intr in a modern neonatal intensive care unit in Berkeley, then reaches back through space and time to a most unlikely setting: the bleak World War II era prison camp at Manzanar in the California high desert. History has largely forgotten what little it bothered to learn about Manzanar in the first place, so Ossola starts with a blank page and fills it beautifully with fragmented flashbacks, contemporary marital drama and dogged pursuit of family history and heartbreak that spans generations.

Ossola's storytelling takes on some of the flavor of a Japanese *kaidan*, or ghost story. She portrays history with an accuracy that speaks well of her journalistic background, but she also understands the *kaidan* approach that a ghost story need not equate to a horror story. What better way to relive the disappeared past."

—**Richard Imamura, screenwriter of** *The Manzanar Fishing Club*

"Ossola walks a wonderful wire here, sculpting a story that's readable and timely. The novel honors its history with austere accuracy, and Ossola captures her characters' complex emotional trajectories in gusts of poetry."

—**Joshua Mohr, author of the novel** *All This Life*

"In lyric prose Cheryl Ossola takes us on an exhilarating journey, as Kira Esposito becomes a relentless detective of her dreams in a search for origins. Readers will time-travel on switchback trails, from Kira's 21st-century life with her husband to a Japanese interment camp in the 1940s—and back again. Ossola's stunning descriptions of the landscape ground us in a vivid a sense of place and the porous boundaries between time-realms create engrossing tensions in Kira's marriage. Ossola is masterful at showing the connection between dreams, quantum labyrinths, and daily life."

—**Thaisa Frank, author of** *Enchantment* **and** *Heidegger's Glasses*

The Wild Impossibility

Cheryl A. Ossola

Regal House Publishing

Published by
Regal House Publishing, LLC
Raleigh, NC 27612

ISBN -13 (paperback): 9781947548626
ISBN -13 (epub): 9781947548701
ISBN -13 (mobi): 9781947548695
Library of Congress Control Number: 2019930300

All efforts were made to determine the copyright holders and obtain their permissions in any cirmstance where copyrighted material was used. The publisher apologizes if any errors were made during this process, or if any omissions occurred. If noted, please contact the publisher and all efforts will be made to incorporate permissions in future editions.

Interior and cover design by Lafayette & Greene
lafayetteandgreene.com
Cover image © by Shutterstock/Senya and Ksusha

Regal House Publishing, LLC
https://regalhousepublishing.com

The following is a work of fiction created by the author. All names, individuals, characters, places, items, brands, events, etc. were either the product of the author or were used fictitiously. Any name, place, event, person, brand, or item, current or past, is entirely coincidental.

Printed in the United States of America

In memory of my mother,
who I'm certain is reading this book somewhere,

and
for all mothers everywhere

ONE

Kira gripped the wheel, focusing on the road ahead. Berkeley awoke in the cool grasp of water—fog unraveling in treetops and blossoming from the asphalt, rain plummeting earthward in ecstatic downpours and gray-blurring the creeping cars and huddled storefronts. California, a place of rain-fueled excess in winter, of choked aridity in summer. You could flee the San Francisco Bay Area, fog-chilled on a summer morning, and end the day watching the sunset in the high desert with sweat beaded on your brow. Wherever you were, the other existence—fogbound or sunburned—would seem like a dream state, a fantasy you'd only imagined.

At the hospital, Kira parked in the employees' lot and killed the car engine. Six forty-five in the morning and the day already seemed long. She yanked her keys out of the ignition. Time to go to work. In some odd twist of logic, the neonatal intensive care unit was the one place where she could block out the unrelenting memories of her own baby, Aimi—the ceaseless thinking, the nagging what-ifs. It was the pace, she supposed, the mental intensity of tending to the critically ill. If the staffing office had allowed it, she'd have worked seven days a week.

After changing into scrubs, Kira went to the nurses' station to check the assignment board. She had Baby Bowen, a thirty-four-weeker, stable and on minimal meds. Not a busy assignment, and because of that she was scheduled to get the first transport, if there was one. Good. The more distractions, the better.

1

"Hey, Teresa," Kira greeted the charge nurse. "Any transports on the horizon?"

"Twins coming from Travis. You've got Twin A. You'll be busy."

Kira checked the board again. "We lost Baby Taylor?"

"Last night, poor little guy."

No surprise. He'd been hanging on by a thread, one of those babies who seemed likely to make it, then had one complication after another. The mother hadn't been involved and maybe that was just as well. At least she didn't have to hear a doctor tell her that her child was dead.

Kira scrubbed in, trying to quell the kicked-in-the-throat feeling the word "mother" gave her. Six weeks since her own mother had died, and Kira still caught herself picking up the phone to send her cat videos or pictures of baby otters, or to set a lunch date at their favorite Sicilian place. Two deaths in less than a year, deaths of the most intimate kind, of people whose tissue she had shared—one whose body she had come from, another she had created. Kira marveled at it sometimes, the malignancy of fate, God, whatever force or power could deliver that kind of cruelty. These days, she turned away when she saw women her age out with their mothers. But young mothers and their babies, she cornered them and asked, "How old is she? What's her name?" or "Does she sleep through the night yet?" If the mother allowed it, Kira would touch the warm, sweet-scented head, close her eyes and pretend the child was Aimi.

Shift report on Baby Bowen revealed a typical preemie scenario: born at twenty-nine weeks, now stable on fifty percent oxygen and moderate ventilator settings, the usual fare of steroids and diuretics around the clock, sedatives and morphine as needed. Lab work was due at eleven; if his next blood gas was good they'd wean the ventilator settings.

"Has he needed much sedation?" Kira asked.

"I gave lorazepam around three; he was a wild man," the

2

night nurse said. "Oh, and the IV in his foot is out; I couldn't get a new one. Sorry. I left you a scalp vein that looks decent. Good thing you're a better stick than I am."

The night nurse left and Kira tested the bedside alarms, adding to the orchestra-gone-haywire beeps and chirps from seventeen bedsides. As usual, the Unit was noisy and crowded, an amorphous, pulsating hive of nurses and attendings, haggard interns and residents, X-ray techs and respiratory therapists, social workers and anxious parents. West Coast Children's, with the biggest NICU this side of the Rockies, was not a place for people who liked things calm and quiet. It got the sickest of the sick, the high-risk babies, and it always had, even before the crack-baby boom in the '80s. The transport teams never stopped.

Baby Bowen looked good. Too tiny and too young, but he might make it.

Kira was taping a new IV in place when Teresa zipped past. "Transport's twenty minutes out," she called to Kira. "The parents are on their way."

The team rolled in five minutes early. Twin A was a micro-preemie, barely bigger than Kira's hand, on a hundred percent oxygen and maxed-out ventilator settings, paralyzed with Pavulon so she wouldn't fight the machine. Eyelids still fused, skin like tissue, body limp as a waterlogged leaf.

"Twenty-two-weeker?" Kira said.

"Yeah, with a head bleed," the transport nurse said. "Two transfusions so far, and *nada*." She gestured to the other transport incubator, six feet away. "Twin B's not much better."

"What about the mom? Drugs?"

"Nope, she's clean. Primipara, bed rest most of the pregnancy."

The transport nurse grabbed her gear and headed out, and Kira began her intake assessment of the baby. She was brittle as hell, her oxygen saturation nosediving, lungs wheezing like an underwater accordion. The blood Kira drew for an arterial gas was so dark she'd have sworn it was venous.

The on-call resident came by, a sleepless second-year. "Uh-oh," she said, looking at the ventilator. "Have you sent a gas yet?"

"Just now," Kira said. "It's going to suck."

The attending swooped in and scanned the chart. "Let's transfuse and do an EEG asap," he said. "She's probably not viable. Let me know when the parents get here."

Packed red blood cells, an exercise in futility. The baby wasn't going to make it and she probably shouldn't. The NICU could work some impressive miracles, but this was one tiny girl with shit for lungs and a vascular system with the substance of a cobweb. As high-risk as they got. Cardiac problems, neuro, metabolic, cognitive, GI—all were more likely than not. If this baby lived, she'd be blind from months of oxygen therapy, probably end up with cerebral palsy. Her only chance would have been ECMO, medical science's best effort to replicate the process of oxygenation, but her gestational age ruled that out. So would a head bleed.

Kira called the blood bank, then the charge desk. "Somebody's going to have to cover Bowen."

Thirty minutes later, Twin A was going downhill. The gas was abysmal. The docs would probably suggest discontinuing support for both babies, if they lived long enough for the parents to get there. And they might. Some of the babies you'd swear were going to die any second managed to wait for their mothers to arrive, and Kira had seen it happen too often to think it could be chance. But most of the babies who did cling to life for those minutes or hours had been out of the womb for a few weeks. Some had known their mother's warmth, held skin to skin against her breast despite ventilators and tubing, the mother's heartbeat going half time in a counterpoint to their own. These moments were all the comfort the babies would get in their brief lives, and they seemed to know it. And waited, hoping to feel that warmth one more time.

Twin A's heart rate spiraled down. "Hang on, baby girl, your mama's coming." Kira stroked the baby's head and the heart rate struggled upward. Placing the bell of the pediatric stethoscope on the tiny chest—it covered the baby from neck to navel—Kira listened. Pitiful breath sounds. Too young, too goddamn tiny. Not viable.

Aimi would have been.

Stop. Kira swung her ponytail behind her shoulder as if the movement would silence the memory.

Ten minutes later the parents arrived, swollen eyes raw in oatmeal faces. Standing next to Twin A's bed, they gripped the side rails with colorless fingers. This child, and her twin six feet away—nothing else in the room existed.

The attending pulled Kira aside. "They agreed to a no-code," he said. The best option, he was probably thinking, but that didn't make it a good one. "God, sometimes I hate this job."

A no-code. Kira looked at the Clarksons, ordinary people now being asked to do the extraordinary. Choosing was worse than having the inevitable forced on you. Even now hope illuminated the Clarksons' faces, diluting their despair. Couldn't a miracle happen now, for them, for their babies?

"Would you like to hold her?" Kira asked Mrs. Clarkson. "Here, let me help you." Baby to breast, if only for a moment. She turned off the monitors; even with the ventilator pumping that tiny chest, Mrs. Clarkson wouldn't need a machine to tell her that her child was dead. And no parent should see the flat line announcing their child's death.

"I'll sit with Jessica," the father said, and kissed his wife.

"I'm here, Jasmine," Mrs. Clarkson whispered. "Mommy loves you." She began to cry, a strangled sound; moments later the father's sobbing echoed hers.

Everything else went quiet, or as quiet as a busy room could get. The parents wouldn't notice. At times like this the world became small, uninhabited. Kira had sat like Mrs. Clarkson did now, holding her dead baby. This mother wouldn't know anyone else was there. This mother was somewhere else, lost. Going on would seem incomprehensible, the future an impossible thought. Nothing mattered but the agonizing emptiness in her belly and the still body in her arms. A universe of two.

Four hours later, Kira sat in her car and cried. That poor woman would never get over the loss. You never did. Lose a baby and you lose yourself. Blood and tissue, yours and your child's, commingled then ripped apart. Images flashed through her mind—Twin A, now a tiny bundle in the morgue; Aimi's body, a rounded weight against her chest. The grief intensified, bloomed like a hot flash. Aimi in her arms, eyes like her father's, hair that promised to curl like Kira's and her mother's—this six-pound proof of family, of bloodlines, gone.

Say the words: Your child did not live.

Kira pressed her hands to her eyes. Her fingers felt oddly warm; within seconds, her palms burned with a dry, fiery heat that reached for bone. Confused, she looked up, thought something had happened outside because everything was monochrome, the pinked orange of raw salmon. It must be late, already sunset—but no, the color was changing, now warm yellow, now cooler, an acid green. Cortisol rushed through her bloodstream, a junkie feeling, hands shaking, a staccato thrumming at her temples. She closed her eyes, opened them again. The green was still there, a watercolor wash. Then it faded, leaving only shadows.

A girl's voice. Kira jerked around, expecting to see someone behind her. The backseat was empty. The voice was in her head.

I hear them coming and pull his arms tighter around me. I can hardly breathe.

Fear like Kira has never known. She sees—or senses, because everything is gray, veiled, lines and shapes mere suggestions of three-dimensional objects—a small interior, rough metal walls, a wooden floor. She tries to open her eyes, but they're already open. She's awake, in the hospital parking lot, in her car. She's not dreaming. Her body shakes. The voice again, compelling yet flat, a monotone so out of tune with the words spoken that Kira's fear skyrockets.

They're closer now; I can hear their voices, my brother's harsh, my father's softer, dangerous. The door opens and I plead with them, but they ignore me. They drag us outside.

A pink breath of air, sage-scented and cool. Kira has no bones, no muscles. No sound but her breath, the wash of blood in her ears. Fear inflames her.

My brother struts like a fighting cock. He's come to right a wrong, of course he believes that. But there is no wrong but him, him and my father. I beg them to let him go. I might as well not open my mouth.

The gun rises and I scream.

In an instant, the scene disappeared. Daylight pierced the windshield, searchlight sharp. Kira sat shaking, fingers digging into her arms, hair glued to her neck. Breathe, she thought. Don't panic. But no one had dreams at four o'clock in the afternoon, wide awake in a car. A hallucination then? No, impossible, she'd fallen asleep, it was a dream, a bizarre grief response. Nothing more.

Kira sat immobile in the driver's seat, afraid that if she moved the world would again lose its color, the voice would invade her head. At last, bloodless with cold, still numbed with fear, she started the car. Key in ignition, spark of life, surge of power—all normal, thank God. As she shifted into first, the engine choked, then shuddered back to life.

Kira stepped on the gas, desperate for home, for wine or whiskey, for her comforting bed. She would burrow into the blankets, pretend that what had just happened was nothing to worry about, cry for Aimi and her mother, feel the weight of their absence flatten her spine. She would dream, wake her husband Dan with her tossing, ignore the chasm widening between them. These were the new rules. They weren't normal, but they were predictable.

TWO

June 16, 1945

Maddalena squeezed Regina's hand as they walked past the Manzanar guardhouse. The day was blistering, hotter than usual for spring, but she didn't care about the sweat and stink. She was here, finally, in this mysterious place she'd seen only from the back of her father's car on the road to Independence, or from the back of her horse, riding on Foothill Road. From either direction Manzanar looked the same—flat, repetitive rows of colorless, dismal-looking buildings and dry streets, giving off an air of despair she could smell from a distance.

The camp had been off limits since the day construction began more than three years ago. Her mother's orders. It was dangerous, Mama said; who knew what the enemy might do? Maddalena had thought about arguing—she'd heard that the camp was going to be home to families, and how dangerous could grandmothers and children be?—but it would have been pointless. Once Mama made up her mind, that was that. Maddalena had kept her word and ventured no farther east than Foothill Road, but that didn't stop her from wondering what went on in the camp, what those people, supposedly so different from anyone else in Owens Valley, were like. So when Mrs. Henderson poked her head into Regina's room, where the girls were sitting on the bed playing Hearts that blistering day, and said she was going to an art show at the Manzanar community center and did the girls want to join her, Maddalena jumped up.

"Yes! I mean no," she said. "I can't. My mother won't let

me anywhere near Manzanar. She thinks it's dangerous. She's afraid of the Japanese."

"She's entitled to her opinion, dear, but I think they're lovely folk."

"You've been there before?"

This was astonishing. Not only was Mrs. Henderson, who wrote poetry and painted with oils, a mellow, indulgent mother—the opposite of fearful, overprotective Mama—she was daring! Brave! Or, if she was wrong about the Japanese and Mama was right, perhaps foolish.

"I go several times a year," Mrs. Henderson said. "Their gardens and art shows put the rest of the county to shame. But we must keep peace with your mother. Oh, don't look so down in the dumps. You're going, and we'll make it our little secret."

Maddalena bounded out of the bedroom and down the stairs before Mrs. Henderson could change her mind.

"Wait up!" Regina called.

In the front hall, Mrs. Henderson tied back her hair and put on a pair of dark glasses. Then she summoned the girls outside and settled authoritatively into the driver's seat of her husband's dark-green Chevrolet pickup. Shaking off her surprise, Maddalena climbed into the truck bed after Regina. It seemed there was nothing Mrs. Henderson couldn't do.

As they bumped along the desert road, Maddalena gripped the edge of the truck bed, stealing glances at the camp through spumes of dust. Such an adventure, made all the more delicious by being forbidden. Little by little Manzanar filled the horizon, creating a rush of anticipation so thrilling that Maddalena wished the trip would take longer.

Once through the gate, Mrs. Henderson parked with a jerk of the brake and Regina leaped out. Maddalena stood in the truck bed trying to absorb everything at once.

Manzanar buzzed with activity. Men and women who had stopped to chat knotted the streets, while others breezed along, all business. Boys in short pants raced by on important missions, laughing and shouting and tussling with their friends, while teenage girls sauntered in groups or sat on barracks steps, heads together, giggling and gossiping like girls did everywhere. The breeze carried evidence of a baseball game—the distant crack-smack of hide against wood, the hoarse cry of a referee, a smoketrail of cheers. Manzanar seemed vibrant, as full of mainstreet activity as any town in Owens Valley—perfectly normal, Maddalena thought with a shiver, if you ignored the guard towers. Eight of them, where men with guns surveyed the camp.

The girls followed Mrs. Henderson to the auditorium, a cavernous building with a stage at one end and an open space dotted with easels and bulletin boards. The only breath of air came from people moving about; the building sucked in the heat and held onto it, suffocating itself. After twenty minutes of studying watercolor paintings and ink drawings of mountains and flowers, Maddalena thought she'd melt. "Let's go outside," she said to Regina. The paintings were pretty, but it was the camp itself that Maddalena wanted to see. After all, she might never get another chance.

"Where?"

"Anywhere. Tell your mother we'll meet her back here in a little while." Outside, the breeze carried whirls of dust and little relief.

"It's so *hot*," Regina said, fanning herself with a flyer from the art show.

"Hotter than Hades."

"Maddalena Moretti, you watch your tongue! That's almost swearing."

"Hotter than hell," Maddalena said, and laughed when Regina shrieked. "Let's follow those girls." She pointed to a trio heading north.

They walked past row after dismal row of meanspirited matchstick construction, squat buildings that looked as if a

11

windstorm would send them skyward. No one had designed them, as far as Maddalena could tell; they were too ugly, too cruel, to have been built with anything but disregard and haste. The only beauty came from things the Japanese had created themselves—colorful curtains, flowerpots on the narrow stoops.

"Look," Regina said, pointing toward a baseball field. "Boys. Lots of them." She poked Maddalena in the ribs and ran to the bleachers. Maddalena followed, and the girls found seats in the front row, across from left field. Shielding their eyes, they took inventory.

"The pitcher is cute," Regina said. "And look at his muscles!"

Maddalena shrugged. "You can have him."

"Well, who do you like?"

"I haven't decided yet."

A few of the boys wore baseball caps, but most of them didn't. How strange to see an entire field of dark-haired boys, when the Lone Pine boys had red hair, or blond, or a million shades of dirt brown. Most of the Japanese boys wore crew cuts. One boy in left field, with glasses, had hair that was short on the sides but long on top, and he kept tossing a forelock out of his eyes. He should have worn a cap, Maddalena thought.

A boy built like a bulldog blasted a line drive and the stands erupted. Regina and Maddalena jumped up, screaming with the crowd, then groaned when the boy got tagged out at second.

"This is almost perfect," Regina said. "All we need is some Coca-Cola and cotton candy."

"I wish," Maddalena said. Still, it *was* a perfect day. No chores, no mother fretting over her, no obnoxious brother making her wish she were an only child. Here she was, on her own with her best friend in this exciting new place. She felt like a tourist in the valley she'd grown up in, seeing things kept hidden from her. And all of it ordinary yet startling.

"I'll be right back," she said.

She walked along the edge of the field, taking in the city around her. That's what it was, a city of more than ten thousand, according to her father, bigger than any other in Owens Valley, built for people who didn't belong there and didn't want to be there. Looking up at a guard tower, the rounded eye of its searchlight puncturing the brilliant sky, Maddalena shuddered. It was easy to forget what those towers meant when you were outside the barbed wire, doing whatever you pleased. At first, when the plans were being made, then when it was built and the first Japanese came, the camp was all that anyone in Lone Pine and Independence had talked about. No one wanted it, and plenty of people were like her mother, afraid of the strangers who didn't look like them. Now, three years later, most of the valley residents had lost their fear, and some, like Mrs. Henderson, considered the Japanese people part of their community. Eventually Manzanar blended into the desert valley's landscape, no more remarkable than the sagebrush and fruit trees born there.

Fifty yards past the ballfield, Maddalena stopped, gazing west. These transplanted people had made Manzanar their home, with art shows, baseball games, and victory gardens. Not the kind of things you'd expect to find in a prison, yet Manzanar *was* a prison.

From here, inside the fence, Manzanar felt wrong in a way it never had before.

A wild cheer rose from the bleachers, but Maddalena couldn't pull her gaze from the the city sprawled before her. It was seconds before she turned. Then, in a flash, everything snapped into place—the game, the ball hurtling toward her, a boy chasing it, hollering, "Get out of the way!" In another flash he pushed her aside, then flung himself on the ball and threw it with his entire body, landing on his shoulder and hip in a whirlwind of dust. The crowd kept on cheering as the ball bounced into center field and rolled to a stop. The batter was home safe.

The boy stood, slapping away dust. "Sorry to scare you. I thought you were a goner." He wiped his face with the hem of his T-shirt.

"What?" Maddalena tried not to stare at the boy's flat, tanned belly.

"I didn't mean to shove you, but I thought you were going to get hit."

"It was my fault. I wasn't..." Maddalena forced her gaze upward. He was a few inches taller than she was, with glasses, hair that fell forward—the boy she'd thought should be wearing a hat. Up close, she could see the fine hairs of his eyebrows, the veins lining his thin forearms. "I wasn't paying attention, I meant to say."

"I know." He smiled, and the delight in his eyes made him look ten years old.

The strangest feeling percolated beneath Maddalena's skin, like warm rain drenching her insides.

"Well, I'm glad you're okay," the boy said. "See you."

It might have been her imagination, but when he was twenty feet away Maddalena thought he slowed his trot as if he might turn around and run back to her, ask her name, put his arms around her, kiss her. Then he broke into a run, headed for the players rushing the field shouting of victory or defeat, and dissolved into the throng.

THREE

February 28, 2011

Kira flicked off the alarm and listened to the pulse of the shower. Dan was up early. The space between them stretched beyond the half-lit room, beyond her body, immobilized in the bed, and his, streaming with soapy water. The thought of him in the shower would have aroused her once, but after Aimi's death, desire had drowned in the wake of despair. As Kira surfaced from sleep, the memory of what had happened in the hospital parking lot hijacked her brain. Panic followed, and she lay there blinking back tears, muscles contracted, trying to figure out what the hell was wrong with her.

The best explanation, the one she wanted to believe, was that nothing was wrong with her, that she'd dozed off and dreamed, the same kind of dreams she'd had every night since her mother's death. Of course weird things would happen after weeks of minimal sleep. And Rosa's death had reignited Kira's grief for Aimi. It had been there all along, buried and unresolved, a constant background thrum with the half-life of uranium, and the dreams forced it to the foreground. Every night they tormented Kira with reminders of what should have been—Aimi crying, Aimi at her breast, Aimi asleep, drooling milk.

Dan said that the dreams were a grief response, and Kira wanted to believe that. It would have made sense if the dreams were normal. What Dan didn't know, and what left Kira disintegrating in fear every morning, was that she wasn't herself in them. She wasn't in the dreams at all, had no presence she could connect to her own psyche. And didn't dreams arise from your psyche, acting out whatever drives your anxieties and regrets, your hopes, your memories? Not these. She'd been ambushed, disappeared by this teenage stranger whose identity now clung to her cerebral cortex, as tenacious as a tumor. And even odder, these dreams refused to fade or disappear with time. They stayed with her, every one of them, tangible, vivid, indelible, as if she were supposed to make sense of them.

Kira couldn't make sense of them. She couldn't make sense of losing both her child and her mother, or of the fact that when she saw Dan sitting at the dinner table or lying next to her in bed she wondered why he was there and whether she wanted him gone. It was a dispassionate exercise. Kira would ask herself if she still loved him, this gentle, clear-headed man, and the reasoning side of her mind said *yes*. She'd been with him for five years now, when she'd left every other guy she'd dated before the one-year mark, bailing when she saw, or imagined, signs of an imminent exit. Better to leave than be left; Kira had learned that lesson at the age of four.

Now, she couldn't remember what love without devastation felt like.

Maybe what happened in the parking lot had something to do with the fight she'd had with Dan that morning. Not that it was anything new. She'd been furious at him ever since Aimi died, because he seemed incapable of losing control, and yesterday she was furious at herself for being furious. Which was probably why she'd overreacted.

Dan had made eggs and toast, and coffee strong enough to shred stomach lining. He sat across from her, pretending, as usual, that neither of them was thinking of the darkened room upstairs, the empty crib.

"I've got a late meeting, but I should be home by eight," he said. "Pizza sound good?"

"Sure." Kira knew what was coming, let him struggle.

"Rough night," he said carefully.

"Sorry I kept you awake."

"It's not that. You know it's not that."

"You're the one who says there's nothing to worry about."

"I know, but you could get something to help you sleep. Some Ambien, or that stuff you took after Aimi—"

"This is different."

She could tell him that she was afraid to take medication, tell him there was something so *wrong* with these dreams that she was afraid drugs would make them worse.

"Maybe you should talk to someone. Or how about a grief support group? I've thought about going."

Kira forked into a yolk as if she might actually eat. She knew that she should reply in a way that matched his love, his good intentions, but saying the words he needed to hear would feel like tendons snapping. She dropped the fork, grabbed her mug and winged it toward the sink, where it crash-landed in a satisfying eruption of china and glass. Leaving Dan stunned, she grabbed her jacket and keys and backpack, telling herself to stop, go back, apologize. At the front door she hesitated, willing him to understand that she *wanted* to apologize, that she needed him to come after her, to hug her and forgive her for being a cruel person she didn't recognize.

He didn't come. And Kira had stepped outside, shivering in the gray grasp of early morning, shaking at the thought of what she was doing to her marriage. And terrified that she couldn't seem to stop it. In the wake of two deaths, love seemed like an abstraction she could no longer grasp.

They'd taken different paths since Aimi died, she and Dan. He tried to normalize things, believing that if they pretended to have recovered for long enough, eventually they would. Kira couldn't do that. Every month she silently marked the single date of Aimi's birth and death, each time wondering if a child who is born dead really has a birthdate, and each time anticipating the stab of agony that followed. Every thought, every memory of that day brought more pain, regenerated the wound that went deeper than Aimi, twenty-one years deep to when Kira was thirteen, pregnant and desperate not to be. She'd never told Dan about that pregnancy, saw no reason to. And after conceiving Aimi, Kira had wanted her baby in a way that was visceral, stronger than any compulsion she'd known. She'd dreamed of their future, her daughter's life tied to hers, imagined the ways Aimi would imitate the past, the ways she would defy it. A world had awaited Aimi, the black-and-white outline of a life that she, this small, wondrous being, would fill in with colors only she could envision. But Kira's body had failed her, and Aimi had died.

Yet Kira couldn't help thinking it wasn't her body but *she* who had failed Aimi. And Aimi had died.

No wonder there was a crying baby in some of the dreams. That girl, whoever she was, rocking a baby at her breast—an innocuous scene in theory; there was nothing frightening about a mother and child. What terrified Kira was the persistent presence of this unknown young woman, her apparent isolation and unhappiness, and the subtext of the dreams, a sense of urgency that screamed, "Pay attention!" And, most of all, the way she, Kira, disappeared.

After Aimi died, Kira and Dan had agreed on one thing without having to say it: their baby was not to be discussed. The practice brought relief, and almost as much guilt. Kira had stopped saying her baby's name—what kind of mother does that?

While Dan was in the shower, Kira dressed quickly, hoping to avoid him. She left a note saying she was having breakfast with Camille. Camille was her oldest friend, the kind of person who always said yes when it mattered, who heard the imperceptible catch in Kira's voice or recognized the desperation buried in a text message.

❧

When Kira walked into Peet's, Camille was waiting, a black coffee and a cappuccino on the table in front of her. Kira shook off the cold-needle rain and hugged her. "You're a sweetheart."

Camille slid the coffee across the table. "Because I didn't buy you a blueberry scone and spared you all those calories? Which you could use, by the way. Anyway, how are you? Besides the usual level of not-good."

Kira shook her head. "I'm…I don't know…just exhausted, I guess." She glanced around the coffee shop, populated by graying women in threes and fours, a tattooed skater hunched over an iPhone, a barefaced young woman with a baby bump who was trying to get her three-year-old to stop blowing milk bubbles. Suddenly the woman smiled and pressed her son's hand to the upslope of her belly.

Kira remembered that feeling, the weird invasion of privacy, the duality of body within body.

"What's going on?" Camille said.

Now that Kira was here, in the reality of rain and coffee, she found it nearly impossible to explain. In the daytime dream, or whatever it was, the girl was the constant, the protagonist; like the nighttime dreams, it was too sketchy to understand. The dreams left Kira with a sense of foreboding, as if there were something about them she should know. Yet she felt the girl's emotions, carried them implicitly with her as if they'd taken root in her own DNA. She was that girl with the baby—and that terrified girl, without her baby, in the daytime dream—but Kira had no context for any of it. No names, no childhood memories, no labels. Trying to make sense of them was like trying to put together a five-thousand-piece jigsaw puzzle when half of the pieces were missing.

The table next to them was empty now, the young mother maneuvering her strollered child toward the door. "You know the dreams I've been having, with the girl and the baby?"

Kira said. "I had one yesterday, kind of. I mean, I guess it was a dream but it was after work and I couldn't move and it was so fucking scary."

"Yeah, I've had dreams like that, when someone's coming after me with a knife or a gun and I can't scream, much less run. I hate that."

"I wasn't asleep, though. I was in my car—Jesus, I don't know, I must have dozed off, right?" Kira told Camille everything that had happened the day before, about the fight with Dan and the twins dying and the terrifying not-dream. Then she was sobbing, Camille's alarmed eyes on her, everyone's eyes on her, and what she was saying sounded worse than when it was trapped in her head.

"Come on, let's go sit in my car." Camille steered Kira to a Subaru wagon strewn with sippy cups, stray socks, and pulverized Cheerios. Kira crumbled into the passenger seat, shaking.

Camille turned on the heat. "With all the crap in this car, you'd think I'd have some Kleenex. Wait, here's a napkin. Okay, listen. First of all, you're going to be fine. Yes, you are. You're strong; look at everything you've been through. I know you had a horrible day and it was really scary, but give yourself a break. Your mom died and you're exhausted and you spent the day dealing with dying babies. That's a lot."

"Babies die all the time."

"But they're not always your patients. And you're vulnerable right now; it's only been a few weeks. Give yourself some time."

"Dan wants me to see someone."

"You told him?" Camille squeezed Kira's hand. "That's good."

"No, he said that yesterday morning. I didn't tell him about the daytime thing. I'm not going to."

"Why not? I know you don't want to hear it, and I'm not trying to piss you off, but he *is* trying, you know. Let him help you get through this."

"I've got you for that."

Camille gave her an exasperated look. "You've got him too. Don't you think he wants that?"

"I've got to go." Kira dug her keys out of her bag. "I'll call you later."

Standing on the sidewalk, Kira lifted her face to the wind whipping the gingko trees along the curb, then walked, jacket unzipped and hood down despite the scattered rain. The skies shapeshifted, gunmetal clouds gathering force.

When a child is born dead, you give up your future, yours and hers, the promise of a blended life. When your mother dies nine months later, when you are still little more than animated cardboard, you forfeit the opposite—your history, your identity, both drawn from the woman who held you, nursed you, comforted you with her body, voice, touch, smell. Kira felt unmoored without the only person who'd known her intimately as a child, who'd shared her memories, who would have had answers if Kira had been allowed to ask questions.

She hadn't been. Don't ask, her mother had said. Betrayal and abandonment are not proper subjects for dinnertime conversation; that message was clear by the time Kira was eight. There were the two of them; that was enough, her mother said. They would do fine without her father, the goddamn son of a bitch. "You were four, Kira, four years old. Who ditches his wife and kid, disappears and never sends a dime?" Kira had tried to make herself invisible when her mother talked like that. A headache, then silence, would follow the rage, and Rosa would retreat to her bedroom, snapping the door shut behind her. To Kira, the door closing sounded like an accusation.

If Aimi had lived, there would have been no closed doors, no child left alone to do her homework and put herself to bed. Aimi could have asked any questions she wanted to and Kira would have done her best to respond, even if she didn't have many answers. They would have been a family of four—if she counted Rosa, and it was impossible to use the word "family" without thinking of Rosa—but on the day Aimi was born and died they became three again, hopeless; two again when Rosa died. Two people joined by marriage, not blood, and it wasn't the same thing. Kira chastised herself for thinking that way, remembered hating that her mother swore by the old saying that blood was thicker than water. Yet she pushed Dan away, and he drifted alongside her on silent currents until he couldn't stand her distance any longer. When he reached for her, she pushed him harder, below the surface, and still he bobbed up, treading water alongside her. She was grateful for his resilience, certain it wouldn't last, incapable of worrying about it.

Dan tolerated her sabotage as if he understood it better than she did. When the dreams started, he'd reassured her that of course she'd dream about a baby after Aimi died; you didn't have to be Freud to figure that out. Kira didn't point out the flaw in his logic—that the dreams didn't start after Aimi's death but nine months later, after Rosa's. Dan promised that all this would fade with time and they would move on. But he didn't feel the rending Kira did, the physical betrayal. The helplessness when her labor started at thirty weeks, she'd never forget that. And when her hope died, an ashen despair buried itself in her muscles and bones.

Kira had been at work when the back pain started, so severe that she couldn't stand. By the time Dan arrived to take her home, the contractions were coming fast.

"You're dead white," Dan said. "We're going to the hospital."

Kira reached for his hand. He was disappearing, getting smaller by the second. How odd, she thought. Is that what fear does? Do we all get smaller until we disappear? Her body enlarged to make room for the pain, dense as clay.

"I'll call an ambulance," the charge nurse said.

"It's ten minutes to Oakland General," Dan said. "I'm not waiting."

They were at the ER in five. Dan jerked the car to a stop and helped Kira out. "Fuck," he said, staring behind her into the car. Kira looked at the tan leather seat, black with blood, and that was the last thing she remembered until after the surgery.

A partial abruption, blood pooled behind the placenta. There was no explanation, no reason it should have happened; Kira had no risk factors. If she'd seen the bleeding sooner, Aimi might have lived. The C-section should have saved her, but the blood loss was too great. *No explanation. Should have saved her.* Meaningless, infuriating words.

Afterward, Kira and Dan held Aimi for hours, Rosa crying next to the bed, looking ten years older. They unwrapped the pink blanket, stroked Aimi's small body, kissed her sweet face, smoothed the hair like black down. Touched the tiny fingers that Dan, at some point in that void, wrapped around Kira's index finger and photographed. Tears like lava. Dan's ravaged face. Rosa's whispered prayers. The pain of breathing. The loss, the memory of loss, hollowed into Kira's body. She had wanted this baby. She wasn't thirteen anymore, worried about shaming her mother, willing her fetus to die.

No, the baby in the dreams wasn't Aimi; she was someone else's. Dan was wrong, despite all his reasoning and good intentions. He would insist that in dream language a baby was a baby, a manifestation of longing. No. Whoever this baby was, she was *someone.* That baby and her mother meant something.

At home, chilled from the rain, Kira took a bath. Thoughts assaulted her—the dreams, the weird daytime thing, Aimi, her mother, the long-ago miscarriage. "Stop, just stop," she whispered. "Please." She sank below the water, stayed there until the knifing pressure in her chest silenced the clamor in her head.

Some time later, a tap at the door. "Kira? You okay?"

Dan was there, worried about her, about them, waiting for her to give him a sign that she was, or could be again, the person he loved enough to marry. She wasn't that person anymore. She wasn't sure she could be.

FOUR

June 18, 1945

Maddalena picked at her dinner, her family's voices floating past her as insignificant as cricket song. Shifting in her chair, she tried to unstick her thighs from the seat. She didn't care about the war, or how many calves they'd have next season, or whether Papa could get a good price for the cattle he planned to sell. She didn't care whether next spring would be a good time to plant alfalfa, or that her mother wanted her to bake three pies for the church social on Sunday. She'd seen the Manzanar boy again—from a distance this time, but she could tell he recognized her. She'd been to Manzanar three times since the day of the ball game and she'd seen him twice, both times on the hospital steps. He'd been wearing hospital clothes, so she supposed he worked there. Her body hummed. He was the one good thing that had happened to her since school got out, something to perk up a long summer of boring chores and loneliness. She didn't get to town very often, and when she did go, she might as well not have bothered, because the Lone Pine kids stuck together like wolves. Doing the shopping was about as exciting as summer got. That, and seeing Regina. But this summer would be different.

Maddalena had already ignored her mother's rules, and she intended to keep ignoring them. Stay on Foothill Road, her mother said; don't go near Manzanar; don't go to town alone. Don't, don't, don't. Her mother overreacted to everything, and now that Maddalena had been to Manzanar she'd seen for herself that it wasn't the dangerous place her mother said

25

it was. Mama *liked* to worry, maybe *needed* to. Mrs. Henderson wasn't like that. "Our little secret," she'd said about their visit to Manzanar, and with those three words Maddalena's world burst open. What her mother didn't know wouldn't hurt her. So today Maddalena had ridden Scout up Foothill Road until they were out of sight of the house, then veered east on one of the old irrigation ditches left over from when the valley was full of ranches and farms, back when there was plenty of water. Before the Los Angeles water thieves, as her father called them, bought up everybody's land along with the water rights. More than twenty years ago, ancient history now.

Marco reached for the breadbasket and Mama slapped his knuckles, giving him a look that made her brown eyes black. "Where are your manners? Maddalena, pass the bread." She got up to refill the milk pitcher, one impatient hand sweeping from forehead to knotted, inescapable bun.

Maddalena couldn't remember when her mother hadn't been impatient or irritable or tired. One time her mother had told Papa that everything was his fault, that their life would have been better if they'd stayed in East Los Angeles. The desert was no place to make a living, she said. But Papa hadn't been happy in East L.A., not with all the Jews and Mexicans moving into their neighborhood. That was why he'd bought this ranch for next to nothing, sight unseen, when a cousin who owned it got deathbed sick. Papa took to ranching immediately, puffed up with pride when he surveyed his land and cattle, his muscles stretching thin the shoulders of his work shirts. He seemed to thrive on the hardship of surviving in the high desert, while Mama grew drier and harsher by the day.

Marco grabbed two rolls without saying thank you and stuffed half of one in his mouth. The boy at Manzanar might be Marco's age, Maddalena thought, but she knew from a thirty-second conversation that he had better manners, and he was a heck of a lot nicer too. Marco had a mean streak as wide as the valley. As a kid, he used to catch lizards and snakes, cut their heads off, and wave them in Maddalena's face. One time he found a coyote pup and brought it home, and when Maddalena went to the kitchen to get some milk for it, he smashed the poor thing's head with a rock. Maddalena had cried for hours, and Marco laughed. Later she buried the pup in the scrub beyond the paddock, where he wouldn't find it and dig it up to spite her.

"Papa, have you ever been to Manzanar?"

Her father studied her as if she were a horse he might buy, flicking specks of cheese from his moustache. "Once or twice. Why?"

"When I ride past it on the way to Regina's house, it looks sad."

"Three years, and you're only now noticing it?" Marco said, snorting.

"Very funny."

Her mother's eyes were sharp. "You're staying on Foothill Road, aren't you?"

"Yes, Mama. You know what I was thinking today? The desert is awfully beautiful, isn't it, in a ferocious sort of way?"

"You're a strange one," Mama said, rising. "Clear the table now."

The men disappeared, Marco out the back door and her father into the living room. The radio clicked on. Time for another war report. Gathering the plates and silverware, Maddalena wondered if the people at Manzanar listened to the news, if the boy did. What did he do besides play baseball and work at the hospital?

"Ferocious," she whispered. She liked the sound of the word, the wildness buried in it.

Mrs. Henderson didn't know it, but she had changed everything. If she hadn't taken Maddalena to the art show, Maddalena and Regina wouldn't have gone to the baseball game, and Maddalena wouldn't have wandered away from the bleachers and met the boy. He was different, not like any boy she knew in Lone Pine, who talked only of pickup trucks and hunting. When he looked at her that day, it was like he *saw* her, in a way one else did. She *had* to talk to him again, and not from the back of a horse.

❧

Akira was halfway down the hospital steps, a trash bag in each hand, when he spotted the girl. She rode as if she'd been born in the saddle, looking more relaxed than anyone on a thousand pounds of animal had a right to. Like she owned the desert.

"There she is," he said to Paul. "The girl I told you about. The one at the game."

"Eh. Pretty enough, I guess," Paul said.

"You must be blind. She's a looker. You should see her up close."

"What do you want with her when you've got Annabelle? Say the word, my man, and I'll take that little lovely off your hands."

The girl was closer now, riding along the western fence. Akira watched her, waiting for the small, surreptitious wave he knew would come when she saw him.

Paul dumped his bags, then Akira's, and slammed the trash bin closed. "Let's go, dreamer, time to get back to work. You're in here, she's out there. Forget her. You playing poker tonight?"

"Sure, if Annabelle doesn't raise a stink."

"So what if she does? You're not married yet."

Inside, Akira stopped to wipe his glasses. The wind was hot today, flinging dust and sagebrush with malicious intent, coating his lips and tongue with the iron taste of desert. Every time the heat returned he thought there was nothing worse; then winter rolled around, cold that drilled right through his wool coat, made his bones and teeth brittle. The one good thing about winter was that the frozen ground held its own against the wind, which meant there was less dirt pelting his eyeballs and filling every pore. In three years he hadn't gotten used to any of it—the desert that alternated between oven and freezer, the dryness, the wind that made his nerves jump. What he wouldn't give to be standing on the fishing pier back home in Berkeley, gazing at the Golden Gate and tasting the salt spray.

He headed for Ward 2, his station for the day. Officially, he and Paul were orderlies, but they did whatever the nurses and housekeeping supervisor wanted done. Only two of the ward's eight beds were occupied, so he'd been told to clean the floors. Slinging a mop was better than being bored, and it earned him twelve dollars a month, enough cash for poker and sodas and smokes.

Akira worked the mop in careful swaths, making sure every inch of the linoleum floor gleamed. He had to admit Paul was right; he was nuts to think about the girl. Not because she was white, though. Her skin was warm, not the kind of white that burned in the first spring sun, but she was whiter than he was, or at least she was to the kind of people who thought the Japanese were yellow. He'd never been called yellow in his life until Executive Order 9066. Then the word was everywhere, in the papers and on signs and posters, on ugly lips and tongues, and everybody with so much as an ounce of Japanese blood was sent to the camps. As if the Japanese were worse enemies than the Germans or Italians.

Three years of being called yellow bastards. Three years in prison.

Apparently the Italians had been sent away too, though not as many—only the ones too close to the coast for comfort, as if living near San Francisco Bay put them in cahoots with "the Japs." *Japs.* Such an ugly word. And ridiculous since many of the Japanese at Manzanar had never even *seen* Japan; they were Americans, plain and simple. And what were people who were born in Japan supposed to do, like his parents? They couldn't become American citizens and they didn't want to go back to Japan. So they'd stayed, belonging nowhere and putting up with it, happy to make a good living and be part of the community. Then the war started, and suddenly they were accused of being the enemy.

Akira submerged the mop and the drowned strings danced, tangling and untangling themselves. No, the problem with wanting the girl wasn't that she was white. The problem was that she was free and he wasn't.

FIVE

June 23, 1945

At Manzanar, it wasn't long before we knew about the girl. In places where the mind is as confined as the body, where privacy is as thin as a brush stroke wanting ink, there is nothing that isn't everyone's business. We took our entertainment where we found it, watching days pass from the hard stoop steps, counting the number of times people walked by, speculating about where they were headed and what they'd do when they got there. Manzanar gave us little to do but wait, and endure, and we distracted ourselves with the imagined intimacies of others.

And so we noticed when Akira watched the desert for the girl. We watched for her too, envied her command of the far side of the fence, her freedom to go where the wind whispered to her, to follow whim or instinct. Freedom made her seem as distant as our old homes—Terminal Island, Santa Monica, San Francisco, Portland, Seattle—homes we would never forget, homes we wondered if we would see again.

The girl rode past Manzanar as if we weren't there, as if she had forgotten about our city wrapped in barbed wire, impossible to miss. The first time, we took her nearness for chance. The second time, her glance suggested curiosity, though the passage of three years, two months, and twelve days since the first prisoners arrived should have made us part of the terrain, not zoo animals to be stared at. The third time, the talk began. Those of us who were less observant wondered why the girl kept coming here alone, why she paid no heed to the guard towers, the machine guns and rifles, the searchlights that jabbed holes in the sky. Those of us who had eyes, who saw how Akira looked at her and how she looked at him, knew why she came. Some would call it love; some were less romantic. On the baseball diamond, in the schools and mess halls, making nets or stoking boilers, we whispered about what we had seen, what we had heard. Or what we imagined.

We knew the girl would keep coming back. We old men who remembered our youth—the recklessness, the blindness of it—we knew there would be trouble.

Six

December 17, 2010–January 14, 2011

Death seldom announces its intentions. Living alone in her house in Martinez, Rosa seemed happy for the most part, at least to those who didn't know her well. Kira knew better. As a child, she watched her mother give way to the darkness that came without warning, sometimes in short bursts, sometimes dominating her for weeks. When the darkness came, Rosa would retreat to her room and a bleak chill would infiltrate the house. Kira didn't know why her mother had these "spells," as Rosa called them, but being abandoned by her husband seemed reason enough. By the time Kira was ten, she'd grasped that if you're seventeen and your mother dies, as Rosa's had, you don't come away whole. By the time Kira was a teen herself, she understood that Rosa couldn't have watched her husband walk out the door, his rigid back signaling his dismissal, without wondering what was wrong with *her*.

The darkness in Rosa thinned when she met Dan and brightened when Kira married him. But it was the promise of Aimi, of a blood-borne through-line, that made Rosa burn with a joy Kira had never seen in her. Technically, Rosa died of pneumonia, an invasion that defeated her emphysema-pocked lungs. But what really killed her, Kira thought, was Aimi's death.

After the funeral, Rosa had gone into recluse mode, and Dan would drive to Martinez every few days to make sure she had groceries and her bills were paid. Kira withdrew too, lying in the darkened bedroom in an emotional coma, wanting her mother—who would understand the loss in a way no man could—to come to her. Rosa didn't come. When Kira surfaced, her body commanding her to drink or eat or go to the bathroom, her dulled brain recognized a pattern of absence, how much agony could come from nothing. The recurrences stunned her—years ago, the silent, shadowed nights of her childhood; the kitchen, forlorn, with only a little girl at the table. Today, the baby's room down the hall, empty and holding its breath. Motherhood—that most essential of human states, a concept of serenity that dominated religions and cultures and tamed violent men—it kept its distance. The physical act of giving birth didn't make Kira feel like a mother; she needed a child at her breast, on her hip, at the table.

There had been no pattern to her mother's retreats, and no way for a child, however determined or desperate, to anticipate or prevent her disappearances. One night they would make hot chocolate and popcorn and play Mouse Trap or Scrabble and the next Kira would be alone, eating Rice Krispies for dinner and telling herself everything was okay, that all mothers locked themselves in their bedrooms sometimes. With her books for company, Kira would read aloud a favorite chapter of *Ramona the Brave* or *Harriet the Spy*, raising her voice to mask the dread creeping into her heart.

These intermittent withdrawals of her mother had happened for as long as Kira could remember. She supposed the resultant loneliness was one reason, at thirteen, she took up with a janitor at school, a chunky blond guy named Buddy. He was older than her friends, so he seemed to offer what they couldn't—the comfort and guidance of an adult— but not so much older that being with him felt wrong. The attention felt good even if the sex didn't. The first time he entered her, pain knifed through her pelvis and she sobbed the whole time he did his business, which she was sure would split her apart. The sex didn't get much better after that. She liked the kissing, the heat and jumpiness she felt when he touched her, but eventually he skipped the foreplay, gave her one rough kiss and shoved her down on the bed. She had been wrong about Buddy, stupid to think that his sweat, his grassy-smelling semen, could drown her loneliness.

When Kira found out she was pregnant, she knew what was coming. She was six weeks along when she told Buddy the news; afterward, while she was in his bathroom, he stuffed forty dollars in her backpack and walked out. For an hour she sat on the bed in his filthy apartment, lit only by a skinny window and a dim overhead light, in case he came back, knowing the whole time that he wouldn't. She didn't want the baby, or Buddy either, and she'd only told him she was pregnant so that he would know what he'd done. If only Cam were there. Cam was the only person besides Buddy who knew Kira was pregnant, and Kira had sworn her to secrecy.

When she got up to leave, Kira grabbed a T-shirt that Buddy had left on the bed and stuffed it into her backpack. Something of his for the baby, she thought, then realized she wanted no reminders of him and threw the shirt into the toilet. She didn't cry, only wondered how it was possible, with this living thing inside her, to feel empty.

At home, Kira stood outside her mother's closed bedroom door, wanting to tell her what had happened, afraid to tell her, hoping she would sense her daughter's presence and call her into the room, pull her onto the bed and ask her what was wrong. The house was silent except for the irritating tick of the cuckoo clock. When her mother's door didn't open, Kira took it as a sign that she should keep her secret. She took a bath and tried to scrub away the scent and memory of Buddy.

Later, downstairs in the kitchen, she made toast slathered with Nutella. From her place at the table, with the lights off and the back door open, she had a clear view of the fishpond and the stony wall behind it, where a statue of the Madonna stood guard over the golden koi below. Everything looked moonlight cold except for the Madonna, whose face radiated kindness. Kira wolfed the toast and went outside. The garden was beautiful and slightly unreal, like a black-and-white photograph. Blossoms glowed white and lilac gray; shadows draped themselves everywhere, black velvet voids. The damp grass chilled Kira's bare toes. A breath in the water, the sigh and gasp of surfacing fish, sleek canisters scaled and feathered and lipped. Kira strained to see the Madonna's face in the darkness, the curve of her cheek and forehead, the gentleness of her mouth, all so familiar and dear. She murmured the only prayer she remembered from the time Rosa had tried to make them both practicing Catholics, said it over and over until her mouth was dry and the chill in her feet had reached her throat. "Holy Mary, Mother of God, pray for us sinners now and at the hour of our death. Amen."

Kira spent the next three weeks willing the thing inside her to disappear and visiting the garden Madonna to pray for forgiveness, though she believed she was stupid, not sinful. Mostly, she wished she'd never met Buddy, never let him touch her, never let his Neanderthal DNA anywhere near her eggs.

Then, late one night, her answer came. Pain cramped her belly, and clots and threads bloodied the toilet bowl. Crouched on the bathroom floor, Kira cried with relief, confusion, sadness. She had wanted this baby gone, and now it was gone, leaving her empty belly blade-cold. She'd wanted her baby to die and it did. The Virgin might have forgiven her for getting pregnant, but Kira wasn't sure she could forgive herself for wishing her baby would die.

She never told her mother. The loss of her virginity, the loss of the baby, the monstrousness of her death wish— three more unspoken truths in their silent house.

Like the first pregnancy, Aimi was an accident. At first

Kira didn't tell anyone she was pregnant. Trying to reconcile her identity with the concept of motherhood, she questioned whether she could love a child with the selflessness all children deserved, whether she had the right to have a child after what she had done. She spun through circles of ambivalence about the pregnancy, her trajectory interrupted now and then by happiness and often by fear. Then, out shopping with her mother one day, Kira bent over to try on some shoes and Rosa noticed the small bulge of her belly. "You're pregnant!" she said, and nearly knocked Kira over with an exuberant hug. "When were you going to tell me?" Kira leaned into her mother, the warmth of her body. As a kid she'd pulled away from Rosa's caresses, the nervous fingers stroking her hair. She'd resisted Rosa's displays of love despite her relief that her mother was back from one of her periods of isolation, being a mother again, visible and overbearing. Now Kira welcomed that smothering, the love that came with a dose of desperation.

Rosa insisted on being present when Kira told Dan, whose joy equaled his mother-in-law's, the two of them as giddy as teenagers in love. Kira watched their normal, uncomplicated response to good news and wished she could be like them. But as the months passed, Dan's happiness infiltrated Kira's defenses, as did her growing belly, and she began to want this child with the same degree of ferocity she'd wished for a miscarriage so many years before.

One day, when Kira was sitting on the couch reading, book propped on her domed belly, she caught Dan gazing at her with a kind of reverence.

"What, you've never seen a pregnant woman before?" she said, laughing. "It's a pretty normal thing, you know. Not like I have a special talent or something."

"I keep trying to imagine what it's like, and I can't. I'm envious, to tell the truth."

"Imagine nausea and heartburn," Kira said.

"You're so romantic." Dan leaned over and cupped his hands on her belly. "Hey, child of mine, your mother isn't as jaded as she pretends to be. Besides, you've got me. We can team up against her."

"Just what I need, you turning my kid against me before she's even born."

"A man's got to have allies. So, any nausea now?"

"No."

He tossed her book aside. "Heartburn?"

"No." Kira laughed. "You're kind of obvious, you know."

"I know." Dan kissed her and started unbuttoning her shirt.

When Aimi died it became clear what having a grandchild meant to Rosa. For her, Aimi would have been more than a wondrous addition to the family, the first stamp of a new generation. A unique distillation of genetics, this baby was part of Kira, part of Rosa herself, part of the mother Rosa had lost at seventeen. And so Kira endured her mother's persistent lament, even when each mention of Aimi seared her brain, when the word "death" made her think of not one child but two. And every day she buried deeper inside herself the hope that with Aimi she would have redeemed herself.

The first inkling that something was wrong with Rosa came on a rainy Saturday in December, eight months after Aimi's death. Kira went to see her mother after work and Rosa came to the door in her bathrobe, her graying hair loose and tangled, eyes capsized with worry. This was not like Rosa, a woman who put on eye makeup when she had the flu.

"Mom, are you sick? Why didn't you call me?"

Rosa pulled away from her daughter's embrace, and Kira followed her to the kitchen.

"I'm frozen," Kira said. "You want some tea? And why aren't you dressed?"

"She should have told me," Rosa said.

"Who should have told you what?"

"My mother. It doesn't make sense." Rosa pressed her fingertips to her temples. "Who *was* he?"

"Who was who?" Kira surveyed the tea in the cupboard. "Chamomile? Earl Grey?"

"You know, the man my mother told me about. The special one. You don't remember anything I tell you."

At first Kira had no idea what her mother was talking about. Then it came to her—the day they'd buried Aimi, on the way home from the cemetery, a distraught Rosa had launched into a tirade about a man she said her mother had known, saying she needed to find him but she couldn't remember his name. Kira, snowed on Valium in the backseat, had let Rosa's hysteria float past her, aware enough only to resent her for worrying about some nameless man on the day they'd buried Aimi.

"You mentioned him once, after the funeral." Kira put three boxes of tea on the table. "I had other things on my mind," she said, and instantly regretted the sarcasm. "I'm sorry, Mom. I thought you'd forgotten about him."

"No," Rosa said quietly.

"So what's the big deal? Why is he so important?"

"I don't *know!*"

"Try to calm down, okay? We'll figure it out. What else do you remember? What did your mother say about him?"

"He has black hair, and he's not too tall."

"Great, Mom." Kira smiled to show she was joking. "That only describes about a million Italian men."

"You don't understand," Rosa said, her breathing ragged. "I'm afraid."

She looked ancient, frail, betrayed. Kira sat for a moment, corralling the anger that always muscled in when she worried about her mother. Her mother had to be okay. Kira *needed* her to be okay. She had no reserves left after Aimi.

"I don't think there's anything to worry about, Mom. Certainly nothing to be afraid of."

Rosa wiped her eyes with a crumpled tissue from her bathrobe sleeve. Her breathing sounded like a chainsaw.

The kettle screamed. Kira silenced it. Time to change tactics, acknowledge, validate. "I'm sorry I don't remember him, Mom. Whoever this man is, or was, I can tell he's important to you." Textbook talk, straight out of Psych 101, but it worked. Usually. "Try to remember something about him. Where did your mother meet him?"

"I told you, I don't know! He's important, that's all." Rosa was wheezing now, her face ghostlike.

"Try to calm down. Where's your nebulizer?"

"I told your father…" Rosa forced the words out. "About him. He…didn't believe me."

The words carried a challenge. After all the years growing up without her father, after all her mother's refusals to speak of him, now Kira was supposed to take sides? Fatigue slammed into her, followed by panicked adrenaline. She found the nebulizer on the counter and gave it to Rosa.

"*I* believe you, Mom. Please don't worry."

If this man was so important, how had Kira managed to get through her entire childhood without hearing about him? And why wouldn't her father believe Rosa? Either the man was real or Rosa was showing signs of early dementia, a thought that made Kira lightheaded. Her mother should see a doctor as soon as possible.

Rosa puffed, hands shaking. "I want you to find him." It was an order, not a plea.

"I'll do my best, I promise. Write down anything you remember about him, or call me. But don't think about him now; you're too upset. Things will come to you when your mind's on something else."

Rosa nodded, her respirations less strained.

"Speaking of other things, remember Kendra Martin,

the micro-preemie we were sure wouldn't make it? She went home yesterday, one year old. How's that for a birthday present?"

Rosa sat with her eyes closed, clutching the nebulizer. Then she spoke as if she hadn't heard a word about Kendra Martin. "He wanted a child. He would have loved our Aimi." She wept again.

Kira took her mother's hand. "I know, Mom. He would have." Her voice fogged with tears. "We all loved her."

An hour later, after convincing her mother to lie down, Kira left for home. She didn't believe they would ever find this mystery man and she was pretty sure her mother didn't believe it either. Once in the car, fatigue dulled Kira's body, but her mind shifted into overdrive. The rises and curves of Highway 4, usually hypnotic, seemed revelatory, each incrementation of the wheel under her hands sending her thoughts in a new direction. Work had been rough that day, with three transports, a cardiac kid who'd coded, and a baby who got discharged to a mother Kira didn't trust. Something was off with her. Plenty of parents had off-the-charts anxiety about going solo after weeks of cardiac monitors and round-the-clock nurses, but this mother was edgy, restive in a way that spooked Kira. Social services had greenlighted the discharge, though, so there was nothing she could do except tuck the baby into his car seat and wish him a good life. A life of love.

Aimi would have had that.

Her phone chirped, announcing a text message. Maybe Cam, who was probably pissed that Kira hadn't called when she said she would, or Dan saying he was going for a run before dinner, or working late—something he did more often lately. He'd always been a runner, but now he was training for a marathon. Kira took his action as a form of condemnation, something he did in order to avoid her. She half expected him to lace up his shoes one day and take off for good, even though he told her repeatedly that he loved her. She believed him. But when she said, "I love you too," it was as if she were standing at the bottom of an abandoned well and her words snagged halfway up its mossy sides. Whether she was imagining this lack of conviction or if Dan heard it too, she didn't know.

At I-80's long decline through San Pablo, she pushed the Fiat's engine, taking advantage of the open road. On the other side of the freeway, the bay rushed to shore under a restless sky.

Kira couldn't shake the image of her mother standing in the doorway with her hair a mess. Rosa had been tough enough to raise a daughter on her own, and she and Kira loved one another with an intensity that came from knowing they were alone in the world. Alone together. But now Rosa seemed frail, as if the darkness she'd fought for years had finally worn her down.

Kira's father had vanished when she was four. When Kira asked where he'd gone, why he left, when he'd be back, Rosa would say he had "grownup problems." Kira didn't know what grownup problems were or why her father couldn't stay home and fix them, but she didn't like the way her mother's pretty face sagged when she talked about him, so Kira would hug her and say she loved her bunches and bunches and bunches, like flowers, careful not to say "and Daddy too." By the time she was six, she'd learned to wait until her mother was in a good mood before asking questions about her father. By eleven, she'd discovered boys and clothes, and she thought of her father less often, decided she didn't love him. Still, every time she brought in the mail she looked for his name on a return address. Frank Esposito, whereabouts unknown.

Recalling what Rosa said about her husband's disbelief

when she'd told him about the mysterious man, Kira flashed on a memory. Once, when she was twelve or thirteen, she'd asked Rosa again why her father had left, and this time her mother surprised her. "He thought I was crazy," she said. Were those things related? Surely her father hadn't really believed Rosa was crazy. Did he think his wife was in love with another man, and it was jealousy that drove him out the door? He must have wanted an excuse to leave, because if something had been wrong with her mother, Kira would have known.

She had only one memory of her father, and that was the nickname he'd given her. When they were alone he'd call her Cara, saying the name was a secret and she wasn't to tell her mother. Her mother had chosen the name Kira, he said, and it meant nothing to anyone. Kira liked having a secret pet name, especially one her father had chosen for her, and she liked it even better when he told her it meant "dear." Proof of his love, she thought when she was older, able to look back on that time but still naïve enough to believe such a thing as proof could exist.

At home, Kira parked the car and read the text message: Dan was out for a run, picking up Chinese after, home by six-thirty. She took a shower and settled on the couch next to The Thieving Magpie, an elongated feline odalisque showing an expanse of white belly, black paws masking her face. Sipping wine, Kira flipped through an issue of the *New Yorker*. There was an article about the opera singer Marina Poplavskaya, and she thought about saving it for her mother, who loved opera. The thought made her realize that she couldn't remember the last time she'd heard opera, or any music, at her mother's house. She tossed the magazine aside and the cat went airborne, then sat on the rug in a patch of sunlight to smooth her fur and restore her dignity.

This mysterious man—how could she find him when they had nothing to go on? If he was a relative or family friend, he might be in one of the family photo albums. Kira had taken the books—four in all, the family archive—because Rosa had said looking at them made her sad. To Kira they were time capsules, their mostly unlabeled contents open to interpretation. Her family history, such as it was. As a kid, she used to imagine the house filled with the people in the photos, an extended family of old and young, living and dead, frozen in time. After Kira's father left, Rosa didn't bother with the albums anymore, just tossed photos into shoeboxes and stashed them on closet shelves.

Kira got the albums from the bedroom. The first one held scallop-edged black-and-whites of stocky, unsmiling Italians in Naples and L.A., plus a few blurry photos of her grandmother Maddalena's childhood home, a ranch in Owens Valley—a horse near a barn, a boy and girl sitting on the steps of a two-story house, a vegetable garden. Other pictures had been taken in Martinez, the family's home since the end of World War II. Maddalena and her husband, Joe Brivio, had lived there with Rosa; then, for a short time after Maddalena's death, Rosa and her father. Then Rosa and Frank and Kira, then Rosa and Kira. Mothers and fathers and daughters. A stream of daughters that ended with Aimi.

Kira paused at a photo of Maddalena as a young woman, her face melancholy, features gentle as a child's. Her death was a suicide, Kira had been told, except for one time, in middle school, when her mother said Maddalena had died as a result of an accident, a revelation she later denied. Sometimes, when Rosa thought she was alone, she muttered to herself about why Maddalena would kill herself and leave her daughter with the man she hated. It worried Kira. All Rosa had left, at seventeen, was her dad and his family—distant Central Valley people, she said, who liked to keep their distance. Rosa had never received so much as a birthday card from them; Kira didn't know their names. And hardly a word was said about Maddalena's family.

If the mysterious man was in any of the photos, Kira couldn't tell. Maybe her mother would recognize him.

She checked the time; Dan was half an hour late. A nudge of dread that he wouldn't come home at all, then she fell asleep on the couch, dreaming sketchily of two-dimensional men in black-and-white scenes, all of them young, their skin pearl gray, hair gloss black, eyes minimized behind wire-rimmed glasses. All of them turning and walking away.

She woke when Dan kissed her. "Ready for spring rolls and kung pao?" Still groggy, she clung to his neck. "Hey," he said, kissing her again. "I could get used to this."

"I thought you weren't coming back."

"What, are you crazy?"

"Maybe." Kira pulled away, thoughts about her mother's odd behavior resurfacing. "I'm worried about my mom."

In the kitchen, Dan set the table and opened bottles of beer while Kira told him about the encounter with her mother. Every few minutes she had to refocus because evening light from the floor-to-ceiling window behind Dan threw him into half-silhouette. He looked as if he'd stepped out of her black-and-white dream.

"Anyway, she wants me to find him, like that's remotely possible," Kira said. "I mean, I don't even know if he's real. I think I should take her to a neurologist."

"Maybe you should ignore her."

"Not funny," Kira said. "I'm really worried. She was still in her bathrobe when I got there. She hadn't even brushed her hair."

"I'm worried too. And to tell you the truth, I don't want to be." Dan took off his glasses and wiped his eyes.

For the first time, Kira noticed the fatigue in his voice. He was struggling too. What would it be like to be happy and spontaneous again, capable of leaning across the counter and kissing in the unstoppable way they used to? They wouldn't bother undressing, just do it right here.

45

Magpie jumped on Kira's lap and snatched a piece of chicken. "I'm going to bed," Kira said, dumping the cat on the floor. "I'll go see Mom after work tomorrow."

❧

The photographs yielded nothing. "He's not here," Rosa said, page after page. "I knew he wouldn't be."

"We'll keep looking. Don't worry, we'll find him," Kira said.

A week went by, then another. Christmas was a subdued event, with few mentions of Aimi. Rosa was quiet throughout the holidays and stayed that way, which was as unnerving as her obsession with the mysterious man. She excused herself from Sunday dinners with Dan's family, stopped calling Kira daily. When she answered her phone, she wouldn't talk for more than five minutes, her voice distracted. Around Dan she was more animated, touching his arm and looking at him lovingly. It was sweet, Kira thought, how her mother had always adored Dan. But given how withdrawn she was now, it was odd that Dan remained the object of her attention.

One day in mid-January Kira stopped by the house and found her mother feverish, barely able to breathe. She was moved to the hospital, silenced by a ventilator. Then she died and everything went to hell.

The day it happened, a doctor swept Kira into the hall as soon as she arrived. Rosa had been hospitalized for three days, making zero progress.

"I'm the attending," the doctor said. "You're the daughter?"

Kira nodded, the floor beneath her unsteady. She put a hand on the wall, surprised by its solidity. "Yes. And I'm a nurse. Neonatal ICU," she managed to say. Her body tensed and coiled.

"Your mother is extremely acidotic," the doctor said. He was tall, too skinny, as if he'd been eaten away by his patients. "I'm very sorry, but I don't think she's going to make it."

The floor dipped and buckled. "What's her pH?" Her hand was there on the wall, seemingly suspended. She could feel nothing.

"Seven point twelve, down from seven point two-five."

"Shit."

"Do you want us to code her?"

Kira stared at him. "God, yes."

She followed the doctor into the room, where her mother was a low-lying ridge under the sheet, still in a way that made Kira go cold. She kissed Rosa's forehead, cool and papery. "I'm here, Mom. I'm here with you." No flicker of eyelids, no tremor in her cheek. "Are you giving her bicarb?" she asked the nurse.

"Yes. She's not responding."

Oxygen saturation eighty-five. *Shit, shit, shit.* She called Dan, left a message saying to come as soon as he could, then took her mother's hand. The cool fingers tightened on hers and Kira squeezed back, hopeful for a fraction of a second. Her mother lay silent, her face the dull gray of concrete.

"I'm here, Mom. I love you."

All at once the room contracted, amplifying everything, as if Kira had lost the ability to filter sensations: her hamstrings taut against the plastic chair, the open weave of the blanket beneath her hand, the bleat of the monitor, the hissing sigh of the ventilator. Her lungs felt tight, too small. The air turned leaden and the room dipped and rose, earthquake sharp. Kira stiffened. The room, the air around her, settled into a slow-stretched suspension, as if time had stopped. Every alarm went off. Oxygen saturation seventy—inhuman, impossible. Rosa dusky, rigid. Heart rate eighty-two, then one-forty, one-fifty.

"What the hell?" the attending said.

"I love you, Mom, please hang on." Kira squeezed her mother's hand again. "I'm here, Mom. I love you."

The cardiac monitor went mute. Then the alarms blared

again, the ECG tracing wild, the scribbles of a child. Rosa's cold fingers softened and Kira's hand grew warmer, then hot, hotter, acid running beneath her skin. She tried to jerk her hand back, but her mother's fingers tensed again, knitting into hers. The heat spread deeper, creeping up Kira's fingers and palm.

"Code blue," a voice blared overhead. "Code blue, Room 225."

"V fib. We need you to clear," the doctor said, paddles ready.

"I can't. I can't let go." Kira leaned forward, her cheek against her mother's hand. Then the heat in her hand vanished and Rosa's fingers opened, the skin unyielding as plastic.

There was no point, no choice to be made. With a pH that low, her mother didn't have a chance. Kira wanted to ask the doctor if he'd felt his hands burn in the chill grasp of a dying person, but she knew the answer.

"No code," she said.

"Time of death, twelve seventeen," the doctor said, and pocketed his stethoscope. He touched Kira's shoulder. "I'm very sorry."

A nurse hit a switch and the ventilator gasped into silence.

Blood was already pooling in Rosa's fingers, her skin rubbery, mottled like blue cheese. As the minutes passed, her mother's face took on the chiseled look of a statue, recognizable but wrong. At some point—she had no idea when—Kira found herself sobbing in Dan's arms.

That night she dreamed about a sad young woman, about oncoming headlights, a crushing impact. It seemed appropriate, a normal manifestation of grief.

SEVEN

June 23, 1945

The barn glowed pink in the seconds before the sun cleared the Inyos and splashed yellow hues over the valley. Maddalena dressed in a rush, trousers and a faded cotton blouse suitable for laundry day. It would be a dreary morning of washing, but the afternoon promised a visit to Regina's house and a ride past Manzanar on the way. A happy prospect, and even if she didn't see the boy she would savor the possibility of *next time*. Each time she saw him she inked a tiny *B* in her calendar; when she found out his name, she would mark the days with his initials.

She tied her hair back with a yellow ribbon, the best she could do to pretty herself without making her mother suspicious. If only her mother were more like Mrs. Henderson. Maddalena could walk into the Hendersons' house and shout, "I'm in love with a Japanese boy!" and she'd bet her bottom dollar Mrs. Henderson would smile and say, "That's nice, dear."

Downstairs, the sharp smell of boiled coffee lingered in the kitchen and the breeze filtering through the screened door promised another scorching day. Her father and brother would be outside already, working the cattle. Her mother was in the vegetable garden, inching down the rows with her gathering basket. Maddalena fixed tea and toast and ate it while watching her mother work. The garden ran the length of the house, territory her mother was determined to defend. Papa wasn't allowed to set foot in it, not that he showed any signs of wanting to. But Mama squabbled at him anyway, and he squabbled right back. Like chickens, Maddalena thought, and sometimes she couldn't tell if they were angry or simply arguing out of habit. She couldn't even tell if they loved each other, though she supposed they must. Maybe after they got married they let their love shrivel up like everything else in this desert. Not her. She was going to have a real love affair with the man she married, and she wouldn't let anything dry it up.

Three hours later the last of the wash flapped on the clotheslines. Maddalena stretched her aching arms overhead, gazing toward Manzanar. A hot wind lifted her blouse, grazed the skin beneath and churned up a feeling of pleasure deep in her belly. In minutes she'd be on her way!

In the kitchen, earth-scented air welcomed her—basil and oregano in the sauce simmering on the stove, freshly shelled peas in a sieve on the counter. She gulped water from the tap, then pocketed a few carrots from her mother's harvest.

"Use a glass, Maddalena," her mother said. "Did you wash your hands?"

"Yes. I'm going to Regina's now."

"Be back before dark."

"I will!" Maddalena called, already out the door.

In the barn, Scout flapped his lips in greeting, snorting softly. "Here you go, boy." Maddalena gave him a carrot and rubbed his forehead. "I know you'd rather have sugar cubes; I miss sugar, too. But these are sweet, I promise."

She couldn't remember the last time she'd had one of her mother's almond cookies or a slice of her brown sugar pound cake. Probably at a church supper, since her mother used up their sugar rations baking for church events. Mama said she didn't miss the sugar, but she guarded coffee as if it were gold dust. Papa complained too, about not having good whiskey anymore. He liked to say bootleg whiskey was criminal in more ways than one.

Rationing was tiresome, and a daily reminder of what was happening so many thousands of miles away. When the war started, Maddalena didn't think it would affect anyone except the boys and men who went off to fight. Then Manzanar was built and thousands of Japanese were plunked down, and people said it felt like Owens Valley had been invaded. The newspaper labeled the Japanese prisoners enemies of the state; the government called them spies and the men who weren't at the front called them Japs and kept guns at their bedsides. Everything Maddalena thought was normal had changed in the first six months of the war.

After saddling Scout, Maddalena jogged toward Foothill Road. Her parents didn't know it, but for her everything was changing again. The people at Manzanar weren't the dangerous traitors she'd been told they were, they were *people*, plain and simple. How could a boy who played baseball be a threat to the country?

The breeze picked up, a few degrees cooler this time. Maddalena took it as a sign; the afternoon would be good, she felt it in her bones. Manzanar lay ahead, a promise on the horizon. Would the boy be there? *Yes, yes, yes,* she thought with every chug-step of the horse. But she hated calling him "the boy." Was he a Mike or a Billy or a Bobby like the boys at school, the ones whose families had been Americans as long as they could remember? None of those boring, ordinary names seemed to fit. A Japanese name would be more interesting, and different too, like hers. She supposed they had that in common, she and the boy—knowing what it was like to be different. At school no one could pronounce Maddalena, so she went by Lena, but they said that wrong too, *Leena* instead of *Lehna*. And there wasn't a thing she could do about her last name. When the teachers called roll, it was all Adams and Bagwell and Kirk and Miller, except for her. Her first two years in school here, every time her teacher called out "Maddalena Moretti," fat-face Stevie Stewart whispered, "Moretti Spaghetti," to his stupid friends and they'd all laugh. When he cornered her on the playground one day, chanting

51

his stupid rhyme over and over, Maddalena punched him and knocked him down. The split lip she gave him earned her a visit to the principal's office and a smack from his paddle, but it was worth it. And eventually everyone got tired of the joke and Fat-Face shut up.

No more than a quarter mile ahead, the guard towers poked their ugly heads into the sky. Maddalena's skin prickled. At night the searchlights shot through the darkness, zigzagging around the camp, visible for miles around. At first Maddalena had watched them from the living room windows, fascinated by the patterns they made, afraid of what they watched over. Dangerous people, her mother said. Everyone said it. Within two months, Maddalena had hardly noticed the searchlights, but now, because of the boy, they seemed brighter and threatening again. And the camp seemed uglier, a scar on the valley made more horrible by the beauty of the mountains. At least the mountains gave the people at Manzanar something pretty to look at. Maybe the boy could see them from his room, like she could from hers, and for three years they'd been looking at the same view without knowing one another existed.

Maddalena kept Scout at a moderate pace, noting the markers along her path to the camp. There—the stink of animals, riding the breeze from the chicken and hog farms. There—the southernmost pass of fence and Bairs Creek, running from the Sierra right through the camp. There—the rock garden, so peaceful and pretty with flowering shrubs tucked among rusted boulders.

Some teenage girls sat in the garden, talking and laughing, and Maddalena wondered if they talked about the same things she and Regina did—boys and clothes and hairstyles, the war, the heat. The girls wore neat blouses and pleated skirts with white bobby socks, their hair styled in bobs and waves. They seemed like anyone else in Owens Valley. If they *were* like anyone else, they must play and study and work, argue and cry and complain. And fall in love. The thought made Maddalena's face flush.

❧

Akira pushed a linen cart down the hall to the Emergency Room, his head foggy with lack of sleep. This time it wasn't the old couple who shared their room, snoring on the other side of a blanket wall, that had kept him awake—it was the white girl, and Paul, who had a lousy track record when it came to keeping secrets. Gossip was a favorite pastime at Manzanar, and if Annabelle got wind of the girl she'd be jealous as all get out. And she'd be right to be jealous. Even though he'd talked to the white girl for all of a minute, and seen her only from a distance since then, she was all he thought about these days.

Of course, his parents would never approve of him seeing a girl like that, and in the old days their disapproval would have bothered him. Now, though he didn't want to hurt them, he didn't give a damn about their approval. Everything was different here, the traditions almost forgotten. With people agreeing to relocate out east in order to leave Manzanar, others taking temporary leave from the camp by cutting beets and thinning lettuces in Montana or Idaho, guys shipping out overseas, and kids running in packs, families fell apart. Akira rarely ate with his parents anymore, spent evenings playing poker or flirting, doing whatever helped him fight the boredom or stoked his sense of outrage. To hell with respect for authority, with being calm and polite when you felt gutted. Every day in this prison siphoned off a little more of who he'd been brought up to be.

Akira stacked blankets on the linen cart, thin from overwashing, coarse from bleach. He thought about the white girl's skin, her hair, what they would feel like. What she would smell like. The taste of her mouth.

❧

Maddalena tightened her grip on the reins, as if she might float up into the air and never return to earth. Maybe that was what love felt like. She'd had crushes before, but it would be perfectly fine if she never saw any of those boys again. This was different. Love or not love, it was something new. She woke up every morning feeling like the day ahead would bring something unimaginable and wonderful, something no boy in Owens Valley could promise her. She felt brighter and stronger than she used to be, as if she'd been reinvented. As if she might have a life that wasn't like her mother's.

Past another guard tower, four more rows of barracks, an apartment where a flowered curtain moved as if someone were spying on her. Then two small boys playing with sticks and marbles abandoned their game and ran parallel to the fence, keeping pace with her and yelling, "Hey, what's your horse's name?" and "Give me a ride!" Suddenly Maddalena felt as if all of Manzanar was watching her.

There—the hospital, as drab and depressing as every other building in Manzanar, made beautiful when the boy stood outside it. There—the plain metal handrail that edged the concrete steps. But no boy, cigarette in hand. No boy to make her throat tighten. Disappointment descended like a darkening sky. Then a keyhole of light—he might still come; the door could open at any moment. She'd count to one hundred before giving up.

Maddalena let Scout graze near Manzanar's cemetery. A small rectangle with barely noticeable graves, it was creepier than most cemeteries. It had taken her a while to figure out why, but then she decided it was because the camp was meant to be temporary. People weren't supposed to *die* there.

When she got to eighty-five, she heard voices. Three girls with white lab coats over their skirts and two boys wearing khakis and green surgical smocks came out the side door of the hospital. One of them was the boy. *Her* boy. He saw her and hung back.

"C'mon, Akira," the other boy said.

"Be right there," Akira replied. "Gonna have a quick smoke."

"Sure you are," one of the girls said.

"Good thing you're not allergic to horses," the other boy said.

"Very funny, Paul."

Maddalena waited, lightheaded, bloodless, airborne. Akira! His name was Akira! His friends walked toward the street, Paul turning to flash a thumbs-up. She flushed, wondering what they would say about her.

"Hello," Akira said softly, pocketing his cigarettes. Even from a distance he could feel her. He walked toward the barbed wire, stopped a few feet away. She was beautiful, like a princess on that horse, the sun coppering her hair.

His voice was low, so quiet Maddalena might have imagined it. Blood was pounding in her ears and something was winging through the air from him to her, as if the fence between them didn't exist, as if Akira could reach out and touch her. She started to reply and he put a finger to his lips, angling his head toward a nearby guard tower. Then he smiled, his face bright and sweet like a little kid's. But the way he stood, tall and straight, he looked like a man, not like the boys at school, all slouched and loosey-goosey. There it was again, that warm, watery feeling under her skin. She couldn't breathe, couldn't move for the longest time. Then she slid off Scout and rushed toward the fence.

The sharp voice of a tower guard sliced the air. "Halt! Move away from the fence!"

Maddalena froze, the barbed wire an arm's reach away.

"Step away from the fence," the voice repeated.

Akira's voice: "Go!"

Her feet had grown roots. A feeling like falling off a cliff, then the crack of a shot.

Maddalena fell to her knees.

EIGHT

March 6, 2011

Dinner at the Kanekos' house had been an every-other-Sunday tradition for fifteen years, non-negotiable as far as Dan's mother, Mariko, was concerned. After Aimi died, Mariko made it her mission to ensure that Kira would be there. The day before each dinner Kira's phone would ring, always late in the morning, and Mariko would say how much everyone was looking forward to seeing her, no need to bring anything. She seemed to think her daughter-in-law would drift away on an ocean of sadness without family to anchor her. She was probably right.

Mariko's vigilance meant staying home on this particular Sunday wasn't an option, no matter how unsociable Kira felt. That morning Dan had gone for a run and she'd stayed in bed, fighting a drilling headache and trying to convince herself she could get through the day. She felt like an ingrate. Mariko, who'd always been a sweet, constant presence, had become extra vigilant, leaving Kira messages when she ignored her ringing phone and stopping by with food she said was more than she and her husband, Kenji, could eat but that Kira knew she'd cooked for her and Dan. She told herself that spending time with Dan's family would be good for her, a distraction, but all she could think about was the daytime dream and whether she'd have another one. A week had crept by, a week of jumpiness alternating with panic, of waking each morning with her jaw clenched, knees drawn to her chest, assessing the temperature of her hands, terrified to open her eyes to what might be a monochrome world. It hadn't happened. No odd color shift, no shadowy murder scene or anything like it, no screaming girl. Whatever it was, it hadn't happened again, and though that was a good sign, it wasn't exactly conclusive.

The headache spidered up the back of her head, aiming for the sensitive spot behind her eyes. The girl in that dream—if it *was* a dream—was the same one with the baby in the nighttime dreams, only this time there was no baby. Then the thought Kira couldn't vanquish pounded in sync with her headache, insistent as a mantra: if this daytime-dream-weirdness happened once, it could happen again. She thought she might throw up.

Fifteen minutes later Dan came home, and Kira shot into the bathroom. She sat on the toilet, sweating and shivering, wishing she could stay home and google "hallucinations" obsessively, trying to find something that didn't mention schizophrenia.

"Can I get in the shower?" Dan said.

"In a minute." She ran the water steam-room hot and let it pummel her head, trying to remember wanting Dan to shower with her. Waterfall sex, they called it. Another pleasure that had become a distant memory, like dinner at the Kanekos'. Kira used to love going, loved being part of the big family she'd wished for as a child. The dinners started at three and went on for hours. Arguments might flare or simmer, jokes might trample on someone's feelings, but whatever happened, it was family time and Kira had treasured it. Now it was a ritual to endure.

She'd gone to her first Kaneko dinner a few weeks after meeting Dan. When he invited her, they'd been at her place in south Berkeley, a cottage planted among apple and plum trees behind an aging Victorian. Halfway through dinner Dan chugged half a glass of wine and said, "Okay, I've mustered my courage."

Kira looked up, alarmed.

"So, we have dinner at my folks' twice a month, my sisters and me. And Jennifer's husband, and sometimes...well, what I mean is, would you go with me? Next Sunday?"

"You want me to meet your parents? Wow, I guess that means we're going steady." Kira laughed. If any other man had suggested she meet his parents so soon, she would have made an excuse not to go and then ended the relationship.

"I *was* thinking of inviting you to the prom," Dan said. "Seriously, Sunday dinner is kind of a big deal for my parents. And I want them to meet you."

"Do you think your mom will like me?"

"Yes."

"How will I know?"

"Leftovers. Especially spam rolls. You'll know you're in if she gives you those."

"Fine, I'll go," Kira said. "I mean, spam rolls—who could resist? But you'll need to brief me. I'm not going without the full low-down on your family."

"You're kidding, right? You're not? Okay, here goes."

His parents were born in the Bay Area, to Japanese parents, he said; he and his two younger sisters, Emma and Jennifer, had grown up in the house his parents still lived in, in the Elmwood neighborhood of Berkeley. His mom used to make chocolate chip pancakes on weekends, and she spent years of her life cheering her children on at Little League games and lessons—piano and gymnastics for him, violin and ballet for his sisters.

"My mom's quiet, but it's because she's shy," Dan said, pouring more wine. "She loves animals. She volunteers at animal shelters, and she's always loved the rejects—senior citizens, three-legged dogs, one-eyed black cats. If Emma weren't allergic, we'd have had a houseful of cats, probably all diabetic or dying of cancer."

His dad, Kenji, used to take him fishing in the Sierra foothills and hiking along the coast. Some of Dan's earliest memories were of spending entire days at the de Young or the Museum of Modern Art. "I learned to love line and form because of my dad," he said. "He never lectured or anything, but he couldn't help talking about how things were put together, the brilliance of it. He taught me that things are more interesting when you look at all their parts, at how the minutiae make up the whole. I remember him pointing out the structure of an oak leaf and then comparing it to another kind of leaf. The day I caught my first fish, he was more excited about showing me the pattern of the scales than he was that I'd actually caught something. Anyway, that's why I ended up going into architecture."

Dan had joined his father's firm the day after he graduated from Cal. For him and Kenji, design was an exercise in finding balance, experimenting with ways to make each architectural aspect the ideal blend of purpose and beauty.

"What kind of things did your dad design when you were a kid?"

"Mostly residential. Now we do some commercial stuff, but we'd both rather design houses. He did a Buddhist temple when I was a kid, but he didn't like it."

"Why not?"

"He thought it was too austere. That's probably why we weren't raised Buddhist."

"Really?"

"No. Are you always this gullible?"

"Yes. You don't know that by now?"

Instead of answering, he slow-danced her to the bedroom.

Kira had spent the next week fighting the urge to back out of the invitation, but disappointing Dan seemed cruel and besides, she was curious. When the day arrived, she emptied her closet trying to figure out what to wear, finally choosing a vintage cashmere cardigan in '50s pink worn over a white camisole and dark jeans. The shoes were easy—ballet flats, because no mother liked seeing her son's girlfriend tower over him. Barefoot, Kira and Dan stood eye to eye.

On the way to the house she said, "I'm terrified. What if I gag on a spam roll?"

"No spam rolls tonight," Dan said. "Dad's grilling. You'll be fine."

Ten minutes later they pulled in front of a brown-shingled bungalow with leaded glass windows. A live oak sentried the yard and dogwoods hovered over the stairs to the front porch. Along the stepping-stone walkway, pink hydrangeas alternated with chubby clumps of Spanish lavender, and milky hollyhocks swayed near one corner of the house. A storybook home, the kind that always came with a mother and father and sisters and brothers. Transfixed, Kira blinked back tears.

"Are you ready to roll?"

"I guess so," Kira said. "Wait a minute—how many women have you brought to these dinners?"

"Can't remember. Forty, sixty? Could be closer to a hundred."

"You'll pay for that later."

As they started up the steps, the front door swung open and a small woman came onto the porch, elegant in lilac silk and black linen, a chin-length bob. Dan took the steps two at a time and grabbed her, swinging her onto her toes. She laughed and kissed him, and when he let her go she turned to Kira, smoothing her silvered hair.

"Kira, welcome, we're so glad you could come. I'm Mariko. Please come in. Everyone is on the back deck."

Two hours later, after feasting on grilled salmon and vegetables and too much sake, Kira had answered innumerable questions about where she grew up, her family, and her work at the hospital. She felt completely at home, though she supposed the sake had something to do with that. It was a premium kind, Kenji said as he filled her glass. "For special occasions," he added, which made her blush. A sweet man, intelligent and pensive, whose controlled exterior seemed to simmer with subdued energy—a mischievous streak, Kira thought, or simply a love of life. She imagined having a father like him, the long conversations they'd have, the walks they'd take, the things he'd teach her.

Mellowed by the alcohol, she watched and listened, enjoying the rush of family, the chatter and laughter, the resurfacing of decades-old arguments. As a child she'd dreamed of sharing secrets, trading clothes and toys with a sister or walking home from school with an older brother. She'd imagined relatives who'd bring food and presents on holidays and birthdays, cousins she'd hide from in the garden, a favorite aunt who'd take her shopping for clothes, a grandfather who'd ride the Tilden Park carousel with her and buy her an ice cream. Instead, she had quiet and loneliness, a mother she couldn't predict.

That night at the Kanekos' she could have sat there forever, already feeling at home. But that was five years ago, and everything was different now. Kira got out of the shower and swiped fog off the mirror. At least she *looked* normal.

Three hours later she'd made it through dinner. When Kira mentioned her relentless headache, Mariko insisted she stay put while the others cleared dishes, set out dessert plates, poured more wine. While everyone else debated the merits of meditation, exercise, or acupuncture for headache relief, Emma brought a cake from the kitchen.

"My famous carrot cake," she announced, setting it on the table. From Kira's vantage point, curled in an armchair, candlelight danced behind the cake. *Like a birthday cake,* she thought, and instantly heat flared in her hands. Then the sudden shroud of salmon-pink shadows, the shift from yellow to nerve-jangling green.

The day is blistering, too hot even for candles. But they blaze before me, sixteen of them on a layer cake with pink frosting. The dining room is hot and stuffy and I long for air, for him.

61

Kira tries to speak but can make no sound. She thinks her eyes are open. There are shadows, figures blurry like those in a black-and-white newsreel shot from a distance at a dead run. Yet she knows the girl is the same one as always, knows she's in a room with a long table and shuttered windows with the curtains tied back.

"Make a wish," my mother says.

"Wish for a husband!" my friend says. She's wearing that dress I like so much, the white one with red polka dots, a full skirt fitted with a red patent leather belt.

My family doesn't know what I wish for. If only he were here, the boy I love. If only I could tell everyone we're in love, make it a real celebration.

They are watching me. I take a deep breath and make a wish, and it is not the wish my mother would have made for me. I blow hard, and all the candles go out but one. A terrible omen. I can't let them see me cry.

A feeling like sand dissolving beneath Kira's feet, rushing to meet the undertow, and the Kanekos' dining room reappeared. Kira was sitting up, gripping the sides of the chair. Dan was kneeling in front of her and Mariko stood as if frozen, a hand at her throat.

"What happened?" Dan said. "Are you all right?"

Kira looked around in confusion, the scene still vivid. *Another one.*

"Should we call a doctor?" Mariko said.

"No—no, I'm okay. I'm fine, really." *Another one.* A sense of empty weightlessness, as if her blood had drained from her body.

"Oh my God, you scared us to death," Jennifer said. "Your eyes were open like you were in a trance or something." Everyone started talking at once, offering tea, a moist cloth for her forehead, a place to lie down.

"No, we're leaving. We shouldn't have come," Dan said. Kenji maneuvered in to help support Kira as she stood, his arms steady, comforting. She wanted them to tell her nothing was wrong, that they would make everything right. *Please make everything right.*

Out the door, down the steps. At the car, the family hovered, a collective mother.

"She'll be fine," Dan said. "She just needs some sleep."

If only. Twice now, wide awake. The emptiness subsided, her body reverberating with panic. You can brush off something inexplicable once, but twice means it's real. Twice means you should pay attention.

On the way home, Dan kept glancing at her. "What was that, a seizure? You looked totally out of it. We've got to call your doctor first thing."

No doctor. Whatever answers a doctor could provide, Kira didn't want to hear them. All she could think of was what her mother had said about Kira's father calling her crazy. What if something *had* been wrong with her mother, something chemical, organic, and she couldn't see it? What if the same thing was wrong with *her?*

"Did you hear me?"

"Yeah."

"Yeah you heard me, or yeah you'll see a doctor?"

Kira made a guttural noise that Dan could interpret however he wanted. Straight ahead, down the seaward slope of Alcatraz Avenue and past the Berkeley flats, the island prison shone, fuchsia-tipped against the crumpled aluminum bay. Then the sun nosedived and Alcatraz disappeared. Kira let out a long breath. Perception was fluid, responsive to time, place, mood, history, changeable in an instant or over a lifetime. The only real truth was that it was impossible to know anything, really. Except, perhaps, that nothing was impossible.

NINE

Get away from the fence!"

Maddalena looked up at the mouth of the megaphone, the man silhouetted behind it. And then somehow she was on Scout's back, urging him on.

The horse hit a canter, dust rising around him. Maddalena's arms and legs were like jelly, her heart a wild bird. She could have been killed; Akira could have been killed. She glanced back, saw him standing on the hospital steps, safe. He was safe, she was safe, no one was hurt. But she said every prayer she could think of, the words in rhythm with the horse's hooves thudding beneath her.

Finally the guard tower was far behind her, its monstrous head and leggy body reduced to a thumbprint. Maddalena slowed Scout to a trot. What an idiot she'd been. She'd lost her head, every shred of common sense. If her mother found out what had happened, she'd be out of her mind with anger, confine Maddalena to the house for weeks, and her father would sell Scout to someone hundreds of miles away who didn't love him. Worst of all was imagining the boy lying face down with a bullet in his back and herself sprawled on the other side of the fence, their blood staining the desert floor.

Slowly her panic ebbed and her mind cleared. Those guards wouldn't have shot her. She was outside the fence, an innocent girl, no threat to anyone. They were warning her, that was all, or having fun scaring her to death. There hadn't been any danger, not for her. Only for the boy, the one on the inside. He had kept his distance from the fence, she realized,

64

and so had the little boys who'd run alongside Scout. Barbed wire and guns. What kind of people put children in such a place?

The wind kicked up, whipped at her hair, slapped her face. Usually an annoyance, today it felt right—like *her,* fierce and unpredictable and crazy. Crazy to think she could talk to the boy through that fence, crazy enough to try. She was sweaty, dirty, exhilarated, alive. Where was the Maddalena who gathered eggs early in the morning without complaint, who arrived at school before the first bell with her dress ironed and her hair neatly braided? She wasn't herself anymore; she was wild and free. Pushing Scout to a gallop, she dropped the reins, her arms outstretched like wings. The sky opened, endless above her, Scout's hooves drumming below. This was what life could be—a risk, an adventure. Her mother could keep her rules and worries to herself. Maddalena would go back to Manzanar and see the boy again. Akira. What a perfect name!

Inside the hospital, Akira wiped his glasses clean, hands shaking. The guard had no right to scare the girl like that. And now there would be talk; there always was when people heard gunshots. Everyone would wonder what happened, ask who saw what. With any luck, nobody had seen the girl, or him, but a lack of facts never stopped anyone from gossiping. People made up stories, and once the rumors circulated at the mess halls and on the streets, they became truth.

Checking in at the supervisor's desk, Akira was told to transport a patient to Ward 4, then clean the floor in Admitting. He was wheeling a spindly old man down the hall when Paul zipped out of nowhere and fell in step beside him.

"Did you hear the shot? Sounded close, this end of camp, I'll bet," Paul said. "You see anything?"

"No," said Akira.

"Now you're gonna tell me you didn't hear the shot. Come on, you were outside. You sure you didn't see anything?"

"You got ears? I said no."

"Right-o. Touchy today, aren't we?" Paul left, whistling.

"Someone got shot?" said the old man in the wheelchair, swiveling toward Akira.

"No. Nothing to worry about." Akira helped the man into bed and traded the wheelchair for a mop bucket. Paul could be a nosy jerk sometimes.

The floor in Admitting was a mess, with dust and dirt everywhere, and a sticky patch of something near the entrance, as if it hadn't seen a mop in about a week.

"Guess you've been busy," Akira said to the girl at the desk. "What happened? Did a pack of dogs run through here?"

The girl laughed, a sweet, musical sound. Before Annabelle, he would have flirted with her. She was small and slim and wore a yellow sweater with pearly buttons. Annabelle had one like it in blue.

Akira scrubbed the floor, wishing it could be as easy to wash away his mounting guilt. A guy couldn't ask for a more devoted girlfriend than Annabelle. They'd started dating last year, right after high school graduation. Sitting next to her, waiting to shake the principal's hand and get his diploma, Akira had tried hard not to think about what graduation would have been like at Berkeley High with all the seniors out on the football field, laughing and yelling and backslapping. Annabelle smiled at him as if she knew what he was thinking, and that was the first time he'd noticed how cute she was. They spent the rest of the ceremony making jokes about what an honor it was to graduate at Manzanar, and afterward, while their parents talked to the teachers, Akira asked her out. They went to a movie that Saturday and started going steady right away. Sitting in the rock garden, watching the sky over Mount Williamson go from blue to orange to pink, they kissed for the first time.

Annabelle was a virgin when they met, but she wasn't a prude. In fact, she was something else when it came to sex, even with dust in her eyes and rocks under her back. But sex wasn't everything. Sometimes Annabelle was funny when she didn't mean to be. Sweet, but not the smartest girl around. The girl he'd marry would have to be someone he could talk to about more than movies and what was for dinner, someone who knew her own mind and wasn't shy about saying what she thought. Girls like Annabelle were obedient and quiet, bending to men's wishes like a sapling to the wind, eager to prove their worthiness as wives, their potential as mothers. She was exactly the kind of girl his parents would want him to marry, someone who had no ambitions other than keeping the traditions alive, raising their children to honor their parents and grandparents.

Akira worked the mop, thinking about the girl on the horse, how different she was from Annabelle. She'd surprised him by coming up to the fence the way she had. Until now, he hadn't thought about seeing her except from a distance—her out there, him in here. But she seemed determined to talk to him. And why not? All they needed was a plan.

By the time Akira clocked out, he knew what to do. The fellas in the Manzanar Fishing Club sneaked out of the camp all the time, and so could he. They went out before dawn, fished the mountain streams from first light till last, then sneaked back under the fence after dark. He'd never wanted to go because he didn't care about fishing, which meant he'd have nothing to do out there but taste the freedom he didn't actually have. Not worth tormenting himself, and definitely not worth the risk. But now a little risk sounded good. The problem was figuring out how to let the girl know.

Lost in thought, he rounded a corner and walked smack into Annabelle. "Geez, I'm sorry!" Akira said, grabbing her arm to steady her.

"You should watch where you're going." Annabelle gave

him a chilly look, one hand clamped on her sun hat. "I'm already a wreck after hearing that gunshot."

"You heard it?"

"Of course, you ninny. I nearly jumped out of my skin."

"Yeah, me too. We didn't send out an ambulance, so I guess no one got hurt."

"That's a blessing." Annabelle took off her hat. "Notice anything different?" She swirled her skirt side to side.

"Well, you look pretty," Akira said. "I mean, you always look pretty, but—"

"I got my hair bobbed yesterday." She tossed her head and her sleek hair swung, barely grazing her shoulders. "Men are so unobservant."

He'd liked her hair long, the way it fell over her face when she was on top of him. "It looks swell. Pretty, I mean." He was getting nowhere. "Say, want to get some dinner? My poker buddies say the new cook in Block 3 is good." Not much chance of that. When people said the food was good, that pretty much meant the cook didn't top the rice and everything else with lime Jell-O.

"Oh?" A tone as brisk as the wind. "You won't be hanging around the fence waiting for someone?"

"What are you talking about?"

"Don't play dumb with me, Akira Shimizu." Annabelle crossed her arms, her lips pouty. "A little bird told me you've got eyes for some girl on a horse. A *white* girl."

"Her? I've seen her ride by a few times, that's all." If only he were a better liar.

"Uh-huh. Well, I'm meeting Jackie for dinner."

"Want to meet at the canteen later, then? Say seven o'clock?" He slipped an arm around her, murmuring into her hair. "You can lose Jackie by then, right?"

"I'll think about it." She left, swinging her hips.

Annabelle wasn't very good at playing hard to get. She'd be at the canteen tonight, and she'd do her best to keep his attention on her and no one else. Not long ago, he would have welcomed that. Funny how when your life takes a turn and your view of the world changes, the people in your life seem to change too. Annabelle was the same girl she'd always been, but Akira no longer thought about how she laughed at his jokes, how her legs moved beneath her skirt, how she made a little "mmm-oh" sound when he pushed inside her. He felt like a louse. He'd never been a guy who hurt people and thought nothing of it, or hurt people at all, at least not intentionally. He'd dated a few girls before Annabelle, back in Berkeley, and he'd tried to be a good boyfriend. The girls had thrown *him* over, not the other way around, and he'd been depressed for weeks, especially after Kaori, the first girl he'd slept with. He knew what it felt like to get dumped, and he didn't want to hurt Annabelle. Still, they probably wouldn't have lasted this long anywhere but Manzanar.

He pictured the girl jumping off her horse, running toward him, oblivious to the guards and their guns, ignoring the fact that he had Japanese blood and she didn't. Because of her, freedom, however fleeting, was something he could imagine again. It was like going back in time, before Manzanar, and remembering what it was like to dream.

The room was suffocating, too hot to sleep. Maddalena tossed the sheet aside. The iron bed she'd slept in her whole life didn't seem right anymore, not when the narrow world of her childhood lay behind her. Her eyes were open now, seeing things that had been invisible, contemplating a future she'd never imagined. All because of Mrs. Henderson and Manzanar, the boy at Manzanar. "Akira," she whispered into the darkness. She flapped her nightgown to cool her legs and belly, and her nipples hardened. She touched them, a tingle shooting through her belly. How lovely to fall asleep touching herself, drifting off all soft and fluid. Her mother said it was a sin, that the pleasures of the body were meant for marriage, but Maddalena had never understood why pleasure was wrong or why it had to wait until certain times in a person's life.

She rolled over, her head full of thoughts that flitted away before she'd finished with them. Getting shot at was enough to make her nerves melt, enough to turn the desert she knew so well into an unrecognizable place, filled with danger worse than rattlesnakes and sandstorms. Why were guns necessary? How could an entire race of people who'd chosen to come to America be enemies of the state?

Most of what Maddalena knew about Japan came from the war reports. At school it had always been America this, Europe that, as if the rest of the world didn't exist—until the "murderous Japs," as her social studies teacher put it, attacked Pearl Harbor. But Maddalena had stood in a city full of Japanese Americans and seen for herself that the world was bigger than she'd thought, that things were more complicated.

The singsong cries of coyotes pierced the air. Maybe they're in love too, Maddalena thought. She went to the window and leaned out, as if breathing in the night air would bring her closer to Akira. The blackness was three layers deep—velvet barn, charcoal mountains, plum sky. High clouds pressed the day's heat into the earth. The coyotes called again and she wished she were with them, the wind soft on her face, her bare feet clouded with warm dust. Whatever this feeling was—wildness, longing, anticipation—she wanted it to last forever.

If she was in love, God help her. The world she lived in had rules that said she couldn't be in love with a boy who wasn't white. Her father wouldn't let a Japanese boy so much as set foot in the door; he was always talking about how the Japs deserved to be locked up. At first she hadn't understood how he could be angry that Italians were being locked up, yet think the Japanese deserved it. Eventually she decided that he needed to look down on someone. He often complained that the northern Italians had snubbed his family, who were from Naples and Calabria, and then he acted the same way himself. He'd scorned the Jews and Mexicans in L.A., and now he thought it was perfectly fine to lock up the Japanese. They looked different, and to him that was bad.

Not to her. Different was exciting. But if it were up to her parents, Akira would have no place in her life. They were so rigid and strict that last spring they hadn't wanted her to go to the junior prom because she wasn't a junior and the boy was a year older. Her mother acted as if the age difference was a crime.

The boy who asked her, Tom, looked like a nervous stork, but he was nice enough, and cute enough in an awkward way, and Maddalena desperately wanted to go to the prom. So she begged her parents until they said yes, as long as he brought her straight home afterward. Her mother altered one of her own dresses for her, a silky sheath in emerald green that Maddalena had never seen and couldn't imagine her mother wearing. It rippled down her body and showed the tops of her breasts. "You look pretty," her mother said when Maddalena tried it on. Then, in a warning tone, "Don't waste it." She tucked up the shoulder straps and Maddalena's hint of cleavage disappeared.

The night of the prom, when she went downstairs wearing that dress and dangly rhinestone earrings, with a green velvet ribbon in her hair, her father stared as if he'd never realized she was female. Then he shook Tom's hand for a good thirty seconds, giving him a look there was no mistaking. When the terrified boy pinned a corsage of pink carnations to Maddalena's dress, he nearly skewered her.

Her parents needn't have worried, because Tom turned out to be any parent's idea of a perfect gentleman. At the school auditorium, made festive with crepe paper and balloons, he fetched glasses of punch, then planted himself a good three feet away from Maddalena. They sipped their punch and watched the dancers, Tom growing paler by the minute. Finally, when the fourth song started, Maddalena said, "Could we dance?" and he gave her a sweaty hand, his face rooster red. They shuffled across the dance floor, his hands barely touching her, both of them apologizing every time their knees bumped. When he stepped on her foot, she yelped and they both bent over, smacking foreheads. Then they both laughed and Tom apologized about a million times, and the rest of the dance was fun. When a slow song came on, Tom's hand crept to the sway of her back and she pressed against him. He turned his head but didn't pull away. Over his shoulder, Maddalena watched couples sneak off to dark corners to neck. Tonight was her chance. She'd always hated that stupid saying "Sweet sixteen and never been kissed," as if it was the girls' fault and boys had nothing to do with it. She was determined not to be one of those girls.

On the way home, Maddalena inched across the truck's bench seat, as wide as an aircraft carrier, until she was within easy kissing distance. Tom drove in silence, while Maddalena tried to make conversation. "That was fun," she said; then, "Did you see Edith and Bennie? I bet they'll be going steady by Monday."

Tom nodded, his eyes on the road. When they got to her house, he shook her hand and mumbled, "Thanks. I had a good time."

"Me too." Maddalena squeezed his limp hand and Tom stared at the steering wheel. "A real good time, I mean. You're a good dancer." Nothing. "Well, good night." She gave him a peck on the cheek, which seemed to turn him to stone, and got out of the truck before he could move again, much less think about walking her to the door.

Hopeless, one hundred percent hopeless. But it was her first date, so that was something. She dried the corsage, then stashed it in her grandfather's smoking stand, a small, square cabinet with a single door atop long, skinny legs. That was where she hid her keepsakes—a cable car ticket from San Francisco, sea glass found on the beach near Los Angeles, a dried baby lizard, and a handkerchief sloppily embroidered with her initials in blue, done when she was eight.

For months after the date with Tom, Maddalena would imagine being in that truck with a different boy, with a handsome boy who wanted to kiss her. Her elegant green skirt would be hiked up and her lipstick smeared. The thought made touching herself even better.

The coyotes fell silent. Maddalena went back to bed.

The simple fact was that Akira made her feel alive, and no other boy had ever done that. When he looked at her, the world seemed as endless as the night sky, full of adventures and surprises. Something had begun, something unknown and impossible. Maddalena thumped her pillow. Even if what she felt was love, she couldn't marry Akira or anyone like him. He had Japanese blood, and that made him more of a fantasy than Clark Gable. Maybe in San Francisco, where real things happened, where people wore beautiful clothes and went to the movies and restaurants and strolled along the bay, it would be permissible for an Italian girl and a Japanese boy to be together. But not here. People in Owens Valley didn't think that way. Her parents already spoke of her marrying one of the boys in town, someone steady and good with the land. There weren't any other Italians in Lone Pine; if there were, Mama would want one of their sons to marry her daughter, even if he was ugly and Maddalena didn't give a fig about him. She might as well forget about San Francisco.

Curled on her side, Maddalena gazed at the night sky and wondered whether Akira was asleep. How could anyone sleep behind barbed wire, trapped like an animal? She imagined him curled up beside her, a coyote no one could catch.

TEN

July 3, 1945

By the summer of 1945, Manzanar had become part of the valley's landscape. Though the war in Europe had ended, Japan remained defiant; in America, we remained prisoners.

Gradually, fear and hatred of us seemed to diminish. Many of the valley's residents came to our festivals and concerts, watched our children graduate from high school and win baseball games, admired our gardens and asked us how we could coax lushness from the earth when their own efforts shriveled in the sun and frayed in the wind. They set aside the guns they'd bought when they heard we were coming. And why wouldn't they have feared us? They too had been lied to.

Some people, though, would always hate us. This we knew. We wondered if Akira and the white girl understood. These people couldn't see beyond their hatred, refused to take off their blinders. We accepted their judgment. *Shikata ga nai,* we said to one another with a sigh or a shrug. It cannot be helped. *Shikata ga nai,* we said when we rose in the morning, when we lined up for the latrine or for the inedible food we had learned to eat. We said that every day for three years, every day since we were torn from our homes. Every day, we struggled to preserve our dignity. A difficult task.

Shikata ga nai. We endured, found beauty in ugliness, patience in work, peace in etching out small pleasures. We worked hard to make Manzanar feel like home, though we knew such a thing was impossible. Time helped. What could never be a home became familiar, and there was comfort in that. Now, linoleum covered the floors we could see through

74

when we first arrived; ceilings closed off open rafters that had carried our whispers and coughs and moans and smells from one end of the barracks to the other; wallboard sealed cracks sought by the wind and covered knotholes once patched with the lids of tin cans; dividers imitated privacy in the bathrooms where the toilets stood inches apart. Bright-colored curtains flapped in our windows.

We endured. We made rock gardens, built a waterfall.

As the years passed, we were given what we had not lacked until we came to Manzanar, as if we should be grateful: schools and churches, a hospital. Laundry rooms and a hair salon, an auditorium with a stage. We were given the chance to work, though it was not work of our choosing. At Manzanar we were firemen and office clerks, cooks and custodians, boiler-room keepers and camouflage net weavers, anything to earn a few dollars, to help to pass the time. Some of us were newspapermen, the *Manzanar Free Press* our mouthpiece. For news of the outside, we old men gathered on stoops, listening to scratchy transmissions from an illegal short-wave radio. It was one way to fight back: hearing what any other American could hear.

We had our ways.

But we had given up homes and businesses, fishing boats and farms. Those who worked shrugged off lethargy, but we held fast to our bitterness. We were not who we wanted to be. We had given up dreams.

A tolerable life does not change an intolerable fact: ten thousand prisoners in the early years. That was before some of us left, forsaking dreams of returning home to accept a conditional freedom, moving to parts of the country where the government believed we would pose no threat. Others, the defiant or rebellious or honest among us, were sent back to Japan for answering "no, no" instead of "yes, yes" to the two impossible questions they asked us about loyalty, questions that could not be answered with a single word, questions that meant different things to different people. And some of us, young men, left Manzanar to join the 442nd, the Japanese American regiment. Dangerous enough to lock up at home, we were trustworthy enough to pick up guns in France and Germany. "Go for broke" was our motto, those of us who became soldiers to defend our country. What did we have to lose?

"Our country." Only those of us who were Nisei, Sansei, born here, could say that. The Issei among us, lacking American blood, had nowhere to set down roots.

Shikata ga nai. The loss of our homes, the indignity and injustice of imprisonment, the desert's brutality—we accepted these things. But acceptance is not forgiveness. We would not forgive the men with guns, nor the men who placed them in towers, ready to shoot for good reason or for no reason at all. In those long years of the war, it didn't matter whom the guards shot at, what flimsy excuse they had. What mattered was that their guns were aimed at *us*. What mattered was that there were shots, and that we heard them and went about our lives.

On a July night with a hot wind blowing, Akira came into the canteen. Four of us, old men with thinning hair and long teeth, were playing cards at a corner table. Young men with round eyeglasses and hair slicked back killed time drinking soda and smoking, wishing for a Coke instead of a LaVida, a pack of Camels or Lucky Strikes instead of the Chelseas we had to make do with. Girls in pleated skirts and buttoned blouses played bridge and tossed smiles at the young men, brash like we used to be, snapping their gum.

Akira went straight to the piano. We watched him; we had little else to do. And we were curious. The shot fired the day before had set women to talking and men to shaking their heads. If the stories were true, Akira was a fool. What business did he have with a white girl, someone who didn't know what we suffered? To her, Manzanar would be nothing more than a blight in the valley, defined by a fence that did nothing to limit her. She would not notice the length of the days as we did; she would not know how cruel the high desert could be when what passed for shelter rattled in the wind, sucked in heat, cracked with cold. The girl would not know the humiliation of living beneath guard towers black against the sky, sun sparking on the barrel of a rifle. She would not understand that their deadly gaze told us we were worthless, subhuman.

We watched him, Akira. Perhaps his parents did not know what he would risk, or perhaps they chose not to know. It would pain them. He was only a boy, unconcerned with risks. We saw it on his face, the excitement, the eagerness. We understood what he did not. Being old, we had little to lose; being young, he had too much. He did not see that. It was no surprise. Most of us had put on blinders—a matter of survival, the acquired apathy of the caged.

That day Akira played scales and tremolos that made us think of waterfalls and fountains. "Play us a song," we called, old men bent and bald with spider-webbed skin. "Play 'I'll Be Seeing You.' " Soda bottles and glasses left wet rings on the scarred table; frayed cards made slapping sounds.

Akira played the song, every note a lament. Afterward, he hunched over, ear to the keyboard, playing a short melody, delicate and lovely. There was heartache in it. Then a single phrase played over and over again, a note changed here or there; the rhythm altered, the tempo. This way, that way, now this again, and again, so insistent we thought we would go mad.

Annabelle walked in, light in her eyes. She stood next to Akira, smiling, and bore his inattention. He paused, began again. She sat next to him on the bench, fluffed and smoothed her skirt. Akira played, his head down. Could she not see his disinterest? We whispered among ourselves, wrinkled faces over wrinkled cards, young smooth faces half hidden behind hands cupping cigarettes. Annabelle's eyes announced her desire, told us what she dreamed of—a husband at her side, a child on her knee. Foolish girl, what had she given up for him? Her pride, her virtue? More than she would have given up at home, that much we knew. A desolate place led to desperation.

The war would not be kind to Annabelle, but she did not know that yet. We old men, having the advantage of maleness and being past the age where loss sears like boiling water on flesh, we could bear the war and its residue. Having already lived long, we would not measure our remaining days against the background of our imprisonment. Annabelle would. The camp, we knew, would take too much from her—youth, pride, hope. It would take Akira too. His mind was elsewhere, his heart not bound by barbed wire. We knew this because we had once been like him.

Annabelle leaned in, her shoulder brushing his. We wished we were young again. The strength of her body, the firmness of her flesh, the clarity in her eyes—we remembered these things, wanted them anew. Nodding to one another, we dreamed briefly of desire. Fanning our cards, stacking our coins, sucking our toothpicks, we let our gaze slide toward the girl and linger. We would never stop wanting.

The door swung open, ushered in a hard wind that smelled of emptiness. Two men entered, one of them Annabelle's brother, Harry. He wore a goatee, a sharp-eyed look, and walked like a mountain lion tasting rabbit in the air. His friend Jiro wore the sleeves of his white T-shirt rolled up, short hair that showed his scalp. He strolled, the world his. They ordered sodas, pulled out cigarettes, watched Annabelle and Akira.

Annabelle's fingers crept to Akira's arm. "Please," Akira said, still playing. Her hand retreated.

Harry sprang to the piano. "What gives?" he said. Annabelle shook her head, eyes pleading. Jiro stood by, ready to launch. Akira said nothing, his eyes and hands on the keys. Harry flicked the keyboard cover and it thudded onto Akira's wrists.

"Harry!" Annabelle said.

"Damn it!" Akira pushed the cover up. "You got a problem?"

"I said what gives? First you take what you shouldn't from my little sister—"

"Harry, stop." Annabelle's face was pale.

"And now you act like she's not worth your time. No one treats my sister like that."

The air lost its emptiness. We angled our bodies in our chairs, took our elbows off the counter, stopped on our way out the door. Everywhere eyes turned toward the piano, faces brightened. This we did not want to miss. This was what we had become.

"Annabelle and I are none of your business," Akira said.

Harry cocked his head. "You're wrong about that. You make her unhappy and I'll kill you," he said. Jiro laughed.

"I don't hear Annabelle complaining," Akira said.

Annabelle stood, a trembling leaf. "Harry, walk me home. You're embarrassing me."

Harry didn't answer, his eyes on Akira.

"Please, Harry."

Akira stood. "I'll walk you."

"Like hell you will," Harry said. "Come on, Annabelle. This loser's not worth your time."

Jiro followed them. "Watch your step," he said to Akira, jutting his chin.

Akira began to play again and we picked up our cards, went back to our conversations. What had happened this night would not be the end of it, that much we knew. Akira saw only the white girl, the freedom beyond the fence. Not the danger inside the cage. Not the danger outside it.

ELEVEN

March 7, 2011

The morning after dinner at the Kanekos', Kira woke up flattened by fear, convinced something was wrong with her, something she couldn't categorize or articulate without sounding like a madwoman. Two daytime dreams. Whatever was going on, she wanted it to fit into the world she understood, a system of protocols, procedures, actions with prescribed effects and projected outcomes, a semblance of order, predictability, control. But those rules proved fallible too, every time a baby died who should have made it, every time a medication or surgery failed. Rules and order were artificial and arbitrary; people did what they had to in order to survive.

Dan came in bearing coffee. "Headache any better?"

"A little."

"Mom called. She's worried about you. So am I."

"I'll be okay."

"We need to talk about this," Dan said. "You need to see a doctor."

Kira stalked to the bathroom and closed the door. From the bedroom, silence at first, then soft footsteps, the click of the closet door, blinds snapping open. Dan was undoubtedly waiting, hoping, for the answer he wanted. She let the shower run and stood next to it on the cold tiles, still in her pajamas, until he called goodbye and left for work. Then she went back to bed and googled "dreaming while awake" and "causes of hallucinations." Failing to find anything reassuring, she pushed her laptop aside and curled up under the covers.

In the late afternoon Kira moved to the couch and flipped

80

through the family albums again. There was her mother in a peasant blouse and bell-bottoms, her chestnut hair cut in long layers, standing next to the koi pond and holding an infant Kira. Kira's father must have taken the photo—Rosa was laughing, her bare arms toned and strong, her gaze suggestive. In that moment, did she have any inkling that she'd be abandoned in a few years, left alone to raise a toddler? She had carried abandonment in her body like she'd carried Kira—herself motherless since age seventeen, and the daughter of a man she rarely mentioned. Her husband's desertion would become a variation on a theme.

What had Rosa dreamed of as a child, a young woman? Motherhood, certainly; she'd often said how much she'd wanted Kira. Surely, as a Cal grad, she had aspired to more than the spirit-drowning secretarial jobs she'd worked for years in church offices and real estate agencies, days spent answering the phone and making order of other people's messes. What had stopped her from achieving more? What darkness of spirit had sent her to her room time after time? Why hadn't she remarried?

Questions with no answers.

If only loving her mother hadn't required so much negotiated silence. Kira could bring up school, clothes, friends, vacations, or what she wanted for dinner, and Rosa would chat brightly, full of ideas and questions. Bring up Rosa's husband, mother, or childhood, though, and she retreated behind a barrier as impermeable as bedrock. Kira had inherited that habit of retreat, both desired and resented it. Yet in marrying Dan, choosing to have a child with him, she'd let her bedrock wall become porous like tufa or brittle like limestone, breachable by absorption or a blow. But that was before Aimi died.

Kira envied Camille, who told her husband everything and trusted him enough to bear three children within five years. What crucial ingredient did Cam have that Kira lacked?

81

The sound of the front door opening interrupted her thoughts. "Dan, come and look at this picture of Mom and me," Kira said. "Doesn't she look like an Italian Farrah Fawcett?"

"Totally," Dan said, looking over her shoulder. He kissed her hair. "She was beautiful. I know how much you miss her. I miss her too."

Kira nodded. Dan had loved Rosa. He didn't define his relationship with her through Kira; he acted more like a son than a son-in-law, stopping by Rosa's house to see if she needed anything, suggesting small home improvement projects, helping her tame the garden after heavy rains. Dan had married into the fragments of a family and tried to make it whole, not realizing that he could never make up for the loss of a father or a husband. Or maybe he did know that, but Kira didn't grant him that grace. She had told him often enough that when everyone got together—their little triad and the Kaneko clan—the crowded table was her childhood dream made real. What she didn't tell him was that the contrast made the emptiness of her childhood resound, reminded her of everything her mother couldn't give her. Of the limits of love.

Last night there had been seven of them at the table. There should have been nine, even ten if Kira's father had stuck around. At any moment there might be six, or five, or four. You never knew. Dan's family seemed borrowed, not owned, as easily taken away as Kira's father, her mother, her child. What if, in losing the parents and child she had loved so intensely—the bookends of her bloodline—she had lost her capacity to love anyone else?

Kira closed the photo album and wept.

"Hey, sweetie, it's going to be okay," Dan said. "We'll get through this, I promise." He kissed her, and she responded at first. When she pulled away, Dan sat quietly for a moment, then put a hand on hers and went into the kitchen.

Kira was pushing him, she knew. The way Dan saw it, love was love—romantic, friendship, maternal, whatever— and if it existed, you couldn't deny it or change it. Some connections are simply there, he said, maybe inexplicable but *there*. He liked to talk about existence as a continuum. One time, in the early months of their relationship, they'd lingered in bed after making love and he'd said he felt like he'd always known her, like they had been lovers in another life, in another spectrum of time, and maybe they would be again someday as different souls, or as the same souls in different bodies. Teasing him, Kira had accused Dan of believing in reincarnation or being overly romantic, which were perhaps the same thing.

"Why do you think anyone knows what's real and what's not?" he'd said. "Can you define truth? Can you prove reincarnation doesn't exist? I can't. You're trying to put things that have no form into boxes that will define them. Let them be what they are. Some things are nameless."

Kira hadn't known what to say to that. Dan thought in ways that were more like water than granite. While he questioned ideas and opinions, he was convinced that something unbreakable bound him to her, something that needed no explanation. Dan believed in love without boundaries. He would give her that, if she let him.

From the kitchen, he called to Kira to come and eat. He'd set out glasses of red wine, leftover pasta, a thrown-together salad.

They ate in silence. Then Kira said, "I'm going to Mom's tomorrow."

"What for?"

"I need to look through her stuff. I want to try to find that man my mom talked about." She hadn't thought about the man in weeks, Kira realized; now she felt compelled to find him.

"It can wait."

"Actually, I don't think it can."

"You are the most stubborn woman on the planet. I really think you should rest, and I'm serious about you seeing a doctor."

"I need to do this."

"I've got a full day tomorrow. We can go Wednesday."

"I'm going tomorrow." Kira wanted the empty house, the privacy. Dan wasn't part of the plan.

Dan drained his wineglass. "You win. But I'm going with you. End of discussion."

He would do that for her. Truth was, he would do anything for her.

"There's got to be something in the house about that man," Kira said. "Or maybe I'll remember something Mom told me about him when I was a kid."

"Yeah, places can do that—trigger memories, the way smells do." Dan put his plate and silverware in the dishwasher. "I'm gonna take a shower."

When the shower was running, Kira went upstairs, past their bedroom to the room that would have been Aimi's. Leaning against the closed door, she pressed her cheek and palms against the cool wood. They'd gotten as far as painting the walls egg-yolk yellow and putting up a Winnie-the-Pooh wallpaper border at crib height, where Aimi could see it as she grew. The bamboo floor remained unfinished, and the crib, the bedding, the changing table, the bouncy chair, the toys and mobiles and onesies and booties that Kira and Rosa couldn't resist buying months in advance—those remained in the closet or stacked in boxes against the wall. Kira hadn't opened the door since Aimi's death, and as far as she knew Dan hadn't either.

She leaned against the door, energy evaporating. This was her ritual, once or twice a day. Usually she ended up sinking to the floor outside Aimi's room and gazing at the skylight, where sparrows or chickadees lined up on its edge, chubby silhouettes in the rectangular sky. They would chatter as if discussing her strange behavior, then fly off, leaving her to stare into the birdless brightness.

She touched the doorknob. Her baby should be sleeping on the other side of the door. In that empty, dusty room, there should be the soft breath of a child, wails and murmurs, the warm scent of life. There should be Aimi, dreaming sweet dreams.

They left for Martinez at eleven the next morning, after Dan had grilled Kira about how she felt, whether she was sure she was up to it, what the doctor's office had said. She had an appointment with her GP in a week, Kira said, the earliest available. It was true, and so was the fact that appointments could be canceled.

Forty minutes later they were in Martinez, rounding the corner onto Haven Street. "What a mess," Dan said as he stopped the car in front of Rosa's white Victorian. Dust and debris dulled the front porch, and flyers bloomed on the screen door. The roses climbing the fence sported fleshy pea-green whips, and two butterfly bushes drooped like shaggy dogs.

"Mom would be—"

"Mortified," Dan said. "I know. According to my calculations, based on frequency of use, it was her favorite word."

Kira laughed. "Thank you for the analysis. I love that you remember that."

"So much for the landscaper I hired."

"Oh my God, the fish!" Kira took off for the backyard.

"They're fine," Dan called after her. "The neighbor is feeding them." He caught up with her and kept going, into the garden beyond.

Kira stood beside the pond, her sneakers damp from the

tall grass. A koi the length of her hand surfaced, flashing golden in the murky water. Ripples fragmented on lily pads and spiraled outward from orange-lipped kisses. The statue of the Virgin Mary peered out from her niche, looking serene despite the splash of bird poop on her pale blue cowl. Serenity, Kira thought. She could use some of that.

She turned to face the house. In the Farrah Fawcett photo, her mother was standing right here at the pond's edge, baby on her hip, smiling at her husband, allure in her eyes. Vivacious and confident, with no sign of the darkness that Kira, as a child, a teen, a young woman, had seen in her. What had happened to Rosa that made her so unhappy?

"Look at this," Dan said, coming back from the garden. "Mint and lemon verbena. It's like a hothouse back there. The mint is overpowering."

Dan's face was alight; he hadn't smiled like this since Rosa died, Kira thought. He was happy to be here with her today, happy that she'd called the doctor. He probably thought they were on their way back to normal, a word she no longer knew how to define.

"I'll make some tea," Dan said, and she followed him to the house.

The back door opened and the airless rooms sighed, then gathered breath. Kira hovered at the threshold. This place that held so many memories, where so much had been hidden, perhaps forever—now the house thrust hope at her, seemed to say *Yes, yes, you are here where you should be.* A path opened through her muddled thoughts, as labyrinthine as the house's narrow hallways, but promising. Promising what? From the layers of fear and doubt that consumed her, a thought emerged: the dreams meant something. Maybe this place of memories had something to tell her. If there were answers—why the dreams, why she was having them, who the girl was, the protagonist of this story Kira didn't understand—maybe she would find them here.

In the kitchen, brown stalks and withered blooms sagged in a green vase on the table. A sugar bowl squatted next to its lid on the counter, and in the sink, petrified cornflakes crowned the rim of a cereal bowl. Evidence of Rosa, a life interrupted.

"Let's air this place out," Dan said. He went from room to room, opening windows and stacking magazines and newspapers. A breeze swept in to dispel the sadness, clamoring of spring, the early bloom of acacias.

Walking through the house, Kira tried to avert her eyes from the omnipresence of loss. In the dining room, a white lace cloth sheltered the oval table's dark wood, and buttery tapers stood in cut-glass candlesticks. Majolica pottery splashed blues, yellows, greens, and oranges onto the white-painted shelves of a built-in cabinet. In the living room, she picked up a CD case from the coffee table—Andrea Bocelli singing opera excerpts, art songs, and Rosa's favorite, "Ave Maria," which she'd instructed Kira, at least a dozen times over the years, to play at her funeral. Kira didn't want to hear the song ever again.

Everything looked familiar and completely wrong.

Dan jogged up the stairs. Upstairs was her mother's bedroom, above that the attic weighted with cobwebs and silence. Kira went into the office, once her bedroom, reminding her of the child she'd been, long before innocence became regret. The desk chair stood at an angle, as if her mother had pushed it back moments before, had gone, perhaps, to the kitchen or bathroom and would return any second. Kira picked up the navy mohair cardigan draped over the back of the chair, held it to her face. A hint of Shalimar, a few gray hairs threaded into the loose weave. Essence of mother.

She straightened the chair and sat, flipped through the bills, shopping lists, and junk mail piled on the desk. Shoved against the wall amid the clutter, a silver frame held a five-by-eight photo of her grandmother Maddalena, her hair knotted low, her eyes sad and distant. The photo had traveled the house over the years, from the mantel to a sideboard to the desk, as if Rosa couldn't let her mother rest. How often had she thought of Maddalena? Had she ever forgiven her mother for leaving her?

Kira dusted the glass with her sleeve and returned the photo to its place. The thought of sorting through her mother's belongings made her want to sleep for a solid year. For today, tidying up would be enough.

Back in the kitchen, she submerged the crusted cereal bowl in warm water, returned the lid to the sugar bowl. Gathering the wilted flowers from the vase on the table, she dropped them, her hands flaring hot. Instantly the room color-shifted and a scene appeared—a small bedroom, a single window, a dresser with a mirror, everything in soft focus as if seen through gauze. Her protagonist, a teenager in a wedding dress, with an older woman standing behind her.

My bouquet is store bought, pink and white carnations and too much baby's breath, stiff like cardboard. I'm glad there's no scent because it would have sickened me. My hair is up, pulled tight like he never would have wanted it, my face in the mirror pale with powder and sadness. My dress isn't my mother's wedding gown, the silk one heavy with embroidery, fitted at the waist, the one she said a thousand times I'd wear someday. This dress is plain, a cheap satin sack from a catalogue, a size too large so that my body floats within it. It's all you deserve, my mother said. Her face is flat, unforgiving. She pins a veil to my hair, tells me to be still. I stand still as death, my eyes on the mountains that guard the desert floor.

Footsteps intruded, drumming down the stairs. Dan's voice, distant but rising. The scene disappeared and Kira leaned on the kitchen table, head in her hands. That shapeless dress, the scentless bouquet—she ached for the girl.

"Did you hear me? I found mouse droppings upstairs. We should—" Dan froze in the doorway, bundled newspapers under one arm. "What's wrong?" He dropped the papers and rushed to her.

Three times now, Kira thought. Not chance, not hallucinations, but something intended. The dreams weren't random; they were a path through this maze of the unknown. The girl had a baby, but clearly she wasn't happy to be getting married. Whom did she love? What did she fear?

"Kira, talk to me."

Dan was worried, frightened, and he loved her; she owed him an explanation, or as close to one as she could get. Yet the urge for secrecy was overwhelming. The dreams seemed to target something deep inside Kira, in her family, her childhood. She couldn't identify it yet, but she knew it was as personal as her breath. She met Dan's gaze. Stay silent, or trust that he would believe her? He would, wouldn't he? After all, he talked about reincarnation, the metaphysical, the intangible force between them.

"I'm okay," Kira said. "I think what's happening is—oh God, this sounds so crazy, but when I picked up the dead flowers to throw them away, I had a kind of a dream, just for a few seconds. But I wasn't asleep."

"You were hallucinating?"

"No, I don't think so. I can't explain why, but this is different. It's happened three times now."

"Three times, and you're just now telling me?" Dan paled. "Shit. This is what happened at my parents' house."

"Yes. They're like memories, but not *my* memories. Someone else's." Realization came as Kira spoke. "I think they're real. I think they happened."

Dan stared at her. "We've got to get you some help, sweetie. Jesus, I had no idea things were this bad. This is fucking serious. We're going to the ER." He ran his hands through his hair, as distraught as she'd ever seen him.

"Wait." If she let him believe the dreams weren't real, that they were something a trip to the ER could fix, then their marriage was over right now. She needed to tell him—no, show him, what she'd seen.

Dan waited, his world collapsing.

"I want you to do something." Kira rummaged in the junk drawer for a pencil and paper. "Here. Sketch what I describe." He started to protest and she cut him off. "Please."

Sitting at the table, Kira talked and Dan drew. When he finished, Kira stared at the sketch, trying to reconcile what he'd drawn with what she'd told him. She'd described the room, the girl's dress, the mountains through the window, and he'd gotten all of it right. But he'd also captured sadness in the girl, judgment in the woman, an overwhelming sense of grief in the room. All true, but she hadn't mentioned any of it.

"Dan?" She put a hand on his arm and his muscles quivered. "How did you know the girl was sad?"

"I don't know. That's how I saw her. Why?"

"Because I didn't tell you she was sad. But she was."

Kira reached for the paper. In the dream, the women's faces were indistinct; yet the girl in the sketch, the planes and lines of her face and neck, they reminded her of Maddalena. Lightning flickered down her spine. "Wait a minute." She went to the office and got the photo of Maddalena. "Look."

"Holy shit. I drew your grandmother?"

Dan had drawn something that existed only in her head, had filled in details she hadn't mentioned. There was no explanation for that. But then, the threads of the universe, the known and the unknown, couldn't be explained either, not entirely. So why couldn't these dreams be truths too, glimpses of a reality that wasn't her own? Maybe, in giving voice to these images, she'd made them real to Dan too, revealed the story they seemed intended to tell. What if the girl *was* Maddalena, and the dreams delivered some as-yet-unknown truth?

If the girl was Maddalena… Kira looked at the drawing

again, fear spiraling through her. That heat in her hands right before the color shift—the same thing had happened when her mother died. Her fear spiked again, then vanished. She didn't understand what was happening, not yet. But she needed to.

Kira stood, pulling Dan up with her. "It'll be okay. At least I think so." Wrapping her arms around him, she fitted her body into the comforting angles and hollows of his. She'd made the right choice in telling him, but he would have to decide what to believe.

It was obvious now, what she needed to do—find out why these images were coming to her, what they meant. And she had to start where she could get closest to Maddalena, here, in this house. She had to enter the maze, alone.

As if he knew what she was thinking, Dan nudged her into a kiss. Kira acquiesced, then released him. Dan wasn't part of this. Already he seemed less tangible, spiraling away from her consciousness as he had when she'd gone into labor with Aimi. Whatever was ahead, she would face it on her own.

TWELVE

July 3, 1945

Maddalena gave the coffee table one last swipe of polish and surveyed the living room. The house was neat as a pin, and any minute now Regina would arrive to stay overnight and celebrate the Fourth of July. Maddalena bounced on her toes with anticipation. She had decided to tell Regina about Akira, partly because keeping him a secret was like trying to hold her breath forever, and partly because she wanted to write him a letter and she needed Regina's help. Neither of them had any experience writing letters to boys, but between the two of them they'd figure it out. Then she would ride into the open desert, away from this suffocating house, and give the letter to Akira. She'd already figured out how to do it. And she had to act fast. The war could end any time now, everyone said it would, and then Akira would go back to wherever he came from, maybe without ever seeing her again. She couldn't let that happen.

"Lena, if you're done in here, help me with supper," her mother said, bustling in and turning on the radio loud enough to hear it in the kitchen. *Amanda of Honeymoon Hill*, as usual. A couple in love, doomed to constant troubles that always ended happily. Predictable, which was why her mother liked it and Maddalena hated it.

"Lena, did you hear me?"

From the radio, the breathy gushing of Amanda, then her deep-voiced beau declaring undying love. Maddalena pictured Akira, his arms around her, leaning in to kiss her.

"Maddalena!"

"Yes, Mama." Maddalena flushed. Thinking about Akira when her parents were nearby made her feel like she'd done something terrible.

Half an hour later Regina burst through the back door, hauling a pink suitcase and waving an issue of *Movie Mirror*. "Lena! Look at my hair!" She spun around.

Regina's hair, which usually framed her face in straight blonde curtains, now swept high from her forehead and curled in soft ringlets around her neck. "It's a Lana Turner 'do. I had to sleep on prickly rollers all night, but it was worth it."

"Awfully fancy for a girl your age," Mama said. "You girls can set the table now."

Maddalena rolled her eyes. "I think you look beautiful," she whispered.

After supper was over, an eternity of talk about livestock and weather forecasts and the autumn apple crop, the girls cleaned up the kitchen and ran upstairs. Maddalena closed the bedroom door, then the window.

"Are you crazy? Open the window, I'm dying." Regina sprawled on the floor, fanning herself.

"It's only for a minute. I have something to tell you." Maddalena sat cross-legged on the floor. "Can you keep a secret?"

Regina bolted upright. "Of course!"

"Cross your heart?"

Regina made an *X* on her chest, and Maddalena told her everything, from her encounter with Akira at the baseball game, to seeing him again on her rides to Manzanar, to getting shot at. The words flew out, and Regina listened with her mouth half open, her face shining like it did when she talked about Robert Taylor. But this was different. This was real life, a matter of life and death.

When Maddalena got to the part about the gunshot, Regina clapped a hand over her mouth, her blue eyes big as an owl's. "Heavens, it's so romantic!" she said. "But *dangerous*! What are you going to do?"

"I'm going to write a letter, and I need your help." Maddalena got a pencil and paper from her nightstand.

"You're crazy! Why don't you go after Rickie Hutchins? I think he likes you. He plays baseball too, you know."

Of course Regina would say something like that. She'd had crushes on at least six boys since eighth grade, and she'd let Frankie Mitchell kiss her at the last sock hop. She probably thought crushes were the same thing as love.

"This is different," Maddalena said. "Don't ask me how I know, but I do. Now think. What should I say? And don't try to talk me out of it."

"All right. Say 'Dear'—what's his name?"

"Akira."

"How about 'My darling Akira'?"

Maddalena shook her head. "That would scare him off."

"Well, say 'Dear Akira,' then. Tell him your name, and how old you are, of course; that's important. And where you live."

"All right." Maddalena started writing, then jumped at a rap on the door. She shoved the paper and pencil under her skirt.

"I'm going out to the garden," her mother said through the half-open door. "There's a casserole in the oven. Take it out when the timer goes off and set it on the stove."

"Yes, Mama. How long should it cook?"

"Forty minutes. Don't forget to close the damper. And open that window before you die of heat."

"Yes, Mama."

When the door closed, Regina whispered, "That was close!"

"Time me," Maddalena said, picking up the pencil. "I have to be done in exactly thirty-nine minutes."

Twenty-five minutes later Maddalena read aloud what she'd written.

Dear Akira,

My name is Maddalena Moretti, and I'm the girl the guards shot at because I got too close to the fence. You talked to me at the baseball game, remember? You saved me from being hit by a ball. I'm fifteen years old. I guess I should say sixteen, because my birthday is next week. How old are you?

"That's good." Regina nodded, her chin on her fist. "But I think you should say he's your true love."

"This isn't a movie, Regina, it's real life. People don't say things like that to someone they've just met."

I live on a ranch near Lone Pine. That's south of Manzanar, if you don't know. I want to see you again. My friend Regina lives north of Manzanar, so I can ride by the camp when I go to her house. Or I can pretend to go to her house sometimes, because everyone around here knows we're friends and they're used to seeing me on Foothill Road. But I have to be careful because people around here have eyes in the back of their heads and gossip like magpies.

Regina giggled. "You told him about me!"

"You're part of this. You're the keeper of my secret now." Maddalena studied the page. "I suppose I should tell him when I'll be back so he'll know to watch for me."

"Say you'll come back two days after he gets the letter," Regina said. "That will give him time to reply."

"Good idea."

The ending was the hardest part. It was too soon to say "love," and "sincerely" sounded stupid.

"Use your initial," Regina said. "That's how they do it in the movies. An *M* with a big swirl after it."

"Good idea."

I'll come back in two days. I hope you'll write to me.

~M~

p.s. My parents would kill me if they knew what I was doing.

p.p.s. I think it's terrible that you're locked up. I hope this stupid war ends soon.

p.p.p.s. I think we are destined to meet again.

p.p.p.p.s. I mean it.

"There. Done."

"It's perfect," Regina said. "He'll be powerless to resist you."

Maddalena wrapped the paper around a rock the size of her palm, using six rubber bands, blue ones to make it as pretty as a wrapped-up rock could be. Everything was ready. All she had to do was wait.

&

Akira squinted into the sun. His back ached from weeding, and there was a ton of work left to do. The beans, running crazy on twisted vines, needed to be staked and the lettuce thinned. The marigolds that were supposed to keep bugs away from the vegetables were nothing but papery skeletons, their heads frayed on broken necks, crumbling at the slightest touch. He would take them out, restore order, simplify. He stretched, and the movement pulled his soaked shirt away from his skin for a blissful second.

Helping his mother in the garden had been a good idea. It made her happy, and that made him feel less guilty—not that she knew about the girl, and not that any amount of gardening would make up, as far as she was concerned, for his interest in someone who wasn't Japanese. But what his parents didn't know wouldn't hurt them. Whether the girl offered adventure or something more, Akira didn't know. Maybe he just liked the *idea* of her, the newness, the distraction. It didn't matter. For now, distraction was enough.

His mother had worked her way to the end of a row of cabbages, her narrow shoulders rounded against the sun. Akira knew that making things grow in this desert soil gave her pleasure, but he couldn't remember the last time he'd seen her smile. She had become as dull and colorless as the gray in her hair.

"Akira!" Annabelle waved, walking toward him, hips like

music. "See you tonight, same time, same station?" she said softly, glancing toward his mother. "We can go for a walk. You and me, alone." She bit her lip and smiled.

"What about Harry?"

"He's not my keeper. I told him so."

"I don't know. I might play cards."

"Oh, you men and your gambling." She tossed her head, then gave him a peck on the cheek. "You know where to find me."

"Sure thing." Akira began staking the runaway beans. He didn't want to see Annabelle, not tonight. The mood he was in, the piano was more tempting than she was. He was writing a song, and he'd only half admitted to himself that it was for the girl on the horse.

That evening Akira offered to have dinner with his parents, and when they responded gratefully he felt ashamed. A neglectful son, that's what he was. At one time he wouldn't have thought that was possible, but everything had changed. His parents used to take pleasure in the smallest things—a ladybug climbing the stem of a cut rose, cold steam rising from a wet railing drying in the morning sun, a Bach cello suite. Now, his parents merely existed. That was Manzanar's fault. Existence wasn't good enough, not for him. He wanted to *live*.

In the mess hall, Akira followed his parents through the line, carrying his mother's tray. His mother refused the hot dogs and creamed spinach, choosing only rice and watery coleslaw. When she picked up her fork to eat, the round bone of her wrist stuck out, a golf ball instead of a marble. His father was thin too, the cords in his neck arching like fishing rods.

They ate silently, quickly. A chore to be completed.

"Can I get you more rice, Mom?" Akira said.

"Yes, please." His mother set down her fork and put her hands in her lap.

97

"Thank you, son," his father said when Akira returned. He held his son's gaze for a fraction of a second longer than was proper.

Akira spooned rice onto his mother's plate. "Eat," he said. "Please eat."

❧

The canteen was packed that night. Someone at the piano was banging out "Shoo Shoo Baby" while a trio of girls sang along. Voices and laughter rose above the music. Tables were strewn with decks of cards and packs of cigarettes, soda bottles and half-filled glasses, and half a dozen couples shuffled around in a semblance of a dance, wet shirts stuck to their backs. The place smelled like a barn.

Akira bought an orange LaVida and wandered over to a poker game in the corner, where four guys sat in a cloud of smoke.

"You want in?" asked the dealer.

"Nah," Akira said. "I'm not in the mood."

It was Gus at the keyboard, and he was damn good, even on a piano so decrepit he claimed it made him want to cry. Before Manzanar, he'd been a music teacher in L.A. He was in his thirties, a short, bouncy guy with lank hair thinning in front, but he was pouring on the charm for the girls tonight, all smiles and jump jiving on the piano bench. He launched into "Don't Fence Me In" and everyone whooped and sang along, cupping their hands like megaphones as if serenading the guards. The girls threw out song titles and Gus played one into the other, from "In the Mood" to "Rum and Coca-Cola" to "Sentimental Journey" with hardly a breath between them. It was clear that Akira would get no time at the keyboard that night.

Lighting a cigarette, he bummed a pencil stub from one of the fellows and sketched a music staff on a napkin. The first few bars of his song were solid, but he couldn't get beyond them, what with Gus's jazzy syncopations and all the noise in the room. After ten minutes of trying he pitched the napkin into a trashcan and left. Striding past barracks, their stoops dotted with bored women and restless men, windows lit in sickly yellow, he headed toward the midnight void of desert and mountains. The girl was out there somewhere, far away and free. Akira took off his glasses and wiped his eyes, pushing hard until the blackness shattered. Somewhere in front of him was the end of the street, the fence beyond it.

Akira put his glasses in his pocket and broke into a run. Near the fence, a flash of blue-white light caught him and his shadow danced in front of him, twice his height. He turned, walked backward, saw nothing but the blinding light, felt nothing but the crosshairs of a gun. Raising his hands, he dropped to his knees and the light swung off him. Laughter drifted from the canteen, distant as another world, as the girl beyond the fence.

Thirteen

March 11, 2011

Kira was leaving for work when Dan's phone rang. He listened to the caller for a moment, then turned to her. "Turn on the news when you get in the car. Dad says there was an earthquake and tsunami in Japan, really bad."

"Oh no! Is his family okay?" Kenji's uncle and cousins lived near Tokyo. Dan shrugged, listening. "Let me know as soon as you have any news," Kira said.

When she got to work, the NICU was buzzing with talk about the disaster, and it didn't let up. But her day passed quietly, with two stable feeders—no vents, no arterial lines, no dicey blood counts, just two babies who were learning how to breathe and eat at the same time. So far both of them were better at vomiting than nippling, but they were getting the hang of it. At midday Dan called to say Kenji's relatives were safe. Kira finished feeding baby number two, and when he settled with a sigh, a lovely weight in her arms, she relaxed too. He would be fine, one of the lucky ones. His mother too.

Kira was changing a diaper when the night nurse arrived, phone in hand. "I've been glued to YouTube all day," the nurse said. "There's this unbelievable video of a whole village being swept away. You've got to see it."

"I'm not sure I want to," Kira said. "Oh, damn it, you pooped again, you little stinker! It's all over your blanket." Holding the baby with one arm, she rummaged for clean linens in the bedside drawer.

The nurse stuck her phone in front of Kira's face. "Look

at this." Surging water and floating cars, a building flicked off its foundation like a gnat off the back of a hand. A British-toned voiceover spoke of thirty-foot waves, entire schools and villages swept away, untold casualties. Then the announcer said "annihilation" and heat shot through Kira's hands. She grabbed the edge of the bassinette, clutching the baby to her chest. *Not here, not now.* She bent over, tucking the baby into the curve of her body. The color shift began, a rush of salmon to yellow to green.

I'm sitting at the dinner table, my sweaty legs stuck to my chair. On the radio, an urgent voice saying something terrible about a bomb, a city called Hiroshima, a certain end to the war. I can't believe my ears. An end to the war! I repeat the words silently, wanting to cry and rejoice. My father lights his pipe, then says, "Goddamn Japs deserve what they got." My brother smiles; my mother nods. I stare at them in horror and shame, disgusted by my father's lips curling around the pipe stem, the yellow of his teeth.

"I've got him," a voice said. "Kira, what's wrong?"

The room came back into focus and Kira zeroed in on the baby, now in the other nurse's arms. Nausea hit as she realized she could have dropped him. He could have *died.* Dizziness followed the nausea, and she seized it as an excuse. "Yeah, I just…I felt dizzy all of a sudden. I guess I shouldn't have skipped lunch. Thank you for taking him."

Kira gave a quick shift-change report and left, her hands trembling as she opened her locker, still trembling when she got in her car, adrenaline surging at the thought of what could have happened. But that wasn't all. The newscast in her dream, about Hiroshima—if she'd had any last doubts, they were gone. World War II. The girl in the dream *was* Maddalena. Her bloodstream hummed.

At home Dan was chopping vegetables, his laptop perched on the counter streaming the news. Magpie squatted underfoot, gnawing on a piece of wilted parsley.

"My parents are pretty shook up, so I spent the day with

them," Dan said. "They wouldn't turn off the TV. It's unreal. Entire villages gone."

"Yeah, I saw some of the footage. It's so horrible—all those kids." Kira sat at the kitchen island, alternately watching the news and reliving the Hiroshima dream. Amid the scenes of walls made of water, cars and buildings afloat, an overhead shot of a pulverized, inanimate town flashed onto the screen. Absolute devastation.

"Just like Hiroshima."

Kira didn't realize she'd said it aloud until Dan said, "Hardly. But I know what you mean."

She hesitated. She could leave it at that, but at this point there was no reason not to tell him what had happened at work. In the three days since they'd been to her mother's house, Dan had been subdued, obviously worried, but he hadn't mentioned the doctor again except to ask whether she wanted him to go to the appointment with her. She said no, omitting the fact that she'd canceled it. Dan hadn't mentioned the sketch either, which she'd brought home and put in one of the photo albums for safekeeping. Another topic on the Do Not Go There list. She was sick of the silence, the deception.

"I had another dream today. About Hiroshima."

"At work? Shit. That's dangerous." Dan's eyes were still on the computer screen.

"Nothing happened." Kira explained about hearing the man's voice on the YouTube video, and in her dream, the newscaster announcing the end of the war.

"It makes sense," Dan said. "The tsunami, the earthquake, Hiroshima."

"It does? How?"

"Think about it. You just said the footage reminds you of Hiroshima. Devastation in Japan, that's the link. The dream was triggered."

A chill flew down Kira's spine. She grabbed the laptop and

googled "Hiroshima bomb broadcast" while Dan peered over her shoulder. "There, that one," he said, pointing to a YouTube link to a CBS news broadcast from 1945. She clicked on it.

"*Tokyo Radio* finally acknowledged…the use of the atomic bomb against Hiroshima, and admitted that extensive damage was done. Apparently the damage was so great that the Japs aren't sure what hit the place…."

Zero gravity, like freefall. "Jesus. That's it, what I heard during the dream," Kira said. "Or something very close to it." She clicked on another link.

"New air attacks have been thrown against Japan. Washington and other capitals are buzzing with speculation about the new bomb and its possibilities."

"Possibilities? I'll say. For annihilating the world." Dan pushed his glasses up, rubbing his eyes. "God, what a day. Honey, I think we're out of our league. If these things are being triggered, they're probably likely to happen again. I don't think you should go to work until you've seen the doctor."

Kira nodded absently, her eyes on the screen. Everything fit. Hiroshima, the earthquake, the tsunami. Devastation. Maddalena listening to that broadcast, blowing out candles, wearing that wedding dress, holding that baby. The dreams were scenes from her grandmother's life—disjointed scenes, but part of a whole. Pieced together, they might tell her something.

"I think you're right; the video caused the dream," Kira said. "It was a fluke."

"I can't believe you're saying that," Dan said. "From what I've seen these things just sneak up on you."

"Fine, I'll put in a vacation request tomorrow." It was a good idea; she could spend more time at her mother's house. Kira clicked on another broadcast.

A few minutes later Magpie jumped in her lap and Kira

realized the house was silent. Dan had probably gone for a run before dinner, she thought, typing in "triggered memories." Of course there wouldn't be anything about triggering someone *else's* memories, but she searched anyway. Maybe it didn't matter if she found out what Maddalena had wished for on her sixteenth birthday, or why she was sad on her wedding day. And maybe it did. For whatever reason, Maddalena was making herself known.

FOURTEEN

July 8, 1945

Maddalena rode into the desert, the note and rock in her back pocket, digging into her hip like a promise. Or a reminder that she'd tried to see Akira three times with no luck and was beginning to think she'd jinxed the whole thing by telling Regina about him. But surely it was only a matter of time. Maybe today he would read her note; maybe today he would sit down to write to her. "Today, today, today," she sang.

At Manzanar people were everywhere, swarming the streets and stoops and gardens. Old men nodded in the sun, and dozens of hatted women worked the vegetable gardens. A policeman on a horse sashayed over to the fence, and Maddalena was surprised to see that he was Japanese. How strange that a man could be both prisoner and policeman! She waved at him, no longer worried about being seen. She had nothing to hide.

The hospital steps came into view, empty again. If she kept riding, it was over—another failed mission. She would *not* give up. Dropping the reins, she let Scout graze. A cloud of dust announced a pickup truck rumbling north on Foothill Road, reminding her that if her father or Marco were to drive by, there she would be, out of bounds and unmistakable. *Don't borrow trouble,* she thought. The road was far enough away that they probably wouldn't notice her.

Ten minutes later, two older women left the hospital through the side door and set off down the street. Then the door opened again—let it be him!—and the chubby boy she'd seen with Akira appeared and sat on the steps to smoke. A minute went by, then another, and another. Heat rose from the desert floor, shimmering the mountains and laying sheets of sweat across Scout's neck and flanks. Maddalena wiped her face on her sleeve, thinking how terrible it was that she'd look sweaty and ugly if she saw Akira now. Then, all at once, there he was, walking fast down the street—and talking to a girl! A slender girl with bobbed hair, sleek and shiny and perfectly framing her too-pretty face. Pretending she hadn't noticed them, Maddalena clucked at Scout, furious with herself for not realizing Akira might have a girlfriend.

"You're late again," the boy on the steps called to Akira. "Better watch out or they'll start docking your pay."

"Get a life, Paul," Akira said.

He spoke loudly, as if he were trying to get Maddalena's attention. She looked up, and the minute she did, the girl gave her a nasty simpering smile and touched Akira's hand as if she owned him, her gaze triumphant. Maddalena glared at her with her best *malocchio*—the evil eye. "Get your hands off him," she muttered, and the words felt good, violent on her teeth and tongue. A minute later the girl left, swinging her hips like a little *puttana*. Akira watched her go, for longer than he needed to.

Paul stood. "I'll punch you in," he said. "You owe me one."

He left and Maddalena took the rock out of her pocket, eyeing the guard towers. This time she'd be patient. Akira was watching her and pretending he wasn't, one foot on the steps, lighting a cigarette. Then a car backfired somewhere on the east side of the camp and the guards turned and Maddalena threw the rock with all her might. It landed close to the steps and Akira startled, then flashed a surreptitious thumbs-up. Maddalena rode off, certain she'd burst from happiness. Her plan had worked!

Akira grabbed the rock and went inside, slipping into a

storeroom to read it. Damn, she was resourceful! He read the letter quickly. Her name was Maddalena—a beautiful name, so musical—and she was almost sixteen. He'd figured her for pretty young, so that was no surprise. He smiled when she mentioned the ball game and the gunshot—as if he'd forget!

She'd come back in two days. He would be ready.

That night, instead of going to the canteen, Akira stayed home to think about the letter he'd write. Lying on his cot sipping cold tea, he listened to the clicking whisper of his mother's knitting needles. The note was stashed in his shaving kit, the only place his mother wouldn't find it. His parents sat quietly as they always did, unaware that his world was about to change. His father was reading, his mother making a scarf from the last of the wool she'd brought from home—good wool, she said, not the cheap yarn sold in the commissary. She knitted to keep busy, not because anyone needed another scarf.

An hour passed. "Akira, please help me," his mother said.

He sat next to her and held out his hands, palms facing inward, fingers toward the ceiling, and she wound the strands of yarn around his fingers, untangling them as she went. Teasing, Akira said, "Is it the wind or the rats that tangle the yarn?"

His mother didn't respond. This was a ritual of hers, one that seemed to calm her. She tangled the yarn herself, to give her something to undo, something to make right, since there was so little else that was right in her world. He understood that. People did whatever it took to get through the days, the endless waiting. For his mother, it was knitting and gardening; for his father, books and daily games of *goh*; for himself, work and Annabelle, and an idea he had about going to law school and helping Japanese Americans when he got out of here. And now Maddalena.

His mother's fingers grazed his, her once-soft skin thick and rough. So many things changed in wartime, in ways a person could never imagine. His parents had wilted, but Akira felt like a live round waiting to blow.

"I'm going for a walk," he said.

The air was crisp, the stars an arm's length away. To the east and west of camp the mountains slumbered, one more barrier between Manzanar and the rest of the world. Berkeley seemed unreal, a dream lost upon waking. Akira followed the line of the fence, dodging the searchlights. Leaving Manzanar to see Maddalena would be worth braving the guards and their guns. The real risk was that out there, with miles of sand and air around him unbroken by any fence, he would remember what it felt like to be free.

FIFTEEN

March 14, 2011

When Kira got up the day of her canceled doctor's appointment, Dan was gone, off to work early according to a note she found with a stack of papers on the kitchen counter. The note continued: *I pulled this info together for you, and I wanted you to have it for your appointment today. Not sure if any of it's relevant, but take a look. Love, Dan*

"Love, Dan." Not a couple of *x*'s or a cartoon heart, but a deliberate, sprawling "love." Kira touched the ink, carved into Dan's favorite heavy paper stock with a calligraphic flourish. He was reminding her of what they'd had, what they could have again. No doubt he thought that if he tried hard enough, and long enough, he could convince her it was possible. Love for him, or the memory of it, flickered in her brain until thoughts of Maddalena and her dreamed life shoved it aside. Immediately the self-recriminations began: Kira was a failure, first at motherhood, now at marriage.

She made coffee, fed the cat twining around her legs, and sat down to read. Camille was due to pick her up at nine-thirty. They'd been texting almost daily, and when Kira mentioned her plan to go through her mother's things, Camille insisted on helping. Remembering how overwhelmed she'd felt when she'd been there with Dan, Kira agreed.

Dan had assembled three sets of papers and written notes in the margins: *memory recall, triggers, recurring dreams, earthquake/tsunami = Hiroshima, woman in dreams, 1940s, WW2 = our grandparents.* The first set was about hallucinations; Kira put that one aside. The next was about ESP, the findings of half a dozen studies, and the last was about something called quantum entanglement, a principle of quantum physics. She started there.

A scientific journal explained that interacting particles can become an indivisible system, connected on a quantum level, even across large distances. Quantum entanglement wasn't ESP, the article emphasized; it was physics, a theory that Einstein had discounted as "a spooky action at a distance." But it was real. Quantum entanglement was the reason birds could navigate the way they did, something to do with the Earth's magnetic field.

Kira skimmed the pages, the science beyond her, until one sentence caught her eye. Scientists were exploring whether quantum entanglement existed in people, on a cognitive level. *Entanglement in people? Holy shit.*

There was no evidence yet that quantum entanglement occurred in humans, the article emphasized, but scientists were testing the psychic connections between people who had strong emotional attachments to one another.

No evidence? What about the dying babies who hung on long enough to die in their mothers' arms? Quantum entanglement came closer to explaining that phenomenon than anything else Kira could think of. If anyone was entangled, it was mothers and their children. Why not grandmothers, then? But that couldn't be true for her; she'd never known Maddalena, had rarely thought about her in recent years. Her excitement fizzled into disappointment. What *did* she know about her grandmother, or anyone else in her family? With twenty minutes until Cam was due to arrive, Kira began making notes.

Maddalena had grown up on a ranch in the middle of nowhere—Owens Valley, east of the Sierra.

1. Find out where the house is/was.

The people at the table in the Hiroshima dream were obviously Maddalena's parents and brother. Kira had forgotten she had a great-uncle.

2. Look up Maddalena's family.

Maddalena's brother died in his twenties, Rosa had said. She didn't say when or how, only that Maddalena hadn't seemed sad about it. "No love lost there," she'd said when Kira pestered her with questions. Kira must have been about ten, because that was when she'd started asking more questions about her relatives, as if they might offer clues to her father's desertion. She kept the one photo she had of her father in a notebook, hidden under some old clothes on a closet shelf so her mother couldn't tear it up. Kira was in the photo too, about two years old, and her dad was smiling and hugging her as if he loved her. Did he? Did he miss her after he left? She'd spent hours studying the picture, trying to find something in his eyes that suggested he was a man capable of deserting his wife and child.

Rosa had told Kira little about her father other than how they'd met and what he did; nothing at all about who he was or why she'd married him. What had her mother, an English major at UC Berkeley on full scholarship, seen in Frank Esposito, a laborer who spent his days wielding a blowtorch? In the few pictures Kira had seen, he looked tough and weathered, with the pitbull neck and shoulders of a man who'd done heavy work for years. Rosa had met him in a coffee shop in downtown Martinez two days after she graduated, and they married a year later.

As far as Kira knew, Rosa had never tried to find Frank after he left. As a child, Kira searched the library for books about families that had been reunited, about heroic fathers. She read *A Wrinkle in Time* until the binding fell apart, wishing she could save her dad like Meg and Charles Wallace saved theirs. Only her dad wasn't a brave scientist. To quote her mother, he was a "goddamn worthless son of a bitch."

Rosa had evaded questions about other members of the family too. Asked to identify individuals in the photo albums, she'd answered with "I don't know," or "I can't remember," her expression becoming blacker by the minute. She hadn't seemed to understand what it was like for Kira to grow up with a family that existed only in photographs.

Kira restacked the papers and got ready to go. She had no idea what Maddalena had been like or how she had spent her days. She didn't know whether her grandmother had knitted or played golf or liked to go to the movies, what her favorite color was, what her laugh had sounded like. She didn't know a damn thing except that Rosa had often talked about how hard it had been to lose her mother at seventeen, when she was on the verge of adulthood and had needed a mother's counsel. Needed her touch.

A mother's touch. If only Aimi had known it. No one should die without knowing her mother's love, the warmth and smell of her skin.

❧

On the way to Martinez, Kira told Camille about the wedding-dress dream, Dan's sketch, and the quantum entanglement theories.

"Damn, that thing with the sketch is just weird," Camille said. For a Catholic, even a progressive one, she swore a lot. "It's got to be a coincidence."

"Come on, Cam. He drew exactly what I saw, even the things I didn't tell him. No way that's a coincidence."

"It's really strange that Dan would even suggest quantum entanglement. He's so practical."

"In some ways. He also says we shouldn't limit our thinking. I made fun of reincarnation once and he got really pissed."

"You don't really think quantum entanglement explains any of this, do you?"

"No, but it's all weird as shit. Listen to this." Kira told Cam about the Hiroshima dream and Dan's theory that it had been triggered by the YouTube video.

"Okay, that's freaky." Camille changed lanes and took the first Martinez exit. "What about seeing a doctor? Maybe a neurologist could figure this out."

"You must be in cahoots with Dan."

Cam parked in front of Rosa's house, now polished and manicured by Dan's second choice of landscaper. Rosa would have been pleased, Kira thought with a momentary glow. Then she wondered what the hell she was getting herself into. What secrets did the house hold? Wouldn't she be better off tending to her marriage than dredging up history?

"Let's go," Kira said, and bolted from the car.

When the front door swung open, the house seemed lifeless, uninterested in its own secrets. Stop inventing things, Kira thought. *Stay focused.*

Camille stashed the sandwiches and bottled water she'd brought, then turned, hands on her hips. "Ready! Where do you want to start?" She had clipped her spiky hair back and wore an oversize T-shirt that made her look shorter than the five-foot-nothing she was. The oldest of seven kids and the mother of three, Cam was a diminutive dynamo, practicality and efficiency personified.

"I don't know," Kira said. "It's kind of overwhelming."

"You think?"

"Smart-ass. Thanks a lot, Sis."

Camille's face lit up at the old nickname. Ever since eighth grade they'd called themselves sisters, after Vera-Ellen and Rosemary Clooney in Kira's favorite holiday movie, *White Christmas.* Camille wasn't a fan of old movies, but she'd agreed to watch it each year, even let Kira persuade her to sing and dance along with "Sisters." They'd laugh themselves to tears, but Kira always cried for real when Rosemary Clooney, wearing a sparkly black mermaid gown, sang "Love, You Didn't Do Right by Me." Camille would say, "How can you cry? It's soooo corny," and Kira would wail, "I know!" It was all part of the ritual. But part of the reason she cried was that at times like these Cam really did feel like the sister Kira had always wanted.

"I guess we should start in my mom's office. That's where she kept important papers."

An hour later boxes and accordion files littered the floor and Camille sat at the desk leafing through shoeboxes stuffed with receipts, cards, and dog-eared photos.

"Look at this." Kira pulled the last box out of the closet, a small hatbox in a faded floral print of blue hydrangeas. "Pretty, isn't it?"

"Pretty old and musty, if you ask me."

Kira made a face and opened the box. "Oh my God." She held up a black pillbox hat with a short veil.

A jolt of memory—a weekend when she was twelve, helping her mother clean out the attic. Kira had complained until she found this hat in a steamer trunk and fell in love with it. She put it on and turned to her mother. "How do I look?"

Rosa's face went slack. "That belonged to your grandmother," she said, her voice pained. She went back to sorting through yellowed linens, then put a hand to her head. "The mothballs are getting to me. We'll finish another time." She went downstairs, and Kira admired herself in a dusty mirror. In the filtered attic light, and with her eyes narrowed, she decided she looked like her grandmother. Her almost-black hair was darker and straighter than Maddalena's, and her nose was flatter and not Italian-looking at all—because she'd slept on her stomach as a baby, her mother said—but her eyes were like Maddalena's, a changeable green that often drifted toward blue. Rosa had them too: three generations of matching eyes.

All these years later, the hat was in perfect shape, just as Kira remembered it. Her mother had stuffed tissue inside it, packed it away in its own special box. A treasured memento, obviously. After she'd found it in the trunk, Kira had taken it for her own, worn it with the veil pinned back, with a vintage skirt or dress, and her mother never said a word, not even to remind her to take good care of it. Maybe she had trusted her with it, this artifact from Maddalena's life. When Kira wore it, she felt sophisticated and mysterious, and from then on she spent her allowance and babysitting money at thrift stores, excavating history. She felt like she found herself in those old things, even though they were someone else's history—a cropped black jacket à la Audrey Hepburn, rhinestone brooches, long ropes of cheap, colorful beads. Her favorite item was the pink cashmere cardigan with seed-pearl trim she'd worn the day she met Dan's parents. As a teenager in the early '90s, she'd worn it with her mother's bell-bottoms, elephant bells with blue-and-green-and-brown stripes. The more incongruous the combination, the more she liked it.

"Hey, Cam, remember when I wore this hat with a red spaghetti-strap dress and cowboy boots?"

"How could I forget? Didn't you get voted best dressed or something in senior year? Crazy."

Kira put on the hat, struck a supermodel pose. "Most Likely to Model for Jean-Paul Gaultier."

"The freaks voted you in, you know. Everyone else made fun of you."

"I kind of knew that. But thanks for not telling me then."

The truth was, Kira didn't care about fashion, never had. She liked wearing old clothes because they made her feel connected to a past she knew almost nothing about. Even now, half of what hung in her closet was pre-1960s. Her favorite pieces, the ones she thought suited her best, were from the '40s and early '50s.

The '40s. World War II. How old would Maddalena have been during the war? Kira added to the list she'd started that morning, now stashed in her pocket.

3. Find Grandma's birth certificate. And death certificate. Mom's too.

At lunchtime they ate Camille's tuna sandwiches at the kitchen table. The sun had faded in a darkening sky, rumors of a storm scenting the air.

"These daytime dream things are getting more frequent, aren't they?" Camille said. "And this woman in them, it's always the same one, right? And she has a baby."

"Yeah. Not very surprising, I guess. Dan says she represents Aimi. He thinks this is like some kind of weird grief thing, but I don't think so."

"How come?"

Kira hesitated. She hadn't told Camille that the dreams weren't hers, that in them she saw scenes from Maddalena's life.

"I think Dan's half right," Camille said. "The dreams probably are about Aimi, but they're about the other baby too. You never really got to grieve for the miscarriage, after all, keeping it a secret from your mom. That's got to be in there somewhere."

"It wasn't even a baby yet. Barely a fetus."

"I know, but you were a baby yourself. I wish we'd told your mother or someone at school. I think about that happening to one of my girls and I go ballistic. The first thing I'd do is call the police and track the prick down. We should have done that. At the very least someone could have helped you. You needed someone to talk to, a grown-up, not just me. Your mother would have wanted to know, I think. Honestly, the more time goes by, the more pissed I get about the whole thing."

"It was a long time ago." Kira stood and put her plate in the sink, her movements as sharp as her tone. "Let's get back to work."

"I'm sorry, Sis. It's just that I'm worried about you."

This time the nickname annoyed Kira. Much as Cam loved her, there was nothing she could do to help Kira, and nothing

116

Dan could do. Or a doctor. There probably wasn't a doctor on the planet who could put a name to what was happening to her. No, Kira was on her own, in a way she never would have been if Aimi had lived. If her mother had lived. But they were both dead, deceased. Ugly words that stalled on the tongue. No wonder people preferred to say a loved one had passed, was lost, departed, gone, no more, sleeping with the angels, with God. Not that a euphemism could disguise the fact that someone you loved had died. Someone who was part of you.

"You know what? Let's get out of here," Kira said. "I'm tired, and I've got a string of twelve-hour shifts coming up." She'd put in a vacation request as promised, but she couldn't get time off until April. Then she'd have two weeks off, and Dan would be happy, and she'd have time to come back to this mess.

Back in Berkeley, Kira said, "Thanks for helping me, Cam. Sorry to waste your day."

"It wasn't wasted," Camille said. "I got to see you, didn't I?"

"You're a sweetheart." Kira hugged her friend, uncertain when they would see each other again, or what might happen in the meantime.

Sixteen

July 8, 1945

Two months since VE Day, and still we waited. With the Third Reich in tatters, we had become impatient. With Hitler dead, we allowed ourselves to dream.

For some of us, those for whom Japan was little more than part of our DNA, for whom freedom meant more than honor or tradition, Japan had become the enemy. Each morning our hopes flew as high as the hawks surfing the Sierra, then shattered at day's end when the war continued. Some of us drank too much homemade sake, sank into lethargy, erupted into scuffles. Others fell silent, fighting the pall of depression, unable to pray for the defeat of our homeland. The thought tasted bitter, no matter the rewards Japan's surrender would bring us—freedom, and home.

We longed for home with the same visceral desire that love brings. Our communities might wait and watch with crossed arms and hostile eyes, but we resolved to reclaim our places there, recognizable or not, and bear the lack of welcome. We would return to the communities we had once called home, to repossessed houses, apartments whose locks had been changed, to boarded-up businesses, to empty docks where our fishing boats once slept. We would open storage sheds to find our belongings gone.

We knew that when we left Manzanar, we would look older than we were, our skin toughened and lined by dust and wind, stripped of oils, darkened by sun. We who had become ditch diggers and net makers would wonder if our broken nails and leather palms would ever again be hands we recognized.

The elderly among us, broken and stripped, knew we would not regain what we had been. The young among us looked far into the future, optimism dimmed but spirits resilient. They refused to believe that Manzanar had changed them forever.

SEVENTEEN

March 21–28, 2011

For the next week and a half Kira avoided Dan. She hadn't convinced him that the doctor's office had rescheduled her appointment, and his disappointment was obvious. She felt terrible about lying to him; hiding things from him seemed cruel instead of protective. The worst omission was the miscarriage. Cam was right—so what if it hadn't been Dan's baby all those years ago? The regret, the unresolved grief, were part of her still, amplifying the pain of losing Aimi.

On Thursday Kira was assigned to Baby Kendall, a stable thirty-six-weeker about to get off the ventilator. One IV, an arterial line, half a dozen meds, a little trouble with his glucose—an easy assignment, assuming he tolerated being extubated. Waiting for the docs to make rounds, Kira changed the bed linens, unsnarled monitor wires and IV tubing, and reorganized the bedside drawers. It felt good to put things in order.

The rounding doctors arrived at ten. "And here we have the well-behaved young Mr. Kendall," Dr. Craig said. "Rumor has it he's ready to solo." He listened to the baby's lungs. "Let's do it. Pop a cannula on him and get a gas in an hour, sooner if he's working hard. Hold his next feeding until you see how he does."

An hour later Baby Kendall was pink and breathing easily; three hours later he was blowing saliva bubbles and fussing. Kira bundled him up and settled in a rocker. "Hey, little guy, let's see if you can eat and breathe at the same time." While the formula trickled through a feeding tube, she smoothed the baby's warm head and allowed herself to pretend he was Aimi. A swiftshattering pain seized her throat, her brain, her heart, as if it knew which were the vital organs and forged a deliberate path. She welcomed it. It was an indulgence to hold this child as if he were hers, to imagine it was her body that created this radiantly complex being, each of its entangled systems necessary for life. An indulgence that, now and then, was worth the pain. She rocked, the feathery scalp warming her fingers.

The doors to the Unit snapped open as a transport team arrived, and a woman's voice shrilled from the hallway. "Where's my baby? Fucking sons of bitches, where'd they take her? Rosie!"

Kira's fingers burned and the color wash swept the room. Instantly, a shadowed scene: an attic, evening; Maddalena, a baby, a rocking chair.

The baby looks nothing like her father, but I see him every time I look at her. I hold his photo in front of her sweet unfocused eyes. "Here's your daddy," I whisper. "Rosa, Rosa, your daddy would have loved you so much." It is not a name my mother would have wanted, had she cared about my child, had she loved her. I chose it myself, the name of no one I knew, a name free of history. It makes me think of a velvet-deep red, a simple kind of beauty. The kind Rosa's father loved.

My husband calls from the foot of the stairs. "You up in the damn attic again? Christ almighty. I don't see no dinner on the table."

"Coming." I kiss the baby's head, wipe a milk bubble from her lips, button my blouse.

An alarm sounded, soft and distant. Then a voice: "Kira, you need help?" Before she could answer, another voice: "Call respiratory stat. And page Dr. Craig." Then Baby Kendall was taken from her, placed on the bed, surrounded, and the room snapped back into focus.

Dr. Craig rounded the corner. "You've suctioned? Good, let's intubate. Chest X-ray and blood gas stat."

Kira backed away from the damage she'd done. In the

hallway, the charge nurse corralled her into an office where she sat and waited, the airless room shrinking around her. She didn't cry, and she wondered why not. Leaning forward, she cradled her head in her hands. The hemostats pinched to her scrub top dangled, their long-silvered jaws indefinably cruel. She wondered why she noticed them, why she could think of anything besides that baby, struggling to breathe because of her. Why what she'd done hadn't killed her yet.

The next few days were a blur of half sleep, too much wine, and the constant torment of *what if, what if?* Baby Kendall was back on a ventilator because of her. She'd harmed a patient, an unforgivable mistake. Every time Kira called the hospital, every hour, she got the same news: "stable on moderate ventilator settings," delivered in a tone that suggested she call less often.

When she told Dan what had happened, she could barely get the words out. "They put me on medical leave," she said, avoiding his eyes. They were standing in the kitchen, the island countertop between them littered with sodden Kleenexes. "What if he—"

"He won't," Dan said. "They got to him fast, right?"

Kira half nodded, half shrugged. He could have said he'd told her it was dangerous, that she should have called in sick when she couldn't get time off right away, that she was selfish and stupid. Instead he said, "He'll be okay." The look he gave her made it clear that he wasn't sure he could say the same about her.

On Friday Kira dragged herself out of bed and found the list of psychiatrists she'd been given. The hospital had ordered a physical, which had revealed nothing wrong; now she needed to see a shrink. The first three doctors she called were booked for weeks, but Dr. Alan Richardson had a cancellation on Monday at two. She had no idea what she would say to him.

The doctor's office was in San Francisco in a homey-looking Victorian on Post Street. Kira sat in a yawning leather chair big enough to curl up in, next to a small table outfitted with a box of tissues and a small sculpture of speckled wood, all maternal curves and warmth. She leaned back, her body buoyed. Lamps tossed out kindly glows that enriched the rusts and ochres, sages and crimsons in the thick rug. Simply sitting in this room, doctor or no doctor, would have been worth the hundred-and-seventy-five-dollar fee.

Dr. Richardson sat across from her, a tall man with a runner's body and a generous smile. "How can I help you, Kira?" he asked, teepeeing his hands.

"I'm on medical leave from my job. As I mentioned on the phone, I'm an RN, neonatal ICU, and there was this incident. I guess the hospital sent you a report? What happened was... well, I've been having these dreams. Well, not dreams, exactly. I'm awake, but I kind of zone out. I had one at work and that's why I'm here." Kira twisted a Kleenex. If the doc had understood any of that, he was a mind reader.

"When you have these dreams, do you lose consciousness?"

"Not exactly. It's more like I go into a trance." Kira told him about the deaths of Aimi and her mother, about the mysterious man, about the nightly dreams that wouldn't stop, then started happening when she was awake. She described the babies who waited for their parents to hold them before they died, how everything she was telling him seemed related somehow.

"And then I had one of the dreams at work and a baby got hurt. Because of me." Kira started to cry. "Why is this happening?" She plucked another tissue from the box. "It's all just so crazy. What's wrong with me? My father left my mother because he thought she was crazy, and my grandmother killed herself, so it's not like I have the greatest genetic track record."

"It sounds like you were afraid to get help."

123

Kira nodded. She recognized the tactic, validation, and was surprised by how good it felt.

"Let's not make any assumptions about your family's track record," Dr. Richardson said gently.

"But I feel so out of control, and I know I'm making bad decisions, and it's hard not to worry about that. And I feel so terrible about Baby Kendall. I know I shouldn't have kept working, and the danger seems so obvious now, but I guess I thought I could be careful. I don't know. Dan, my husband, he thinks the dreams are being triggered, which makes sense." She paused. "I just didn't think it would happen again. Not at work."

"Why does your husband think the dreams are being triggered?"

Kira explained about the video and Hiroshima and the doctor took notes. "Interesting," he said.

"What do you think is happening? When I had the first daytime dream, I thought I must be hallucinating, but now I don't think so."

"Why not?"

"Well, wouldn't I hallucinate stuff that's part of my world? With me in it? The dreams don't happen like that; the real world goes away entirely. And I'm not in them—well, I kind of am, but I'm not *me*. I'm someone else. Kind of." Kira shredded a tissue. "God, that sounds worse, doesn't it?"

Dr. Richardson smiled again. "Tell me about the dreams. Let's go through them one by one."

Kira went through the list. When she finished, she was on the edge of the chair, her toes knotted and her fingers dug into the leather. "There's something else. The girl in the dreams, the person I am in the dreams—I think it's my grandmother." She laughed, it sounded so ridiculous. "Actually, I know it's her. It's my grandmother in the dreams. I'm her. And I never even knew her."

"Interesting," Dr. Richardson said. "Let's start with that next time."

"But what do you think is going on?"

Dr. Richardson stood. "We've just begun, Kira. I'll see you next week." He opened the door and beckoned to his next patient, a man with the sad eyes of a basset hound.

Kira watched the office door close behind them. Now that drooping man was in there, telling his story, hoping the doctor could make sense of his life. How many screwed-up people did Dr. Richardson try to make sense of in a week, how many strange stories did he hear? She'd bet none were as weird as hers. Still, it was a relief to tell Dr. Richardson about Maddalena.

Kira stepped into the sweet afternoon sunshine feeling better than she had in weeks. Lighter. Then she remembered Baby Kendall and plodded to her car as if she were made of stone.

EIGHTEEN

July 10–11, 1945

The rock landed six feet in front of Scout. Maddalena nodded at Akira, watching from the hospital steps, then slid off the horse, grabbed the rock, and was on her way, all in twenty seconds. The guards didn't see a thing. Her plan had worked! She couldn't wait to tell Regina.

Maddalena headed toward a nearby apple orchard where she could read the note safely out of sight of anyone on Foothill Road. Finally, she would learn something about Akira—maybe how old he was or where he came from, though what she most wanted to know was whether that pretty girl she'd seen him with was *his* girl.

Ten minutes later, an absolute eternity, Maddalena guided Scout into the shelter of the trees and tore off the yarn that bound the letter to the rock. The paper shook in her hands.

Dear Maddalena,

What a beautiful name. It suits you.

A beautiful name! Her heart was thundering like rocks on a tin roof.

Thank you for your letter. I didn't think I'd see you again after the baseball game, so it sure was nice to see you ride by. I remember thinking that I'd never seen eyes like yours before. I can't decide if they're blue or green—you'll have to tell me. Or better yet, I'll judge for myself.

Judge for himself? How?

My name is Akira Shimizu and I'm seventeen. I'm an American. My parents are from a village near Kyoto, but I was born here. I live in Berkeley with my parents—or I used to, before the government locked us up. I don't know what you think about Manzanar, but what they did

126

to us is horribly unfair. When I get out of here I'm going to law school so I can stop this kind of thing from ever happening again.

I'd like to see you. Can you sneak out of your house at night? If you can, meet me in the grove of trees I can see to the northwest when I stand on the hospital steps. I think it's an orchard. Maybe you're wondering how I can get out of the camp, but it's not that hard. Lots of guys go under the fence at night to go fishing. One of them is crazy enough to sneak out in broad daylight, inside an empty trashcan that his friend sets up for him on the garbage truck.

I'll be at the orchard at ten o'clock. Please come.

Akira

Maddalena read the note twice more, then pressed it to her chest. Akira Shimizu, age seventeen, answered her letter! And he remembered her eyes! He wanted to see her again! He didn't mention the little *puttana,* but maybe that was because she didn't matter. Maddalena threw her arms around Scout's neck, laughing when he rolled his eyes. If feeling lightheaded was a symptom of love, she was sick with it. But tomorrow night! How on earth was she going to manage that? And what an odd coincidence that he wanted to meet her here, where she was this very minute! He had to mean this orchard, the only one to the north within sight of Manzanar.

On the way to Regina's, with Scout in an easy canter, Maddalena saw the desert as if she'd never been there before. It was like a long, dry river hemmed in between the mountain ranges but running forever, to the oceans, through Oregon and Washington and Canada to the north, through Mexico to the south. The air tasted of sweet sage, bitter earth, her own tangy sweat. Ahead was Regina's house, and it looked different too, like a dollhouse with a tiny door and tiny windows with tiny curtains, and a toy truck parked nearby. The house wasn't far off, but neither was dinnertime, and if she wanted to stay in her mother's good graces she had to be home in time to help. But first she had to see Regina or she'd burst.

"Hurry up, Scout," she said, urging the horse into a gallop. No time to waste.

❧

Akira spent the rest of the afternoon restocking the supply carts, his mind on his big adventure. Now that he'd made up his mind to go under the fence, it had better be worth it. First of all, there was Annabelle to consider. She'd been clinging to him like a leech ever since she'd seen Maddalena. Girls sure did make things complicated.

As for Maddalena, he supposed there was a good chance she wouldn't show. Maybe it would be hard for her to sneak out of the house, or maybe she wasn't the kind of girl who'd do something like that. Or maybe she wanted to but would decide it was too risky. He wouldn't blame her. She had no reason to trust him, and no reason to be reckless, not like he did. The way he saw it, why worry about the future when you weren't sure you had one?

It would be an adventure, whether Maddalena showed or not. And if she did, he might find out that she wasn't worth losing Annabelle for; he had to consider that possibility. But he wanted to find out because if he did have a future, he couldn't spend it wondering whether he'd made a mistake in passing her by. He was going; the question was how. Maybe with the fishermen. Those guys knew what they were doing, and even *they* almost got caught every so often. One time a military police jeep had appeared out of nowhere and the guys had to dive into a gully to avoid being seen. You never knew what might happen.

No, going alone would be better. The guys would ask him why he was going with them if he didn't fish, and he couldn't think of a story they'd believe. And the more people who knew what he was doing, the more talk there'd be.

He asked himself again if he wouldn't rather stay home and stick with Annabelle, but it took him only a few seconds to scratch that thought. There was no point in playing it safe, not anymore. He could live his life, risks and all, or he could sit at home drinking tea and wondering why he existed. If Maddalena didn't show or he didn't care to see her again, at least he'd have stood in the desert with open space between him and the mountains, knowing that if he headed north or south for long enough he would walk right out of Owens Valley, leave Manzanar behind to rot and crumble. So what if he'd never make it? It was the kind of fantasy that kept him going when he was lying on a prison cot in the middle of nowhere, thinking his life was nothing like he thought it would be, and half wishing he'd die in his sleep.

The next day Maddalena fidgeted all through dinner. Sneaking out of the house wouldn't be easy, and there was only one way to do it—from her bedroom window, second story or no second story, because the floorboards in the upstairs hallway squeaked. And what if a door slipped out of her hand and closed too quickly? The noise would wake the dead.

"Can I take the truck tonight?" Marco said, wolfing down applesauce. "I want to meet up with some fellows in town."

Papa nodded, which he wouldn't have done if he knew what Maddalena knew, which was that Marco was lying. He was going to town because he was courting Becky Adams, the police chief's daughter. Maddalena knew this because Regina had told her, and Regina heard it from her mother, who heard it from her hairdresser, who knew everything that went on in town. Papa didn't like the police chief and he'd be none too happy if he found out it was the chief's daughter Marco was seeing. But good riddance, as far as Maddalena was concerned. She needed rope, and he would be safely out of the way when she went to the barn to get it.

After dinner Maddalena jumped up to do the dishes

before her mother could tell her to. Marco slammed out the back door, waving off their mother's instructions to drive carefully. Papa turned on the radio and settled into the wing chair with the Sears catalogue and a glass of whiskey, and Mama sat opposite him with her sewing basket and a stack of clothes to mend. The war report was on as usual, no doubt with the usual news—more fighting, more people killed. In Europe the war had been over for two months, and that was wonderful news. But the war wasn't over everywhere. Not where it mattered most.

Maddalena dried the dishes and put them away, her thoughts on Akira. Tonight! She would see him tonight! But if she got caught—her stomach flipped—she'd find herself facing the unimaginable depths of her parents' fury.

After hanging up her apron, Maddalena announced that she was going to feed Scout and then go to her room to read. "I'm almost done with *The Clue in the Jewel Box* and I *have* to find out what happens. Nancy is trying to find a pickpocket, and a prince, and I *know* they're related somehow. It's so exciting," she said, then escaped to the barn.

In the storeroom, amid pitchforks and shovels and spools of wire, she found a big coil of rope. Dirty and frayed, it must have been lying around for a while, which meant there was a good chance her father and Marco wouldn't notice that some of it was missing. Maddalena cut off a thirty-foot length, tucked it into a rolled-up saddle blanket, and ran back to the house. She hurried through the kitchen and dining room and up the stairs, and her parents never even lifted their heads.

An hour later the rope was ready, anchored to the dresser with knots tied every few feet. The only thing left to do was wait for her parents to go to bed and for Marco to get home. If he stayed out late she'd be up a creek, because she couldn't chance running into him in the yard. Maddalena paced, looking out the window every few seconds, then worried that her parents would hear her footsteps. Reading was out of the question, so she changed into navy slacks, a blue-flowered blouse, and a gray cardigan, then sat on the bed to fix her hair. An Artie Shaw song wafted up the stairs. "Dancing in the Dark," one of her favorites. How perfect. Tonight she would be with Akira, in the dark. Every inch of her skin tingled.

At nine, her father went to bed. Half an hour later the truck pulled into the yard, the back door slammed, and Marco pounded up the stairs. Ten minutes later, her mother's weary steps sounded in the hall. The house fell silent.

Maddalena was ready. She'd pulled her hair back with tortoiseshell combs, one on each side, which wasn't the most practical hairstyle for climbing out windows, but after all, who wore a ponytail or a braid on a date? And that's what this meeting with Akira was. If they were in a movie, like Clark Gable and Carole Lombard, they would call it a rendezvous and it would be someplace fancy where Maddalena could wear a dress that showed her shoulders. And silk stockings, if it wasn't wartime. And they could glide across the floor to "Dancing in the Dark."

If only the war would end.

Carefully, silently, she lowered the rope out the window. Down she went, one knot at a time, quiet as a cat. With each movement, her knuckles and knees scraped the wall and she had to bite her lip to keep silent. The whole time she expected to hear her father yell, "Who's there?" or see him glaring down at her from the open window. But nothing happened. When she reached the end of the rope, she waited, listening and gathering courage. The silence held. She dropped to the ground and ran.

Scout greeted her with a fluttery breath. Elsewhere in the barn, the cattle shifted, hooves clacking against the floorboards. Normal sounds, but tonight they seemed deafening. Maddalena slipped a hackamore over Scout's head and climbed onto his bare back. "Let's go," she whispered.

❧

Akira spent an hour at the canteen working on his song and making sure plenty of people saw him there. The old guys who did nothing but play cards were in one corner and a slew of giggling girls were in another, making eyes at the fellows across the room. Annabelle wasn't there, but Harry was, staring at Akira with snake eyes. Let him stare. Soon enough, Harry might not have a reason to defend his sister anymore, or at least not from Akira.

Just before nine, Akira slipped away, and ten minutes later he was at Bairs Creek, where the drop-off to the creek gully created a crawl space under the barbed wire. On the other side of the fence, cottonwoods lining the creek bank offered shelter.

Crouching behind the end barracks in Block 6, Akira watched the searchlight move lazily, as if the sentry's heart wasn't in it. The fence stood a good thirty or forty feet from the picnic area, cast in low shadows from a half moon. A light swept by, and he counted off the seconds before it returned—a generous twenty. Piece of cake. Akira edged along the building, toes curling in his shoes, nerves sparking like frayed wires. He might be dead in a few minutes, but right now he felt every nerve, every muscle, every hair. He was alive, on the verge of something exciting and dangerous. No going back now.

The searchlight swung past and Akira bolted. Another guard broke the pattern, speeding his light toward the fence, and Akira dropped to the ground. The light swooped past and he was up again, running—one, two, three, four, five, six, seven—his footsteps deafening—eight, nine, ten, eleven, twelve—into the creek bed on all fours, under the fence. Seeing a light race toward him, he dove into the underbrush, exhaling with relief when the light veered north.

He was out. Safe. Free.

Akira followed the creek bed west, then headed north

toward the orchard. The air seemed cleaner outside the fence. Sweeter. He broke into an easy run.

≈

Maddalena shivered. How odd to be alone in the valley at night, with only the moon and stars to light her way. The Sierra crouched across the horizon to her left, while far ahead Manzanar glowed. Searchlights crisscrossed the camp in long, slow streaks, looking for prey. Akira might be dodging them this very minute! "Be safe, be safe," she whispered.

Forty minutes later, a hundred yards from the orchard, Maddalena reined in Scout, suddenly afraid. Akira was there waiting for her, but what did she know about him? Her mother would say she was foolish, reckless, risking her reputation for a boy she didn't know, asking for trouble. Maybe her mother was right. Then Maddalena saw Akira walking toward her and forgot about her mother.

"You're here!" he called. "I wasn't sure you'd come."

Maddalena slipped off Scout's back, could think of nothing to say but hello.

"Come on, under the trees," Akira said. "No one will see us there."

Maddalena hung back. The orchard looked creepy at night, the trees twisted and streaked with moonlight. No one *would* see them. If she cried out for help, no one would come.

"Don't be afraid. Say, what's your horse's name?" Akira offered his hand and Maddalena took it, warmth surging all the way to her toes.

"Scout. He's ten years old and I've had him since I was eight."

After tethering the horse, Maddalena turned to Akira, unsure what to do or say. All she'd thought about was the excitement of the adventure, the fact that Akira wanted to see her again. She'd had no idea what would happen when they got here.

Akira spread his jacket on the ground. "Come and sit," he said, and she did, wrapping her arms around her knees. "I can't believe you're here. Actually, I can't believe *I'm* here. Look at this place! Smell it! I swear, the air is different out here, everything is different. Except you. You look as beautiful here as you do when you're riding that horse of yours. Queen of the desert."

What to do, what to say? The boys Maddalena knew didn't talk like this, like men in the movies. He made her feel giddy, and she wanted this moment to last forever, but everything was moving too fast. She was sure the stars would disappear any minute and the sun would rise and her mother would call to her to get out of bed. What if she went into her room and found her gone?

"Was it hard to get away?"

"Not terribly. I tied a rope to my dresser and climbed out my window."

"Ah, an adventuress—I like that. Tell me everything about you."

"Like what?" All she could think about was the fact that the two of them were alone in the dark in the middle of the desert and no one knew she was here. Except Regina. For a moment that was a comforting thought, until she remembered that she'd made Regina promise to keep her secret, and she wouldn't say a thing to anyone until Maddalena turned up missing the next day. And if that happened, it would be too late.

"Anything. What you like to do, your school, your friends, your family. What you dream of. Your secrets."

The way he talked! "*You're* my secret," she said. "My parents would skin me alive if they found out I sneaked out of the house at night to meet a boy. But you're the one who's brave. Aren't you afraid you'll get caught?"

"No," Akira said, then laughed. "Well, sure, a little. But like I told you, people go under the fence all the time now. It's risky, but the guards aren't as careful as they used to be.

I think some of them wonder why we're here anymore. Still, you never know when they might get a little trigger-happy."

"It's strange being here at night. Scary," Maddalena said. The ground was cold, littered with stones and sharp-edged stubble. "I can't stay long. I'm worried that my mother will find out I'm gone."

"I don't want you to worry. Now that we know we can do this, we can do it again. Can you come again tomorrow?"

"No, not so soon. We have to be careful." He was so eager and dear. The way his hair fell over his forehead, he looked like a kid, but when he talked he seemed grown up, serious. A grown-up man who had risked his life to be with her.

"Are you scared? You're safe with me, you know," Akira said. "I won't so much as hold your hand if you don't want me to."

What to do, what to think! His body so close to hers she could feel his heat—it was like rolling down a hill, the world spinning past, her dress twisted so tight around her that she couldn't breathe.

"Have you had a lot of girlfriends?" The words were out before she knew it, and she clamped a hand over her mouth. What a thing to say!

Akira laughed. "No one that matters. Listen, Maddalena, I—never mind. I can't see you very well, and I want to. Here." He took her hand and held it to his face. A bristle of sideburns, the bony line of his jaw. Then his palm on her cheek. "Is this okay?" he said.

She nodded. Copying his movements, she smoothed an eyebrow, explored the hair at his temple, ran a finger down his nose. His skin was smooth, what she imagined vellum would feel like. Did most men's skin feel like this, or only his? Then his fingers found her lips and she caught her breath. Again, that sweet feeling of warm water running beneath her skin.

"You are very beautiful," he said.

It was silly, this kind of talk. Then why did she wish he would kiss her?

"So soft," he said, smoothing her hair. "Did you know that in the sunshine your hair is like a halo?"

He leaned forward and Maddalena waited for the kiss, wondering what to do with her mouth, where to look. Instead, Akira rested his forehead against hers, his arms on her shoulders. It seemed odd to sit like that, but when he pulled away and sat next to her again, her skin felt hot where his forehead had been, her shoulders empty.

"It's strange, isn't it, being here together?" he said. "And all because of a baseball game. If I were free we could see each other anytime, but I'm not, and who knows when I will be. *If* I will be. It makes me sick." He picked up a rock and pelted it into the darkness.

"Don't say that! You'll be free, I know you will!"

"You don't know that."

She turned away, her face burning. Of course he was right.

"I'm sorry, I didn't mean to snap at you." He took her hand again. "It's hard to explain, but being locked up when you've done nothing wrong is worse than anything you can imagine. It makes you feel like an animal, less than an animal. Worthless."

"I hate it that you're there," Maddalena said. "It's so unfair."

They gazed at the desert, the searchlights restless in the distance. Finally Akira stood and pulled her to her feet. "You should go," he said. "Can I kiss you?"

Maddalena raised her mouth to his. Chapped lips, then a sweet, spreading warmth, like floating in a shallow lake with the springtime sun on her face. She wondered if she would ever see again. Hear again. Think again.

"Perfect," Akira whispered.

Maddalena pulled one of the combs out of her hair and pressed it into his hand. "This is for you. Don't lose it."

Nineteen

March 29–April 4, 2011

Waiting for her next appointment with Dr. Richardson was like being thrown into Dante's First Circle of Hell. Kira spent the week worrying about Baby Kendall, hating herself, and spinning through a perpetual thought cycle of Maddalena - Rosa - Kira - Aimi - Kira - Rosa - Maddalena. Quantum entanglement. Connections across great distances. If time was a continuum, then there was nothing linear and impermanent about it. It was a form of distance that could be backtracked upon, forward, reverse, forward, reverse, like a highway or hiking trail. The dreams were a road, a bridge, connecting present and past, linking her to Maddalena. They bypassed Rosa and stopped short of Aimi, but Kira couldn't help including her mother and daughter in the cycle. Doing so diminished, in a small but significant way, the emptiness she felt in the wake of their loss.

Dan hadn't tried to disguise his relief that she was seeing a doctor. She didn't say much about the session, only that Dr. Richardson was kind and smart and gave her hope. She and Dan spent the week in a careful truce, a low-frequency sharing of affection, the kind you might feel for someone you had loved once and hadn't seen for a decade. If anyone had asked her to describe her marriage at this moment, she'd have said she and Dan were two fish in a suffocatingly small bowl, swimming in opposite directions and grazing fins now and then.

The fact that she had a husband at all was strange, really. Marriage wasn't a choice Kira had expected to make, but being with Dan had felt more like a compulsion. She'd kept her distance from other men she'd dated, was happy when they did the same. Then she met Dan and it was as if her ovaries had gone into hyperdrive, screaming *baby-baby-baby* in tiny droid-like voices. She'd been thrown off her game.

They'd met at West Coast Children's, when he showed up with the mother of one of her patients. Kira mistook Dan for the father and told him he could hold his child. He replied, "She's not mine. But I do hope to be a dad someday," and looked at her with an intensity that made her feel drugged. After he and the mother left, Kira found a piece of paper on the bedside table with his name and phone number and "Call me" written on it in a bold, angular hand. For a week she picked up the note several times a day, studied the handwriting, and put it down. It was no big deal, she told herself, only a date. If he got serious, she could make her escape as she always did. But something told her it wouldn't be that easy, that if she got involved with Dan there'd be no half-assing the relationship. Her brain said *don't-don't-don't* and those goddamn little ovarian voices said *yes-yes-yes* and she did it, picked up the phone and called him. They met the next day, talked over coffee for three hours, moved on to an Indian place for dinner. Within a week they were seeing each other daily. He was an irresistible high, both mentally and physically; just looking at him aroused her. She would remove his glasses and he'd say, teasingly, "Again?" and she would nod and strip. Within a month they were a couple, an impossibility for her until now. The fact that she could be in such an intense relationship simultaneously warmed and chilled her.

The day before her doctor's appointment, Kira was restless, wandering the house, googling "quantum entanglement," examining Dan's sketch of Maddalena. He'd gotten every unspoken detail right; how was that possible? Then she called the hospital again, and this time, finally, the news about Baby Kendall was good—he was stable on decreased ventilator settings. After texting the news to Dan and Camille, Kira grabbed her coat. She needed space for her exhilaration, the life-affirmation of fresh air.

Kira walked to Aquatic Park, where a path circled an estuary. Wind snapped across the black water, sculpting it into skidding tufts and peaks and fringing the neck feathers of poised egrets. She thought of Dan, as she always did when she came here. After the first night she spent at his place, they'd walked this path hand in hand, the lengths of their arms touching, a memory so distant now it seemed like a story she'd been told. Dan had zeroed in on her with an intensity that enthralled and frightened her, offered her the kind of love she wasn't sure she believed in. She did her best, loved him carefully. If he saw the wall she'd made— which she retreated behind in moments of panic, checking incessantly for cracks in the mortar—he didn't show it. He accepted what she could give, as if having three-quarters of her was like having all of anyone else. As if being with her, and someday having the child he so clearly wanted, and wanted with her, was his reason for being. And, she discovered, he was willing to wait. The first time she went to the office he shared with Kenji, a pristine tin-ceilinged space where wooden tables held rolls of drafting paper, boxes of pencils and calligraphy pens, she asked what the sign above his desk said. It was written in kanji.

"Stumbling seven times but recovering eight," he said. "It's about perseverance. Some things take time."

❧

The next day, sunlight adorned San Francisco like gold dust, ricocheting off glass and metal, warming wood and vegetation. Kira took the fineness of the day as an omen promising, if not answers, at least some reassurance from Dr. Richardson. When he called her in, she shot into the room and perched on the leather chair.

"Have you come up with any theories? Besides hallucinations, I mean."

"Not yet, Kira, we're just getting started."

"Have you ever heard of quantum entanglement? Did you know they're studying whether it happens in people?"

"That's an interesting thought. Granted, there's plenty we don't know about the human mind, but any evidence of that is a long way off."

"Yeah, but if it's my grandmother in the dreams, couldn't they be *her* memories? And now I'm living her memories— that's a kind of entanglement, right? Maddalena's memories are tangled up with mine."

Dr. Richardson thought for a moment, tapping his pen on his notebook. "All right then, for the sake of discussion, let's say you are dreaming someone else's memories. Why your grandmother, whom you never met? Why not your mother?"

"I've thought about that," Kira said. "Remember how I said my father told my mom she was crazy? Suppose it was because she had the dreams too, and she told my dad about them and that's why he thought she was crazy. Maybe that's why he left."

"And she passed the dreams down to you? That's a very romantic idea."

"But when she died, this weird thing happened." Kira told him about Rosa's death, the bizarre heat fusing her hand to her mother's.

"That sounds like a very traumatic experience. I'm not dismissing your theory; I can understand why it appeals to you. For the moment, though, let's just say it seems unlikely. I want to go back to your husband's idea, the possibility that the dreams are being triggered. What were you doing immediately before each one?"

"The first one was in the hospital parking lot, after work," Kira said. "I was exhausted, just sitting there in the car."

"Did anything unusual happen that day?"

"Not really. Twins died, and one of them was my patient. It was a rough day, but not unusual. The twins were too young to survive. It's the parents that get to you, watching them suffer."

"And you've seen plenty of parents go through that?"

"Yes."

"And there were no babies in the dream?"

"No."

"Describe the dream again."

"The main thing was fear, pretty overwhelming. Like being hunted." The images resurfaced, as vivid as the day she'd seen them—voices barbed with hatred, the swagger of boot heels, the chill desert air. The acid smell of fear. A sense of foreboding, black and dense and endless. "There was a gun," Kira said. "A shotgun."

Dr. Richardson raised an eyebrow. "The twins died, and then you dreamed about being hunted. Do you see any connection there?"

"The trigger was death?"

"It certainly seems possible." He scribbled a note. "What about the birthday party?"

"That one's easy. I remember thinking the candles on the table behind the cake made it look like a birthday cake."

"And the wedding dress dream?"

"Well, we were at my mom's house and I was in the kitchen. I was cleaning up, and I picked up some dead flowers. Oh! That makes sense, because the girl—Maddalena, I mean— was holding a bouquet. Baby's breath and carnations, with no smell."

"Good."

"The Hiroshima one we already know about. And then the one when I was holding Baby Kendall." Kira wiped her eyes. "Sorry. You must think all I do is cry. He's doing better, thank God. Anyway, in that dream Maddalena was thinking about why she named her baby Rosa. The trigger must have been the woman who was yelling for her baby. She kept yelling, 'Rosie!'"

"All right, I think we can make a pretty good case for the dreams being triggered. Which means you could try to trigger them."

"Why on earth would I do that?"

"I think we have two options here, Kira. We could put you on an antipsychotic, probably haloperidol to start with—"

"No way."

"Don't rule it out. But let's say we're not looking at something as conventional as hallucinations. Why are you having the dreams? Especially if, as you theorize, your mother had them too, or similar ones."

"But you said that was wishful thinking. Now you're agreeing with me?"

"I didn't say that. Medication might stop the dreams. However, if you had more of them, they might give us more information. We might find a pattern or gain some insight into why they're happening or what they mean. Bear in mind I'm not saying they mean anything, or that you'll find out any more than you know now. But I admit I'm curious." Dr. Richardson looked at her over his reading glasses. "It's entirely up to you. I can write a prescription, and if the dreams stop, we'll assume there's a brain chemistry imbalance. You'll have to keep seeing me until we know it's safe for you to go back to work, of course. But if you think it's worth exploring why this is happening to you, then you should wait on the meds. I don't think you're in any real danger, though you shouldn't drive. And of course you can't work. Think about it, and we'll discuss it next time."

"I don't have to think about it. If there's an explanation, I want to know what it is."

Dr. Richardson smiled. "So do I."

Kira left the office with two prescriptions, an antipsychotic and an anxiolytic. In case she changed her mind, the doctor said, but he needn't have bothered. If there was a chance the dreams could give her some answers, she was ready. Her mother's house—Maddalena's house—was her best bet. The house held memories, so maybe being there would trigger the dreams. No, "dreams" was the wrong word. They were Maddalena's memories, pieces of the past, like scenes in a TV episode. Fragments of a life.

Kira stepped outside into radiant sunlight, a gentle breeze. Of course there was a good chance nothing would come of this. But every cell in her body urged her to try it: search for the tangible in order to find the intangible. Follow the road to the past far enough and she might find her grandmother. Beyond that it was anyone's guess.

On Post Street, ginkgo trees stood tall, leaves fluttering, and carefree rhododendrons splashed magentas and lavenders onto the sidewalk. A woman jogged toward Kira pushing a stroller, a toddler tucked inside, a shepherd panting next to her. The stroller was the three-wheeled kind Dan had wanted for Aimi, so he could take her on runs from day one and get her addicted to the sport before she could even walk. They'd run marathons together someday, he said.

The woman jogged past, smiling, and Kira turned to watch her. Even her back looked happy. A happy family.

It wasn't until she cut the engine at her mother's house that Kira remembered she wasn't supposed to drive. But she was here now, and no harm done. The landscaper had been back, judging by the deadheaded rosebushes and sculpted grass. The place was neat as a pin, she thought, because that was what her mother would have said, and she'd probably said it because her own mother had. From Maddalena to

Rosa to Kira, phrases filtering down through generations, words stamped on psyches like sealing wax on an envelope.

Kira opened the screen door and a nickel-sized spider dropped to the porch floor, a trail of sticky thread catching the afternoon sun. Inside, that familiar feeling of held breath before the house relaxed around her.

A text message popped up, Dan asking about her appointment. She texted back, said it was fine, she'd tell him about it at dinner. Then she turned off her phone and got to work.

In the living room, framed photos that had become invisible to her over the years jostled one another on every surface, calling for attention. In one small photo on the mantel, she and her mother were hugging, Rosa's lips pressed against Kira's hair. Kira thought she looked about two, so her mother must have been thirty-three. Maddalena, if she had lived, would have been fifty. Kira tried to picture her at that age, but it was Rosa she saw, her beauty softer, graceful with age. She moved on to the others—her graduation from nursing school, various Christmases and birthdays, her wedding portrait. How happy she and Dan had looked then, how oblivious. As far as she knew, it was the only wedding picture in the house. Her mother had torn up her own, along with the photos of Kira's dad. If any pictures existed of Maddalena's wedding, Kira had never seen them.

She sat on the couch and tried to picture her grandmother in this house. Maddalena would have been quite young when she married and moved to Martinez, where her husband, Joseph Brivio, worked in an oil refinery. Joseph was Maddalena's cousin, a distant one, and older. That was all Kira knew about him. She'd never thought to ask why Maddalena had married a cousin, and someone who lived far away from her home. Were there not eligible young men in Owens Valley?

Upstairs, Rosa's bedroom held only a double bed, an oak

dresser with a beveled-glass mirror, and a small nightstand. On the dresser were two pictures of Kira, one taken when she was eight, with jaw-length hair and crooked bangs. Wiping dust off the glass, Kira remembered the silkiness of Aimi's hair against her cheek, the terrible coolness of her head. She turned the photo face down on the dresser and climbed to the attic, where the thin air tasted of old wood and cobwebs, the stale perfume of decades-old fabrics and sun-warmed dust.

A rocking chair stood in the corner, wool tufting out of the seat's quilted cover, evidence of the mice Dan had found. Kira shivered, her skin prickling. She hadn't seen the chair since she was a teenager, but it was the one in her dreams, no doubt about it. More evidence that the girl with the baby was Maddalena, rocking the infant Rosa.

Chilled, Kira dragged the chair into a patch of sunlight and began to rock. What comfort had Maddalena found here in the dusty attic? How did she end up here, married and unhappy? Kira closed her eyes, listening to the rhythmic creak of wood as she rocked, hoping the sound or motion would trigger a dream. A fragment of Maddalena's life.

Kira woke to a darkening attic, chilled, her throat dry. No fragments, no answers, nothing but a waste of time. She rocked to her feet and the chair's cushion flew off, landing near a small cabinet, a cube of dark wood with a single door, perched on skinny legs. She'd played with it as a child, forgotten it completely. It was the perfect hiding place for whatever had been precious to her then—rocks and marbles, a snow globe of San Francisco, plastic horses, wild-haired trolls in various states of undress. She opened the cabinet door, revealing dust and mouse poop, and disappointment flashed through her. Honestly, did she expect to find her mother's photos and letters, answers to all her questions? She swatted the door closed. Time to go home.

In the car, she called Dan to say she was on her way.

145

"Are you still in the city?"

"No, Martinez. Dr. Richardson said—hang on, I'm putting in my earphone. I'm in the car." Kira turned on the headlights and a row of eucalyptus trees flashed into view, forbidding as sentries. "I'm trying to put some pieces together. You said being in the house might help me remember."

"Right. But what did the doctor say?"

"I'll tell you when I get home," Kira said, merging onto the highway. The road was empty, the hills dark and silent. "It's just—maybe all this is happening for a reason."

"He said that? Shit. I get that you've got stuff to work through about your mom, but that's nuts. What about medication, getting back to work? I want our life back. I want—" Dan's voice thickened. "I can't help thinking, when all this is over, we could try again. Have another baby."

Another baby. The first time either of them had said the words aloud. The road ahead blurred and Kira wiped her eyes. The miscarriage, Aimi, baby Rosa in the attic with Maddalena, the Clarkson twins, Baby Kendall. So many babies. It was hot in the car. Kira cracked open the window, wiped one sweaty palm on her jeans, then the other. Then her fingers flared with heat and the darkness exploded into salmon, yellow, glaring green.

I'm on my back, my legs open under the sheet, the midwife there, my mother too. They're too close to me, both of them, talking and talking, and I would give anything for them to be quiet, to stop touching me. There's a light above me, white glass, too bright. I close my eyes and push, push, the pain red and black. The women's hands hurt, insistent as flies, and I think of him, wish he were there. I twist on the bed, taste my sweat, each second elongating into a force I couldn't have imagined. The pain grabs me, lifts me, fills my mind, my blood, my muscles. I think I might die.

Kira hit the brake and the car veered off the road, the steering wheel twisting from her hands. A sickening impact, and she pitched forward. A baby cried, then nothing.

Twenty

July 17, 1945

At Manzanar, the wind made us crazy. Days when it never stopped, days when it came in sudden bursts, a desert storm flaunting its power. Infernos of sand and fragmented sage flailing our skin, worse than the creaking cold, more relentless than the lingering sun. The wind tormented us, ruled us, shaped our days.

When the wind blew hardest, flinging dust and grit in our eyes and mouths, we knew something would happen. It might be a lovers' spat, or two drunk men arguing with their fists. It might be despair muting the voices of the Issei at dinner or keeping them at home, their hopes and appetites worn down. It might be a guard jumpy enough to swing his gun at someone for getting too close to the fence. Though the sentries' vigilance had eased, we did not trust a man with a gun.

It was blowing hard the night we heard Akira was asking for trouble, going outside the fence for more than fish and a taste of freedom. We saw defiance in him, recklessness. The fishermen went for the trout, the peace, the rhythmic air-slice of a fishing line, the satisfaction of a well-placed cast. And they went for the pleasure of thumbing their noses at the government. Akira went for another reason, and for him it would prove more dangerous than machine guns, searchlights, rifles with bayonets. Akira went for a girl.

Those of us with eyes and experience pitied Annabelle. She'd staked her claim, but the look in Akira's eyes told us she stood no chance of keeping him. To the Issei among us, his behavior was incomprehensible. He'd been well raised, schooled in our traditions, taught to respect his parents, brought up with a proper sense of duty, of *on* and *giri*. In turning away from our ways and traditions, he brought dishonor to his family.

Or it could be that the girl, and whatever would happen because of her, was his fate. *Shikata ga nai*. It cannot be helped.

One night soon after the rumors started, Akira came into the canteen. There was an edge to his gait, a restlessness that uprooted our calm. He walked over to Annabelle, glancing at the piano with an expression that told us he wanted it, not her, under his hands. If she noticed, her face did not show it. She smiled, crossed her legs, sat up straight to fill out her blouse. The girls sitting with her drifted away with knowing looks.

Annabelle sipped her soda straw. "There you are."

"I said I'd be here, didn't I?"

"These days I'm never sure." She patted the chair next to her and Akira sat, hands on his knees. "Did you hear about the picnic on Saturday?" Annabelle said, her voice too bright. "A bunch of us are going to spend the day at Bairs Creek. Jackie and Hiroki already have dates."

Akira struggled. We knew what he should say.

"I might have to work on Saturday," he said, avoiding her eyes. "Someone asked me to trade shifts."

"So tell him no."

"I don't like to go back on my word."

"Or maybe you have other plans."

Akira stood. "Come on, let's blow this joint."

"What's the rush? Have a soda."

"Are you coming or not?"

"All right, keep your hat on. Let me say goodbye to the girls."

He nearly dragged her out of the canteen. The tension between them paralyzed us.

"Where are we going?"

"Doesn't matter. Anywhere." Akira propelled her up the

street. Some of us followed, strolling as if we weren't trying to eavesdrop.

"You're acting awfully strange," Annabelle said. "It's that girl, isn't it?"

Akira swung her around and pinned her against a barracks wall, kissed her hard while she struggled. Some of us paused in the shadows, debated whether to stop him. Then Annabelle grew still and Akira caged her, his palms on the wall.

"Happy now?" he said. "That's what you wanted, wasn't it? You want more? You want to screw right here?"

"Stop it."

"You know you want it. Why wait for the picnic? We can go to Bairs Creek right now and do it there. Then will you believe what I say? I said forget that girl and I meant it."

"You're being mean. I thought you liked me." Annabelle began to cry.

"I like you fine, and you know it. But don't tell me who I can talk to and who I can't. We're not married, for crying out loud."

Annabelle twisted away. "Well, you can keep your pants zipped, mister. I wouldn't go with you tonight if you were the only man in camp."

"Fine by me." Akira turned to go.

"Some gentleman you are."

Akira bowed his head, then looked west, beyond the fence, before turning to Annabelle. "Look, I'm sorry, I'm being a Class A jerk. Let me walk you home."

Annabelle pushed ahead of him, arms crossed. Akira caught up and took her arm. A tumbleweed whirled past them, then settled in the dust as the wind died. The street was suddenly still, the air thick and cool.

On the barracks steps, we sucked our cigarettes. They walked past us, Annabelle staring at her feet, Akira's eyes on the horizon. Both of them looked miserable, like dogs left out in the rain.

Twenty-One

April 4–5, 2011

Kira woke up splayed over the steering wheel. Pain pulsed through her head and torso, and blood sweetened her lips. She tested her fingers and toes, assessing for spinal cord damage. Movement possible, sensation intact. Thank God.

"Are you all right? Hello? Can I help?" In the driver's side mirror, the image of someone hurrying toward the car, silhouetted in headlights. "Should I call an ambulance? Oh, don't try to get out, let me help you." The woman opened the car door and eased Kira out.

"Thank you. I need to call my husband. Can you find my phone? It's in there somewhere. And my purse." The car was nosedown in a shallow ditch. Luckily there were no trees around.

"I'm calling 911."

"No, I'm okay, really—I'm a nurse. But you could call Triple A for me." Kira lowered herself to a grassy patch of ground, careful not to overtwist her aching neck. The woman brought her the purse and phone, which showed four missed calls from Dan. It rang again and Kira picked up the call, said yes, she was all right, she didn't know about the car, someone was there with her, he shouldn't worry.

"Of course I'm going to worry," Dan said. "Jesus, Kira, I've been picturing you dead. Where are you? Did you call an ambulance?"

She said she didn't need one, and he said nurses were crappy judges of their own health and would she at least stay put and not try to drive the car. As if she'd be that stupid. But the edge in his voice told her to stop at yes.

"I'm on my way. Where are you?"

"On 4, a little west of Alhambra."

The woman got off the phone. "Triple A is coming. And you're shivering, poor thing." She draped her sweater over Kira's shoulders and sat next to her, peering at her in the darkness. "Your face looks pretty bad, honey. I really think I should call an ambulance."

"My husband is on his way." Kira pulled the sweater tighter. The urge to sleep was overwhelming, but she knew she should stay conscious in case of a head injury. What a fucking idiot she'd been, driving when Dr. Richardson said not to. Just as she'd kept working after the Hiroshima dream. Denial at its finest.

Dan arrived twenty minutes later, armed with antiseptic wipes, bandages, ibuprofen, and a flashlight. "You forgot the vodka," Kira said, but Dan didn't smile.

"God, look at you," he said, and the love and dismay in his voice made Kira want to collapse onto him, cry and apologize. But he turned away to talk to the woman, who retrieved her sweater and left a few minutes later, wishing Kira well.

A siren screamed and Kira looked at Dan accusingly.

"Yes, I called 911," he said. "And if you had any sense you would have too."

Kira succumbed to the paramedics, avoiding Dan's eyes. The EMTs were worried about a concussion and wanted to take her to the hospital, but she convinced them she could monitor herself. Besides, she added, her husband would be with her. While they were telling Dan what symptoms to watch for, the Triple A guy showed up.

"There's a body shop on Alhambra, right off the highway," Kira said. "I can't think of the name, but it's the only one there."

"I know the one," the driver said. Dan said no, he should take the car to their Berkeley mechanic. The driver shrugged and said, "Your call."

"Martinez is closer," Kira said. "And I want to go back to my mom's house."

"I am not going to argue right now," Dan said, his voice steely. He told the driver to go to Martinez, then helped Kira into the car. At the house, climbing the porch stairs, he gripped Kira's arm so hard it hurt.

Kira lay on the couch with a bag of frozen corn over her eyes. "Rest for a while, then we'll go home," Dan said. "I'm going to leave a message for the body shop to call me in the morning."

"I'm staying here."

"No, you're not. You can't be alone tonight, and I've got an early meeting in Menlo Park tomorrow."

"Reschedule it," Kira said. "I need you to stay here."

"We need to go home."

"I'm staying."

Dan swore under his breath and went into the kitchen. Kira heard him on the phone, his voice low, edged with worry and something darker. Fear, she thought. Guilt simmered in the back of her mind, then vanished when she snapped back to the scene in the car. Childbirth, the absence of free will, a nonnegotiable biological drive. A loss of control she knew all too well these days.

Dan came back with some ibuprofen for her and a glass of bourbon for himself. He left the kitchen light on and they sat in the semi-darkness and said nothing.

Kira woke up at first light, her body stiff and her mind a vacuum. No dreams, or none that she remembered. That was a first. Dan's side of the bed was empty, but before she could do more than register his absence she fell asleep again. When she got up two hours later, she moved as if her body were a single ambulatory bruise. It was a mistake to look in the mirror: nose spongy and bloodcrusted, raccoon eyes dark and shiny as eggplants.

She inched downstairs to the kitchen, and Dan abandoned his phone and papers to reheat the oatmeal he'd left on the stove. "You slept, so that's good," he said as if he didn't give a damn.

"Yeah. Where's the ibuprofen?" Kira took a bag of peas out of the freezer and molded it to her face.

"You crashed the car because you had a dream, didn't you? I can't believe I let you drive."

"I don't recall asking for your permission."

Dan slammed a cup of coffee, a bottle of ibuprofen, and a bowl of oatmeal on the table. "So what did the doctor say?"

The aroma of coffee made it past the frozen peas, earthy and spicy, the most desirable thing in the world at that moment. Kira lowered the ice pack to sip it, braving Dan's unhappy gaze, his perfectly justifiable concern. She contemplated lying, which would make her feel like shit and add more wreckage to their marriage. The truth would infuriate Dan, but it would be better in the long run. She tossed the ice pack on the table and downed four ibuprofen tablets and half the coffee.

"We talked about trying to find out more about the dreams, you know, the stuff that happens in them. It's that or try meds, and I don't want to do that because if they work I won't have the dreams anymore, and—"

"Isn't that the point?"

"It was, but if it really is my grandmother in these dreams—fragments, I mean; that's what I call them now. I think they're fragments of her life. If it really is her, I want to figure out what's going on. So I need to be here to go through Mom's stuff, to see if more fragments happen, and I can't go back to Berkeley because I can't drive. Obviously."

"Let me get this straight. You're going to stay here and look at old papers and shit and hope you'll have more dreams instead of taking meds and trying to put our life back together."

It wasn't a choice, not really. The hammering in her head intensified. "Yes. For now. I think they're happening for a reason and I need to know what it is. Dr. Richardson thinks you're right about the triggers, so I'm going to try to trigger them."

Dan was staring at her in disbelief.

"This is about my grandmother, Dan. It's important to me."

"More important than our marriage, obviously."

"I'm talking about a few days. A week at most."

"Suit yourself." Dan took out his wallet and tossed a stack of twenties on the table. "This should keep you in takeout for a while. Do me a favor and promise you'll see a doctor if you feel worse tomorrow. Although why I think you'd do anything I suggest is beyond me."

He gathered his things and left. No kiss, not even a goodbye, an omission she'd thought Dan incapable of. The thought crossed her mind without weight, left her sitting in welcome silence, the childbirth fragment replaying in her head. The abandonment of will, the sublimation to a biological force, a feeling of hurtling toward something wonderful and terrifying, of trying to control a runaway horse. *Hands like flies. An unimaginable force.* Two pregnancies of her own, and it took her grandmother's laboring to show her what childbirth was like.

Leaving her oatmeal untouched, Kira went into the office. An hour later she gave in to fatigue and pain, took a nap and a long bath, and lay on the couch listening to her mother's opera CDs. When her phone rang, it was Cam.

"Ignore whatever Dan told you," Kira said. "I'm fine."

"Shit, Kira, you could have been killed."

"I know, it was stupid of me to drive. I learned my lesson, I promise. So I'll be at my mom's for a while."

She turned down Cam's offer to come over, promised

to call the next day, then slept. When she woke up, she remembered Baby Kendall and called the hospital. The charge nurse spoke in the careful tone she used with parents whose anxiety rattled the phone. Baby Kendall was doing well; they'd weaned the vent again and started feedings. Relief swept through Kira, dissolving as her mind snapped back to Maddalena.

Kira hobbled to her mother's office and picked up the photo of Maddalena: collarbones as delicate as nasturtium vines, hair knotted low on her neck like an old-fashioned ballerina's. A few wayward curls suggested a woman free of care, perhaps playful, but her eyes said something else. They were grave, distant, as if she could see something the photographer couldn't, as if she didn't see him or his camera at all. As if she wasn't really there.

What was so important in Maddalena's life that it had to be relived in her granddaughter's head?

Kira took the photo to the kitchen and placed it in the center of the table. It looked solemn in its silver frame, commemorative, like the pictures of dead relatives some Italian families put on small altars in their homes, their loved ones side by side with the Virgin Mary or Jesus. Maddalena deserved an altar, Kira decided. She placed white tapers in cut-glass candlesticks on either side of a white linen placemat, then decided to add flowers. The pruners were where her mother always kept them, on a shelf by the back door.

Outside, sunlight streamed pain into her eyes. A koi nosed the edge of a lily pad, drawing Kira to the pond. Orange torpedos in black water, silent and sinuous. The fish had made a ruckus the day she and Dan got married, right here by the pond, thrashing about as if they'd been celebrating too. Four years ago. Were these the same fish from her wedding day, still swimming in unending circles, constant and serene in their confinement?

It had been an intimate ceremony, family and a few friends

semicircled around the pond. Dan had designed their rings, gold bands etched with kanji that said, "I love you." His suit was of pale gray linen, her dress an off-the-shoulder sheath of creamy raw silk, its simplicity sparked by spiraling sapphire earrings. She'd carried a bouquet of white roses, accented with irises that matched the blue of Dan's shirt. Her vows were minimalist, his poetic. His words had lingered in her mind for weeks afterward. He cried when he said, "I do," and Kira hadn't. Did that mean she didn't love him enough?

Dan had never proposed, had simply spoken, from their earliest days together, as if their marriage was a given. No question about their future, no discussion of whether they were right for each other. A truth not worthy of doubt. And now look at them. On that June day four years ago, neither of them could have imagined losing a baby, or a mother.

Kira went to the garden, where the light was more forgiving, filtered through rhododendrons and skeleton trellises tagged with new green. As a child she had spent hours here, lying in the damp shade and listening to the rumble of bees, the mechanical growl of lawnmowers. The garden offered a peaceful kind of solitude, an antidote to the loneliness of a house too big for two. Sprawled on her back, the blue sky umbrella above her, she used to imagine her blood racing in circles, from her head to her toes and back again. With her hand on her bony chest, she'd feel her heart thump, soft and constant, a gentle reminder of something her child self couldn't identify but that she was convinced connected her to the world.

Now the rain-softened earth beckoned, as if time had stopped. Kira lay down, head boomeranging, hand on her chest. Same heartbeat, same sky, same shaded silence. She imagined Aimi running on the garden path, grabbing peonies and tulips with her chubby hands, bringing the crushed blossoms to her grandmother, the two of them laughing together.

Time hadn't stopped. Aimi was gone, Rosa too. Only the garden was unchanged.

Kira moved deeper into the garden, to the back fence smothered in white flowers from an early blooming jasmine. Cutting the blossoms, she breathed in the perfume, sweet as raw honey on her tongue. As she reached forward, her vision dimmed momentarily, sudden traffic in her ears. She leaned against the fence, waited for the heat, the wash of orange.

Nothing happened. Kira laughed, tears stinging her swollen eyes. Here she was expecting a goddamn tell-all fragment and instead she'd nearly fainted. Suddenly the brightness was too much. A wave of loss, so sharp-edged she caught her breath. Aimi, Rosa, Dan. Time hadn't stopped.

TWENTY-TWO

July 20–24, 1945

Akira slid the "Friday" rock out of the lineup he'd placed on the windowsill in the hospital storeroom. Seven rocks in a row, one for each day of the week. If a rock was missing, it meant "Meet me tonight."

It was Maddalena's idea. "North to south, Sunday through Saturday," she said. "When you can meet me, take away the rock for that day. I'll put seven rocks near the fence—"

"Not too close," Akira said.

"No, not too close," she said, smiling. "If I can meet you, I'll match your pattern."

"What if you can't come by to check for my signal?"

"Then I can't meet you, silly. Make sure the rocks are big enough that I can see them from a distance."

It was a good system, and better than anything he could have come up with. "Awfully sneaky," Akira said. "I bet you've done this kind of thing before."

Maddalena answered in a voice so grave it was impossible not to believe her. "No, I never had a reason to until now."

That was nine days ago, and not a glimpse of her since, and no row of rocks anywhere near the fence that Akira could see. Either she had changed her mind about him or something else was keeping her away. Either way it wasn't good news.

Akira went outside, the third time that morning. He could still smell her hair, feel her mouth against his. He liked the substance of her, strong and sturdy, not balsawood like Annabelle. Tapping out a cigarette, he searched the horizon

158

for an approaching horse. Nothing. No cloud of dust, no rocks, no sign that Maddalena had ever been there.

He went back to his task of organizing the supply room, trying not to think the worst. Maybe it was just as well that Maddalena had gone AWOL today. Friday night was movie night, and he'd promised to take Annabelle to see *Two Girls and a Sailor*. It wouldn't be easy to come up with an excuse to ditch their plans. He'd liked movie night better in the old days, though, before the auditorium was built, when a screen would be set up in a firebreak and everyone lounged around on blankets. Out there in the dark, you could do some serious necking. There was no such thing as privacy at Manzanar, so you made do however and wherever you could; any of the fellows and their sweethearts would swear to that. There wasn't a dugout under a barracks or an out-of-the-way corner in the boiler room that hadn't seen some action.

The door opened and Paul poked his head in. "Any luck?" he said.

Akira shook his head and yanked a box from one of the shelves.

"You taking Annabelle to the movie tonight?"

"Looks like it."

Annabelle hadn't been easy on him since the night he'd pinned her to the wall, and he couldn't blame her. She'd kept her distance for three days, and when he asked her friends where she was, they sniffed and said things like, "Home crying her eyes out," or "What do *you* care?" They had it all wrong. He didn't like hurting people and he felt like a creep for doing it. Annabelle didn't deserve to be hurt. She hadn't done a thing except fail to be Maddalena.

Akira hoisted a box of antiseptics onto his shoulder and climbed the stepladder. Making order out of chaos gave him a sense of control, of creating harmony. That was probably why his mother liked working in the garden. A day or two ago, helping her tie up plants, he'd told her about his storeroom project and her eyes brightened, as if she recognized him in herself. "Working meditation," she'd said, tugging at a weed.

Once Akira had decided on a system, the storeroom work went quickly, and now the boxes and canisters and bins stood in neat rows. Up the ladder again, shoving another box into place, aligning its corners with the one underneath. The next person who unloaded supplies would undoubtedly mess up his system, but it felt good to set things right, even for a short time. After growing up watching his father at his workbench—the care he took with his tools, the precise way he fitted edges of wood together with exactly the right amount of glue—Akira found it impossible not to try to put everything in balance.

Thoughts of his father carried guilt. When was the last time he'd had a real conversation with his father? Or his mother? He should stay home in the evenings more, but it was hard to sit around and watch his parents shrink and fade into people he could see through. They had given up, and seeing the change in them was like taking a knife to the gut.

Paul appeared again. "Cake ahoy," he said, jerking a thumb toward the nurses' station. "Ellen's leaving tomorrow."

"Where to?"

"Ohio, I think."

So, Ellen was going east to freedom. Akira was glad his parents didn't want to go. Berkeley was home, and he'd be damned if he was going to live in Ohio or some other landlocked place because the government said it was okay. Too far from Japan to do any harm, that was how those idiots figured it. All of them were about as bright as General Dimwit, the nickname he and Paul had given to DeWitt, the moron in charge of Western defense who'd convinced Roosevelt that every person of Japanese descent on the West Coast was a threat. Roosevelt signed Executive Order 9066, but it had all started with Dimwit. Then again, maybe Ellen had the right idea. Starting over somewhere new might be better than going home, because who knew what going home meant? His parents had been forced to give up their apartment, his father's woodshop; his father had no money, no lumber, no tools. What would he do for work now? .

Akira shoved the last box into place, thumped it twice to flush it with its neighbor. It stuck out an inch and wouldn't budge. "Son of a bitch."

At the nurses' station, Paul was leaning on the counter, chatting up the ward clerk. Spotting Akira, he slid a paper plate heaped with white cake and blue frosting across the counter. "Saved you a piece. You're welcome."

Akira poked at the thick pink filling oozing from the center. "This isn't Jell-O, is it?"

"What's dessert without Jell-O? What are you, anti-American?" Paul laughed. "Let's go outside; I need a smoke." He slapped a hand on the counter, making the ward clerk jump. "Back in a minute. Don't go away now." The clerk smiled, blushing.

Outside, Paul sat on the top step and lit a cigarette. "She's a doll, isn't she?"

"Who?"

"The ward clerk, oblivious one. I do believe I'm making fine progress with her. Maybe I'll take her to the movie tonight. Nice tits."

"Yeah." Akira tossed the plate aside, staring at the horizon, willing a horse to appear.

"Man, you are no fun anymore, mooning around after Horse Girl all the time."

"Her name is Maddalena."

"Righ-tee-o. And you, my friend, are an idiot."

Akira punched Paul's arm, then dodged a return blow.

"Well, well, well, fancy meeting you here," said a voice from the street. It was Harry and his henchman, headed right for them. Akira got up. "Hold your horses. I've got news for you, Akira my friend," Harry said.

"Bug off," Paul said.

"I'm not talking to you, lard-ass." Harry smiled, thumbs hooked in his pockets.

"Lousy timing, Harry," Akira said. "Duty calls."

"Hang on, I've got a very important message for you from my sister. You remember her—Annabelle? Sure you do. She said to tell you that someone else invited her to the movie tonight. Which means he's in like Flynn and you're on the outs." Harry flashed a sarcastic smile. "A shame, isn't it?"

"Since when does Annabelle ask you to talk for her?"

"Since she can't be bothered with the likes of you, that's when. C'mon, Jiro. Our work here is done." Harry strutted off, breaking stride to smash a scorpion with the heel of his boot.

"Let's punch his lights out," Paul muttered.

"Nah, he's not worth the effort."

"Aren't you sore about Annabelle? Jeez Louise. Cocky bastards."

"Why should I be sore? Harry's lying," Akira said. Good thing he had no plans with Maddalena after all. "Screw him. I'll be the one taking Annabelle to the movie tonight."

"Yes!" Akira said. Marching parallel to the fence, a good ten feet out, was a row of rocks. Six rocks, because the Tuesday slot was empty. At last! After all this time, he'd see Maddalena again. It'd been ten days with no sign of her, ten nights of lying in bed thinking about her until his body ached. He'd almost stopped hoping. Annabelle could tell something was up because when she'd finally let him touch her again, after he'd taken her to the movie and proved Harry wrong, he went a little crazy. "Well," she said when he rolled off her, "if that's what saying no does to you, maybe I should say it more often." But she knew that wasn't it. She stopped by the hospital more often now, came looking for him in the mess hall. She was watching him, and he'd bet her friends were too. He couldn't chance running into any of them tonight. Lie low at work until nightfall, that was the best plan. As long as Annabelle didn't come looking for him, he'd be fine.

That evening he clocked out and slipped into the storeroom to wait. Tucked into a corner behind some shelves, he dozed off, jerking awake every so often to check his watch in a panic. Finally it was eight-thirty, time to go. In the locker room he exchanged his scrub top for a sweater, then stuffed a blanket into a duffel bag.

Half an hour later Akira stood in the shadows at Bairs Creek. A full moon would make going under the fence riskier this time, but he felt invincible. Watching the searchlights, he waited for an opening, then ran. Perfectly timed. Under the fence, out, safe.

At the orchard, he didn't have long to wait. When Maddalena appeared in the moonlight, he ran to meet her.

"Are you a sight for sore eyes! I thought you weren't coming back!" Akira lifted her off the horse and she clung to him, surprisingly fierce.

"I know, I'm so sorry! I knew you'd think I wasn't coming back. But Mama kept such an eagle eye on me I could barely breathe, and I didn't dare try to sneak out. I swear she knows something's going on."

"It's all right, you're here now. Come on, I brought us a blanket to sit on."

"Thank you." Maddalena sat, feet tucked under her, while Akira tethered Scout. "It was awful, not seeing you and not being able to tell you why. After we met, the next day at breakfast my brother Marco said he'd heard something thump against the side of the house during the night. It must have been me! I thought I'd die of fright. After breakfast I ran upstairs to see if the rope was still where I'd hidden it, and of course it was. No one goes into my room except Mama, and she was in the kitchen all morning. But all I could think about was Marco finding it and telling Mama. I've never been so scared!"

"I bet," Akira said, sitting next to her.

"So then Mama decided someone must have been trying to break into the house, and whenever she gets scared she gets even more protective than usual. Every time I said I wanted to go riding or go to Regina's, she said no, and I didn't dare disobey. Finally she calmed down, and last night I stayed over at Regina's. I set up the rocks this morning. They were in my saddlebag the whole time."

"I missed you."

"I missed you too."

Akira kissed her and it was exactly as she'd remembered it. In his arms, she could feel him the way she felt Scout when she rode bareback, the horse's long muscles moving under her thighs, her rhythm matching his. But this was different. She felt shimmery inside, but also perfectly still.

Akira traced the curve of her ear, watching her reaction. Her eyes were closed, her face changing in small, quick ways. So different from Annabelle. How much did she know about sex? He pushed her back gently, and she didn't resist. "I won't hurt you." He found her tongue, the rippled edge of her teeth.

Maddalena turned away. "Wait. Please." He rolled onto his side, head propped on one hand, watching her.

How was it possible to feel so many things at once? With him next to her, the world was made right. Everything inside her, everything in the universe—the trees and the wind and the moon, even Scout dozing nearby—settled into place, the way the world collected itself after a storm. But underneath the glow, in the back of her mind, an alarm shrilled like an air-raid drill. She glanced at Akira, who was clearly waiting for her to say something, probably wondering why she wouldn't let him kiss her. She wanted to, wanted that delicious sense of sinking into his body, but her thoughts were in a jumble—

the rope slapping against the house, her mother's fear, barbed wire, the towers, the searchlights. Akira was risking too much. He could die because of her. She should tell him they shouldn't see each other again until this horrible war was over.

"Talk to me. Tell me about when you lived in Berkeley," she said. "I want to know everything."

He sat up. "I'll tell you anything as long as you promise to meet me here again. Soon."

"I promise." She kissed him quickly. "Tell me about coming to Manzanar."

It seemed odd to speak of things he'd only carried inside him. Until now there'd been no need to talk about the day he and his parents had left home, what they'd left behind. Everyone at Manzanar knew the story; it was theirs too, a shared shame.

It happened so fast, he told Maddalena. The notices went up on April thirtieth and they had a week, one lousy week, to settle their business, pack what little they could, say their goodbyes. Each family was given a number, like they weren't good enough to have names. Then the waiting at Tanforan, sleeping in horse stalls, the long train ride, the bus to Manzanar. On the train, at first, Akira felt like they were on an adventure—the rocking cars carrying them off into the unknown, the windows covered as if to withhold a surprise. He was only fourteen; what did he know? Only the ashen faces of his parents kept his imagination in check. And then, the disbelief when they arrived—the shock of the desert, the naked land, the makeshift buildings of Manzanar. No trace of kindness or welcome, only wind and dust and rock, mattresses of straw, endless lines for every need. Bells that called them to eat, whether the food or the hour suited them or not. Food that made them sick, vomiting and shitting in a room filled with other groaning people, lined up like pack animals. Manzanar was a place where you threw

165

away everything you knew about how people should live, a place where you tossed your expectations, your standards, your pride into the toilet along with the indigestible food. Nothing would remain recognizable in a place like that.

As a child, Akira had never imagined hardship. The apartment his family rented in Berkeley was spacious and warm, and he'd had his own room, plenty to eat, good schools, friends he'd known all his life. He liked where they lived on Tenth Street, in a neighborhood called Ocean View with the bay shining in the west, where the toy-sized bridge braved the ocean winds and tides, and forested hills guarding the east. His father never lacked for work. The pieces he made were simple but fine, his attention to detail uncompromising. His mother cooked and mended, sang songs from her childhood, padded silently past on hardwood floors while Akira practiced piano.

"Berkeley sounds wonderful," Maddalena said. "It must have been awful to be taken away and locked up."

Akira shrugged. How could he begin to explain? Of course she was curious, but curiosity had its ugly side. He'd seen it in the early months at Manzanar, when valley residents came by to stare at them, looking none too friendly. "I don't like to talk about it much," he said. "I will if you want me to, but not right now. Let's not ruin tonight."

"I don't mean to pry. It's only because…"

"Because what?"

"Because if it's about you, I want to know it, whatever it is. Everything, good or bad. That's all."

For a moment Akira couldn't speak. "Thank you," he said when he found his voice. "You're something else, you know it?"

Maddalena blushed. He acted like she'd given him a hundred dollars. "How about playing the piano? I wish I could play. Is it okay to talk about that?"

"Much better." Akira kissed her lightly.

He was five when he started taking lessons, on a neighbor's piano. His mother had taken him to the neighbor's house one day, and while the women chatted he sat at the keyboard, fascinated by the cause and effect: push a key, hear a sound. The woman noticed his interest and told his mother to bring him back on Wednesday, when her son had his lesson. "Let him try it," she'd said when Akira's mother refused. Not because she didn't want him to play, but it was a matter of *giri,* indebtedness. Akira didn't know what the woman said to change his mother's mind—there had been some transaction that evened the score, of that he was sure—but on Wednesday he sat at the piano again. Already the ivory keys, silky and cool, felt familiar, part of him. His feet dangled beneath him, inches from the pedals.

It was agreed that he would study, that he had talent. Three years later, his parents stood smiling when he came home from school one day and saw the piano they'd bought him, a Steinway baby grand, gleaming and gorgeous, impossibly expensive. At eight, he'd been thrilled and unquestioning, but when he was older he understood the sacrifices his parents must have made to buy it.

"You had to leave it behind," Maddalena said. "That's so sad."

"I try not to think about it. Anyway, when I was in sixth grade I decided I was going to be a concert pianist. Play at Carnegie Hall and the top opera houses in Europe."

"I thought you wanted to be a lawyer," Maddalena said.

"I do now, but that's because of what they've done to us. Back then, all I cared about was music. And baseball."

"I want to hear you play."

"I'm not very good anymore. But I'll get back to it someday, when I have a piano worth playing again. There's one at Manzanar, in the canteen. It's a real piece of junk, but I play it sometimes. I'm writing a song now." *For you,* he thought.

"Have you written many songs?"

"I've always tinkered. A few songs, and part of what I thought might be an opera one day. Nothing very good."

"An opera!" Maddalena laughed.

"What's so funny?"

"My grandfather likes opera, but I don't know any boys who do. In Lone Pine it's all sports and trucks and fishing. I bet the boys at my school don't even know what opera is. What's yours about?"

"It's based on a very old Japanese story about samurai—those are warriors. It's called 'Chushingura,' which means 'The Forty-Seven Ronin.' It's about loyalty, dishonor, and revenge—good stuff for an opera, right?" Akira laughed. "What kind of music do you like?"

"I hear Artie Shaw and Tommy Dorsey on the radio sometimes. I like them."

Akira nodded. "Big bands, yeah, good stuff. I like classical music better, though it's not as popular with the girls, that's for sure. I almost quit playing because of that, when I was twelve. I had a crush on a girl who thought musicians were sissies, and I didn't practice for a whole month. I dishonored my parents by not working as hard as I could—that was my duty, to pay them back for buying the piano. After I missed two lessons, they made me pay for every one I missed, and pretty soon I had no spending money. Anyway, the girl I liked started going steady with a jock, so I gave up on her. Eventually I figured out that any girl who didn't like my music wasn't the girl for me."

"I like classical music too," Maddalena said.

Akira laughed. "Good. Now it's your turn to talk."

"Next time. I should go."

"When is next time?"

"I don't know," Maddalena said.

They kissed again, lingering this time, and she wanted to crawl inside him, blend her breath and blood and muscles with his. Finally she pulled away, and Akira helped her onto the horse.

"Please be safe," she said.

"Don't worry. Dream about me, okay?" He grabbed her hand and kissed it.

When the thud of hooves had faded, Akira set out for Manzanar. Crouched among the cottonwoods, he tracked the searchlights. One beam skimmed past, then another. He ran, slid underneath the fence and stumbled, his mind screaming *run run run run!* A beam grabbed him, tracked him. He dodged sideways and nearly fell, startled by a high-pitched zing. Then another zing, dirt spraying just ahead, and he rolled, hands over his head. The light swung off him and he ran again, reached the barracks and slipped into the shadows, his muscles quivering.

Warning shots. If that guard wanted him dead, he'd be dead.

Shoving his shaking hands into his pockets, Akira headed home. He'd done it. He'd been outside twice now and nothing could stop him, not Executive Order 9066, not barbed wire, not searchlights or machine guns or rifles. He could survive Manzanar. With Maddalena to dream about, he could survive anything.

Twenty-Three

April 5–6, 2011

Kira spent the afternoon and evening in a funk. Twice she almost convinced herself to call Dan, and when she finally managed to do it he didn't pick up. She left him a message about Baby Kendall and skipped the apology she'd rehearsed in her head. At nine, when she was in bed icing her eyes and nose again, he called back.

"Got your message. Good news about the baby." His voice was flat.

"Yeah." She bit back a remark about how long it had taken him to call her. "How are you? Did you go for a run?"

"No, I had dinner with my folks. Mom wanted to know if she could do anything for you, but I told her you were at your mom's and wanted to be alone." He sounded either hurt or pissed. Probably both.

"Look, I know you don't get why I'm doing this. I understand. But I need you to try to understand too. There's something about the dreams I never told you. And the fragments. It sounds kind of nuts."

"So what's new?"

"You're not making this any easier." Kira went downstairs, tossed her veggie ice pack in the freezer, and poured a shot of brandy.

"Sorry, go on."

"You know how when you dream, you're, like, the protagonist? Well, in these things I'm not, my grandmother is. I'm not in them. I mean, I *am* in them, but I'm her. My grandmother."

170

Silence. Then: "So when I drew your grandma, I was drawing you? You were her?"

"Yeah, kind of. It's hard to explain. I guess the best way to describe it is that I'm in her head. There but not there. I know what she's feeling in the moment and I can see where we are, but I don't know much else. Anyway, the point is, what if these things aren't dreams? What if they're my grandmother's memories, and I'm *living* them?"

"You're not serious."

"Jesus, Dan, you're the one who was researching quantum entanglement. I know it's not that, but it could be *something*. Dr. Richardson says there's stuff we don't know."

"Please don't tell me you think you're channeling your dead grandmother."

"Not funny."

"So how many dreams have you triggered so far?"

His tone stung, but what hurt most was how unlike himself he sounded. Kira heard water running in the background, the scrape of the teakettle. He'd be puttering around the kitchen in his favorite Cal Bears T-shirt, the one he'd worn so often it was nearly transparent. He was trying, this beautiful, sweet man she'd married. He always did. Her mother used to say Kira didn't appreciate Dan enough, and every time Kira had felt defensive. Which meant her mother was right.

"I miss you," she said.

"Right."

"I'm just distracted by all this, can't you see that?"

"You probably don't even remember what I said the other day."

"About what?" she said at the same time the words hit her. *Have another baby.* "No, of course I remember. It's just—I'm not ready to think about that yet."

"Obviously."

"Please don't be mad. It's not that I don't want to. I just… not now."

"Listen, I've got to get some work done. I'll talk to you later."

"Can you come over tomorrow? And bring the photo albums and my laptop?"

A beat. "Sure."

Dan hung up, and Kira spent the rest of the evening sitting at Maddalena's shrine and wandering around the house, her childhood flooding back. There was so much she'd never told Dan—about her mother's pendulum swings from loving to neglectful and back, her own loneliness as a child. The miscarriage.

She texted Cam. *Do I take Dan for granted?* The message whooshed away, and twenty seconds later a *yes* pinged back. Then the phone rang.

"Thanks a lot," Kira said to Cam.

"Well, you asked."

"Do you ever think you shouldn't have married Kip?"

"Of course, every time he acts like a jerk," Camille said. "What's going on?"

"I don't know, things just feel so one-sided. Sometimes I think I'm faking it. Our marriage, I mean."

"I don't think you are."

"I can't worry about it right now," Kira said, "but if I don't, I might lose Dan. And I almost don't care."

"You want me to talk to him?"

"And say what?"

"Reassure him, I guess. After all, he and I are kind of in the same boat." Kira started to protest, but Camille cut her off. "I get it—you've got to take care of you right now, and that's fine. I'm here when you need me, and so is Dan."

"I hope you're right."

Kira hung up, remembering what it was like to be thirteen, alone and confused, praying for something she didn't understand. Not much had changed.

❧

The next morning brought good news: Baby Kendall was on full feedings, and if he held his own for twenty-four hours, they'd extubate him. If her head hadn't weighed a thousand pounds, Kira would have danced a jig. She texted Dan and Cam, got a string of heart emojis back from Cam, and tried to still a jangle of panic when Dan didn't reply.

After sorting through the last of the boxes and files from her mother's office, she'd found nothing. No journals, no letters that might explain the mysterious man, nothing that triggered a fragment. At lunchtime Kira sat at the kitchen table eating cereal, staring at her grandmother's photo. "I'm here," she said. "You can do your thing anytime now." Maddalena gazed at nothing, as cryptic as the goddamn *Mona Lisa*. Kira rinsed her cereal bowl and headed upstairs to the attic.

In the womblike space under the eaves, sunlight bored through grayed windows, casting warm stripes on dusty floorboards. *See, Dan, perfect for channeling dead grandmothers.*

She started with the steamer trunk where she'd found the veiled hat all those years ago. Nearly three feet tall, the trunk had dark leather skin that curled at the corners and "Moretti" stenciled in patchy white capital letters on each side. It had probably come from Italy on the boat with her great-grandparents, but Kira had never thought to ask. Inside were towers of folded fabric, curtains and runners and tablecloths bearing the toxic smell of mothballs. A small white cloth bore the initials M.M.B. embroidered in dark blue. Maddalena Moretti Brivio. Joe Brivio, another man who'd left faint footprints in the family's past. Kira thought of Maddalena in her rocker, the man calling to her from downstairs with a snarl in his voice. If the fragments were real, Maddalena hadn't loved him. How had she felt about taking his name?

At the bottom of the trunk was a shallow cardboard box with a housedress in a cabbage rose print, faded red on a dark blue ground, and a silver comb and brush set, browned with age. A small oval box in burgundy leather held a necklace of three twisted strands of beads in rose, sapphire, lavender, and white, plus matching clip-on earrings. In another small box, tortoiseshell hair combs, turquoise costume jewelry, a pale pink rosary.

Kira sat in the rocking chair and fastened the beads around her neck. Maddalena had sat here, in this chair, rocking her baby. Rolling the orbs between her fingers, Kira thought about Maddalena's life: growing up on a ranch in Owens Valley in the 1940s, married young, the move to Martinez, a child right away. Then dead at thirty-four. Her own age now, Kira thought, the realization a blow. She should look for Maddalena's obituary, not that it would tell her much. Obituaries emphasized the positive and the sentimental and avoided unpleasantries like suicides. Death certificates might have more information, but their facts often hid the truth.

Kira rocked, and the beads grew warm under her fingers. *Yes.* Warmer still, and she was sinking, sinking into the salmon and yellow and green. *Concentrate.*

There. Maddalena is in a bedroom with a single window, an iron bed. It's the same room as the wedding-dress fragment. The little cabinet with the spindly legs is there, and the necklace Kira is wearing now is piled in a rainbow heap on top of it. Maddalena's breathing is fast, her motions quick and nervous. She's wearing a shapeless dress, her hair in a braid. She wedges the back of a chair under the doorknob, pulls the curtains closed, and kneels in front of the cabinet.

No one can see what I have, so little, so precious. I cannot let them take it away from me. I wonder how I can breathe, my throat is so tight, and my eyes ache from crying. I check my pocket—yes, it's there. Hide it, quickly.

A door slammed. "Kira?" Dan called.

Kira clung to the image of Maddalena poised in front of the cabinet, but it was gone, *gone,* goddamn it. She wiped away tears of frustration. Dan's footsteps drummed through the living room, the kitchen, up the stairs. Then the attic door opened and Kira rocked to her feet. "You ruined it! You fucking ruined it!"

Dan froze, his hand on the doorknob.

Kira stared at him, her hand at her throat, the beads still warm, willing herself to speak. *Say you're sorry, go to him, forget the fragments. Make dinner, make love.*

Kira turned toward the cabinet. Dan went downstairs, closed the front door, started his car. Kira heard the sounds as if from a great distance, dismissed them. If she'd triggered one fragment, she could do it again. Kneeling, she opened the cabinet door.

Twenty-Four

July 25, 1945

It took no time for word to spread. We heard it in the mess halls, the beauty parlor, the newsroom, the latrines. Someone had been shot at, not going outside the fence but coming back in. A warning: don't tempt us, don't push your luck. The war is not over yet.

Who was it, who saw it? Akira Shimizu, that boy asking for trouble, that's who it was. No one knew who said it, but everyone believed it. There was talk of the white girl, the one on the horse, that Akira went outside to find her. A fool's errand. He denied it, but the truth was on his face. The others who went under the fence to fish or taste freedom had no reason to hide what they did; they took pride in their adventures, competed to see who would stay out the longest, come home with the coveted golden trout. Akira's lie revealed the truth. We saw the change in him, the restlessness, how he ran hot and cold with Annabelle. And Annabelle—we saw the stoniness in her face, how she used it to crush her sorrow. She let her anger rise and surface. We understood. Better anger than devastation, than humiliation, than grief.

The day after the shot, Akira and Annabelle argued, their shoulders hunched, their voices hushed, then rising. We saw wildness in him, need, frustration. And, in the softness of his mouth, the desire to spare Annabelle the pain he had inflicted on her. But he had made his choice. Her sapling body became an ancient pine before our eyes.

"My brother was right," Annabelle said. "He saw you for what you are, but not me, oh no, I was too stupid. I thought you loved me." Tears in her voice, her face made unlovely by suffering.

"You're making it worse than it is," Akira said.

Annabelle turned on him, her instincts sharp. "Do you think I'm blind? You're a selfish pig!"

He tried to answer, then gave up and drifted away. Annabelle remained, her body bowed.

At Akira's barracks, we overheard his parents speak to him about honor, respect for tradition. Akira offered apologies, asked for forgiveness. But he made no promises. He did not say he wouldn't leave again. He did not say there was no white girl. Although he would deceive Annabelle, he would not lie to his parents. The truth was in what he did not say.

Some of us called him reckless, foolish, a bad son. Some of us remembered youthful passion, the body's tempestuousness, and we understood. Not one of us believed Akira would stay inside the fence. All of us wished for his safety.

Twenty-Five

April 6–7, 2011

The cabinet was empty, of course, as it had been the last time Kira had looked, as it had been for years, and opening the door hadn't triggered a damn thing. Yet she could still feel her grandmother's urgency, her need to hide whatever she had in her pocket, her blackness of spirit, as if she had lost everything.

Go there. A thought as piercing as a voice. Kira spun around. "You're imagining things," she mumbled into the silence, and turned back to the cabinet. It wasn't much of a hiding place; anyone could open the door and see what was in there. Unless... She ran her hand along the interior. The top surface felt rough, as if it hadn't been sanded. Or maybe something had been stuck there? Kira took the cabinet to the kitchen and laid it on the table, found a flashlight in the junk drawer. There—the outline of a rectangle, dried glue or the fossilized remains of tape.

"Way to go, Grandma!" Kira said. Then her excitement trickled away. So what if the cabinet had been Maddalena's hiding place? Whatever she'd kept there was gone, removed or discovered decades ago.

Kira put the cabinet in the bedroom, collected the necklace and earrings and housedress from the attic and laid the dress on the bed, smoothing its wrinkles. It slept there, a keeper of secrets, smelling of regret, stale darkness, and neglect.

&

The next morning Kira woke before dawn, naked and cold. Crumpled on the pillow next to her, the housedress lay like a deflated torso. She must have worn it to bed, taken it off during the night, though she didn't remember doing either. She did remember drinking too much whiskey, pinning her hair back the way Maddalena wore hers in the portrait, and trying on the housedress. Lit only by the glow of a bedside lamp, she saw what her mother had seen, all those years ago—Maddalena in herself.

She couldn't remember getting in bed, but she remembered dreaming. This time she was herself, riding a horse on an open plain surrounded by mountains, flying between ecstasy and foreboding. "Stop!" she cried, but no sound came out, and when she pulled on the reins, they flapped on the horse's neck, slack and lifeless.

Kira sat up, and again the thought penetrated her brain: *Go there.*

She left an apologetic voicemail for Dan, showered and made coffee. With her hair coiled like Maddalena's and makeup caked over her bruises, wearing the matching beads and earrings and a white silk shirt from Rosa's closet, Kira took a cab to the Contra Costa County Clerk's office. One form to fill out, a reasonable amount of waiting, and voilà— her grandmother's death certificate. "Cause of death: trauma to the head and internal injuries, car versus pedestrian." The words gutted her. She'd known how Maddalena died, of course, but the impassive words lent brutality to her death. "Place of death: 1100 block of Haven Street, Martinez, California. Time of death: approximately eight p.m." After "Witnessed by," an illegible scrawl that she assumed was Joe Brivio's. How much had her grandfather known that this paper couldn't tell her?

Back at the house, Kira left another voicemail for Dan, then texted him. It occurred to her that he was ignoring her because she didn't sound convincingly repentant. She made coffee again, went outside to feed the fish while the machine hissed and spat. With each tossed pinch of food, the golden bodies surfaced and disappeared. Maybe the women in her family weren't meant to stay married, weren't capable of loving the men they had. Or of letting the men love them.

Wind rustled in the trees and the afternoon light dimmed as if preparing for rain. In the house, the air felt heavy, the kitchen subdued but vigilant. Kira half expected to see something change—a shift in the texture of the paint, perhaps, or in the color of the countertops. Wind stirred the top branches of the towering eucalyptus trees, exuberance bordering on violence, and pink plum blossoms flung themselves onto the lawn, misshapen polka dots against the green. Dan loved storms, called them nature's power trips, and if he were here he'd go outside and watch. Kira rushed to the front porch, watched the sky laboring under low clouds, pressure building. Thunder groaned in surround-sound, and seconds later lightning roadmapped the sky. Then, with a roar, rain slapped at the street, pelted the parked cars and raced through the gutters in instant streams, an over-the-top display of might and will. Ten minutes of torrential excess, then the clouds drifted east, thinning into tendrils, moisture rising like steam. Kira hugged her arms, suddenly chilled.

Let go. She stopped breathing. *Let go of me.*

A hand on her wrist, so hard it hurt. Fear. And rage.

She waited, ready for more. But her hands remained cool; the porch, the street, empty; the world rainwashed.

Another chill, rippling through with high voltage. That hand on her wrist—Maddalena had run into the street here, died here. Had someone attacked her? What was the date? It was 1963, but when? Kira rushed inside, grabbed the death certificate. It said March, not April, the seventeenth, not the seventh. Not today. She didn't know whether to be relieved or disappointed. The paper shivered in her fingers.

Those iron claws on her arm. Someone had been with

Maddalena right before she died. She was trying to get away.

Kira charged through the house, closing blinds and curtains and flipping on lights. The buzzing continued, an internal alarm. *Go there.* Where? She felt like screaming, turned on the CD player to let the music pour out, Gounod's *Roméo et Juliette,* one of her mother's favorites. Had she loved opera because Maddalena did? What else didn't Kira know?

Go there.

"Go where?" she shouted. "For what?" She charged into the kitchen, where a box from the attic sat on the table. She rifled through it—stacks of pictures, herself as an infant, a toddler, dozens of cards. A box of birth announcements, pale pink card stock topped with a slender bow of yellow satin. Kira exhaled, slowed herself. Her birth announcements: Kira Madeleine Esposito, born at ten a.m. on December 12, 1977, six pounds, eight ounces. Half a dozen cards unused, one a reject with a note, a few crossed-out words, no signature. Her mother's handwriting.

Dearest Helen, I am overjoyed! Our sweet little girl is healthy and so beautiful, with dark brown hair that stands up straight and eyes that remind me of my mother. She always told me I would have a daughter one day and I was to name her Kira, and so I have, in her memory. I don't know why she chose that name, but she was quite insistent, and I think it suits our little love perfectly. Her middle name is for my mother, of course.

What? Her grandmother had named her? Maddalena, who couldn't possibly have known she'd have a granddaughter one day, had chosen a name for her?

The wind chimes outside the back door erupted into a mad dance and Kira jumped. The dream from last night, the horse beneath her like an unstoppable train—she was on the verge, she could feel it. On the verge of something she had to give in to. The thought again, snakebite fast: *Go there.*

She grabbed the announcement again. Its deckled edge, linen finish—it was something she might have chosen

181

herself, for Aimi, whose name meant "love" and "beautiful" in Japanese. What joy there must be in announcing the arrival of a child. The tears came without warning, and with them memories of that devastating day in the hospital, her belly too flat, the bedsheet pulled taut across her knees and feet so that she could barely move. Her mother and Dan next to the bed, crying. The nurse taking Aimi away. Sunlight filling the window, pretending it was a beautiful day.

They'd stumbled through the paperwork, the decisions, the funeral, all of it surreal. In the weeks that followed, Dan pretended to be strong, handled everything because Kira couldn't. But she knew how destroyed he was. He startled at the slightest sound, went running and was gone for hours, came back looking half dead. In the evenings he sat looking over his drawings, then abandoned them without ever having picked up a pencil.

Kira and Dan had gone silent, but Rosa spoke of Aimi incessantly, going on and on about her beloved daughter's first child, her darling grandchild, such a loss, it was more than anyone could bear. Kira wanted to scream at her to shut up, and Dan knew it. He would steer Rosa into another room, tell her Kira couldn't talk about Aimi just now. He would sit with Rosa, listen to her like he always did, which was one reason she adored him. She had from the moment she met him.

Kira had taken Dan to her mother's house for dinner, and Rosa had watched from the doorway as they approached, her face the flat white of porcelain. "Excuse me, what's your name?" Rosa said in a breathless voice. She'd looked startled, a mixture of excitement and alarm.

"Mom, this is Dan." Kira nudged Dan and said, "I told her your name. Really."

Dan smiled, unfazed, and offered his hand. "Dan Kaneko. Nice to meet you, Mrs. Esposito."

"Oh, of course, forgive me. Kira told me all about you.

I just—I thought—for a moment you reminded me of someone." She smoothed her hair back, a nervous habit. "But never mind that, please come in. And call me Rosa."

"He reminds you of someone? Really? Who is it, Mom?" Kira followed Dan and Rosa to the kitchen.

"Someone my mother knew. I don't know his name. Please sit, Dan, and have some wine. I've made my mother's lasagna, Kira's favorite. I hope you like artichokes."

"I do. It sounds delicious," Dan said.

Rosa beamed. All through dinner, she smiled and looked at Dan with what Kira could only describe as love. After lemon cake and coffee, while Dan took out the trash, Rosa grabbed Kira's hand. "You'll marry him," she said as if stating the obvious.

"It's kind of early for that, Mom. But I'm glad you like him."

They left at ten, after Dan promised to visit again soon. On the way home Kira said, "My mom really likes you. It's kind of a miracle, actually, since you don't have Italian blood. I'm half kidding," she added, "but only half."

"I believe it," Dan said. "My parents are the same way, but they had to get over it a long time ago. When I told them I was taking a blonde to the senior prom, they nearly stroked out. Both of them. Simultaneously."

Kira laughed. "At least I've got dark hair."

"I'm glad your mom likes me, but tell her not to get any ideas. I'm already taken." Dan stopped at a red light and kissed Kira until the driver behind them honked.

The birth announcement slipped out of Kira's hands as she stood, her head a dandelion gone to seed. The wind had quieted, but the air in the room felt thick and charged. Dan had reminded her mother of someone Maddalena knew. Maddalena had named the grandchild born after her death.

Go there.

"I'm trying," she said. Talking to herself was becoming a habit.

Dan had brought her laptop and left it on the dining room table. A quick search for Maddalena's obituary and there it was, a brief accounting of her death, attributed to a tragic accident, with the usual dates and survivors and funeral plans. A few other sites carried the same article. Then Kira saw a link to someone's blog, something about racism. She clicked on it.

The blogger had posted a scan of an article in the *Inyo Register* with the comment: "Found at the Eastern California Museum while doing research for a school paper. Unreal."

The headline screamed, "Jap Killed by Lone Pine Rancher." Below, in smaller type, "Love Nest Discovered, Girl's Father Takes Revenge." Kira scanned the story and froze at her grandmother's name. What the hell? Maddalena was the girl, and the man who was killed was a Manzanar internee named Akira.

Akira? Then it hit her. Akira, Kira. Her grandmother had named her for the boy she loved, before Kira was even born. This was it, the beginning of an answer. Hope percolated, bumping up against fear. Was this a path into the maze or a step into an abyss? How could any of this be real?

Kira zoomed in on the black-and-white photo that accompanied the story, what looked like a school picture of a teenage boy with hair that fell forward, wire-rimmed glasses, a smile that broke her heart. She knew instantly that it was the photo in the attic dream, the one Maddalena showed to her baby. Akira was the mysterious man Rosa had spoken of—dark-haired, yes, but Japanese, not Italian. That was why Rosa had stared at Dan when she met him; he'd reminded her of Akira. She seemed to understand that, yet she knew nothing about Akira, not even his name. But she knew he was important to her mother. If Rosa had had the dreams, what else had they told her?

Kira searched for a date on the article: August 23, 1945. Maddalena had been sixteen.

Tears blurring the words, Kira read the piece again. The *Register* had gone for the lurid, editorializing about the blast of a shotgun, the splattering of blood, the screams of the girl. It said Maddalena's brother, Marco Moretti, discovered the lovers' hideout and fetched his father. "We didn't ask any questions," the article quoted Marco as saying. "It was plenty clear what was going on. My papa wasn't going to let a Jap have relations with his daughter."

Those poor kids. They were *kids*. By the third reading Kira was able to skip the gore and look for facts. Akira was from Berkeley—from Berkeley!—born there to Japanese parents, a carpenter and a housewife. They'd been sent to Manzanar in the spring of 1943. Akira worked as an orderly at the hospital. Manzanar—Kira remembered it from school, a World War II internment camp. Racism in the guise of national security.

A wave of sweat and nausea hit her. Opening the back door, she breathed in crisp air until her skin cooled. Peppermint tea would calm her stomach. She was filling the kettle when the sounds of a baseball game drifted from a nearby park. Heat seared her hands and the kettle clattered into the sink. The color shift descended, swift as winter nightfall.

A figure shimmered into view. Maddalena, a small, hesitant figure in slacks and a white blouse, halfway up the stairs to the bedroom, her hand on the railing.

The radio clicks on and there's the crack of a bat, the cheers of the crowd. I should have gone to the attic earlier, before he got home, but there was the laundry, the market, the cooking, the baby. But there is time—his mind is on the game, and he won't leave his chair in the kitchen and come looking for me, ask why I'm going upstairs, what I need up there. It will take only a minute to get to the attic, only a minute to look at his picture, his dear face. One look, then I will be able to go on.

Downstairs, the baby begins to cry. I lean against the wall, my hand at my breast. There is no time. I will have to endure another meal listening to him complain that dinner was late, that I don't understand how hard he works, how hard he works for me, for the baby. My baby, not his. He finds every chance he can to remind me of that. The tingling in my breasts becomes a burn, wet circles bleeding into my blouse. The baby—I have to go to her. Later, I will take her with me to the attic, hold the picture up so she can see it. She looks too much like me, too Italian. If only I'd had a boy, his small round face a mirror of his father's.

Kira couldn't move. The late afternoon sun angled through the screen door, a silent dust storm swirling in the light. That baby was Akira's. Akira was Rosa's father, Kira's grandfather.

"Akira," she whispered. "Kira."

Kira. Akira. Kirakira.

TWENTY-SIX

July 27–29, 1945

At four o'clock, when dinner was prepped and the kitchen was clean and her mother had turned on the radio and "put her feet up for a minute," as she always said, as if not working required an explanation, Maddalena saw her chance. "I'm going for a quick ride," she said. "I'll set the table the minute I get back, I promise." Her mother nodded, eyes closed, and Maddalena ran to the barn.

As she headed north, the wind was fierce, hurling dust and sand like Zeus pitching lightning bolts. Within minutes Scout's black eyelashes looked like pale, crocheted fringe and Maddalena was coughing. She pushed the horse hard. There would barely be time to get to Manzanar and back before her mother raised a fuss.

Today Manzanar was quiet—the fields empty, a lone policeman making his rounds, people scurrying between buildings, heads down. For a moment Maddalena wished she were home, listening to the ghostlike gusting of chimney drafts and watching the weathervane whirl atop the barn. At the hospital there was no sign of Akira, but the Friday rock was missing from the windowsill. Maddalena moved her rock, matching his, banishing the fear that she might be too late. Surely he would check for her signal before dark. *Tonight, tonight, tonight.* She galloped Scout all the way home.

"You call that a quick ride?" Her mother sat at the kitchen table with the silver chest and a bottle of polish, scrubbing a platter engraved with pomegranates and pineapples. She nodded toward a stack of silverware. "You can start on those. And no more dillydallying."

"I'm sorry, Mama. I didn't mean to be gone so long, but Scout needed a good run. I think he's getting fat." Not true, but her mother knew nothing about horses. "The wind was awful! The whole time I was wishing I'd stayed home." Maddalena dabbed polish on a serving fork. "Is that a new apron? It's very pretty."

"I won it in the church raffle." Her mother glanced down at the blue-and-yellow-striped fabric. "It's pretty enough, I suppose."

"Why are we polishing the silver? It's not a holiday."

"I told you two days ago that your father's cousins are coming. You have a mind like a sieve."

This was news of the worst kind. The women would stay up late talking, which would make it hard to sneak out. Maybe impossible.

"I hope I don't have to give up my bed like last time."

"Francesca will sleep on a cot in your room. Your Uncle Aldo and Aunt Jo will stay in the guest room."

There went her plans, up in smoke. Francesca wasn't here yet and she was already a pest. And Akira would risk his life tonight for nothing. If only she could go back to Manzanar and put the Friday rock back in its place. Maddalena's eyes burned, but she absolutely could *not* cry in front of her mother.

"Can't Francesca sleep with her parents?"

"Put a twelve-year-old in the same room with her father? Perish the thought."

How would she survive the night? It would go on forever, all the boring conversations and the stupid, boring games she'd have to play with Francesca, worrying about Akira the whole time. How would her mother feel if *she* couldn't be with the love of her life because of some stupid relatives she didn't care about?

The timer dinged and her mother peeked into the oven.

Maddalena took the cleaned silver to the sink and doused it with hot water from the kettle.

Cleaning and cooking and shopping, that was all her mother did. And worry about everything being exactly right. Worry, worry, worry. Maddalena tried to imagine her mother as a flirtatious girl or a bride in love. It seemed impossible that she'd ever been anything but a dried-out worrywart with lines around her pouchy eyes and a scrub brush in her hand. She and Papa never kissed, unless you counted an occasional peck on the cheek, which Maddalena certainly didn't, and that was usually after her father had his whiskey. Maybe they gave up kissing like they'd given up playing Bingo on Saturday nights after Marco was born. The ranch was their whole world, but it wasn't going to be hers.

"When will they be here?"

"After dinner. I want the kitchen spotless."

There was nothing she could do, nothing but endure the evening and think of Akira every single minute. And worry, exactly like her mother.

By ten-thirty Akira had figured out that Maddalena wasn't coming. He told himself it was something minor, inconvenient but harmless, like a stomachache, but he couldn't help imagining one dire scenario after another. She could have gotten caught leaving the house, or Scout might have stepped in a pothole and thrown her. Maybe she was lying unconscious somewhere in the desert. After waiting ten more minutes, he set out on a search.

It was slow going, even with the moon nearly full. Cutting west to Foothill Road, Akira walked south, calling Maddalena's name. His voice carried across the desert, then faded, absorbed by the distant mountains. The valley had never seemed so vast.

It must have been after midnight when he came to a

driveway running straight as an arrow toward the Sierra, ending in a glow of lights. Definitely a ranch, but most likely not Maddalena's. If he remembered right, she'd said hers was six or seven miles from Manzanar, and he couldn't have gone that far. He cut through a field, brush snagging his trouser legs, and circled wide around a two-story house and a barn twice its size. The soft bleating of livestock, shadowy shapes of vehicles. Then a porch light clicked on and a sharp voice from the house brought on a chorus of barks. Akira threw himself to the ground, breathing hard. A woman came onto the porch, asked someone named Henry if he knew how late it was, and didn't he know morning would be here before he knew it. "Coming," the someone named Henry said. Boots scraping on a stoop, the muted thunk of a door closing, utter blackness when the porch light died.

Akira waited a full minute before he moved again. Not far from the road he found a small outbuilding, a storage shed with corrugated metal walls and a slanted roof. The door sagged on its hinges, but it closed well enough. If he couldn't make it back to the camp before dawn, he could hide out here. He noted the shed's location—a quarter mile southeast of the barn, west of a clump of trees about a hundred feet from Foothill Road. If he had to, he could find it again.

An hour or so later he came to another barn, its paddock sharp-scented with manure. Between the barn and the house lay hard-packed dirt, a few skeletal pieces of farm equipment. Convinced that this was Maddalena's ranch, Akira sat with his back against the barn, fighting to keep his eyes open. A glimpse of Maddalena, proof that she was safe, was all he needed.

A soft clocking of hooves, a muted chorus of lows and grunts from the cow barn startled him awake. He glanced at the upstairs window. There! A flicker of white through the open curtains, the backlit shape of a nightgowned girl. Maddalena. He'd know her anywhere.

Akira stood and stretched, the weight of worry gone and,

in its place, the ache of longing. He wanted to climb up to that window, slip through it into Maddalena's arms. But the lightening sky told him dawn approached.

By the time he reached Manzanar, the eastern sky had paled to warm lavender. Hidden in the trees along Bairs Creek, Akira debated whether to chance it or go back to the shed. Then, voices in the guard tower closest to him, two silhouettes instead of one, the searchlights idle. Shift change.

He went low and slow this time, a shadow in the semidarkness. Under the fence silent as a snake, move and wait, move and wait. Well clear of the fence, Akira walked briskly, swinging his arms, a guy out for an early morning stroll. A magenta glow crested the Inyos. He pictured Maddalena in that upstairs room, in her bed, himself curled behind her, his face in her hair and his hand on her breast. *If only.*

The cousins left on Sunday after church, and Maddalena had never been so glad to wave goodbye to anyone in her entire life. Two endless days with Francesca-the-pest and not a single chance to get to Manzanar. She had wanted to take Francesca riding in hopes that Akira would see them and understand why she hadn't shown up, but her aunt would only let Francesca ride around the paddock, and only if Maddalena kept an eye on her. What a joke. Francesca rode Scout in circles, waving and shouting "Giddyup!" like an idiot while Maddalena wished with all her heart that she could smack her. Manzanar seemed as far away as Canada.

After the relatives left, Maddalena cleaned up the kitchen and put the good china and silver away. When she thought there couldn't possibly be anything else her mother would want her to do, she asked if she could go to Regina's house. To her shock, her mother said yes, and thanked her for being nice to Francesca. Maddalena hugged her and dashed out the back door. *Please, please, please let Akira say he'd be at the orchard tonight.*

In the yard, her father and Marco were working on the pickup, dust and grease on their coveralls. Marco glanced at her with a look she didn't like, smug and superior like the boys at school who lied about skipping class and got away with it.

"Riding again, huh?" Marco said. He had their father's thick body and ropy arms, black hair coarse as a Brillo pad. Both of them always stank of cows and sweat and dirt.

"What does it look like?" Maddalena said. As if Marco cared what she did. She felt like smashing a cowpie in his face.

Minutes later, her father appeared in the barn. "Doing a lot of riding lately, I hear," he said, watching her saddle Scout. "You staying on Foothill Road like your Mama wants you to?"

"Yes, Papa." Maddalena tightened the saddle cinch. "Foothill Road to Regina's house, like always. I wish she lived closer."

Since when did her father care how often she went riding, and where? It wasn't like him to be suspicious; he was too busy with the ranch to notice her. Girl business was Mama's business, he always said. So why was he paying attention to her now? Had someone seen her near Manzanar?

Maddalena rode off, certain that her father and Marco were watching, their eyes boring holes in her back. What if Marco had seen the rope? *Don't be silly,* she thought. Marco had no reason to go into the yard late at night, and he wouldn't notice the rope in the darkness if he did. Still, the thought spooked her, and the feeling dug in, tick-deep. What if her father followed her and dragged her home and locked her in her room forever? Or what if he and Marco went snooping at the Hendersons'? She'd have to warn Regina to cover for her and say of course Maddalena had been there whatever day they were asking about, she was there all the time. Mrs. Henderson never paid much attention, so she'd take Regina's word for it and back her up.

Half an hour later, Manzanar rose in the east. As nervous as she was, going there now was out of the question. Maddalena kept her eyes on the road ahead, her knees tight into the saddle, certain that her father and Marco could see her from miles away. Akira might be there on the steps, wondering why she didn't stop. *Don't look. Not even a glance.* Keeping her gaze on the narrow patch of desert between Scout's ears, she whispered, "I'm sorry I can't stop now, but I'll be back. Meet me tomorrow night. I love you."

She meant it. Life without him seemed impossible, and she couldn't imagine feeling this way about anyone else. Right or wrong, she loved Akira. Tomorrow night she would prove it.

At Regina's house, the girls sat cross-legged on the bed, knees touching, heads together, the door locked and the dotted-swiss curtains drawn.

"You have to help me, I'm desperate," Maddalena said. "I need to stay here tomorrow night so I can meet Akira at the orchard. Papa and Marco think I'm up to something, I know it, and I don't dare sneak out of my house now. But if I'm here, no one will suspect a thing. Oh, and this is important! If anyone comes here and asks your mother or you if I was here on a certain day, any day, say yes, even if I wasn't. Make your mother say yes. Promise."

"I promise. This is so exciting!" Regina bounced, her ponytail swinging. "Have you kissed him yet?"

Did she dare say what she was thinking, that she'd decided to prove her love to Akira? Give herself to him, that was how Mama would say it, and she'd make it sound wrong in every way, like Akira would be cheating Maddalena out of something she didn't want to give. And that wasn't true, because she *did* want it, and he would be giving her part of himself too. Wasn't that what love was—two people wanting to be together in every way, understanding each other the way starlings did, swooping around like a single bird?

"Of course I've kissed him. This is serious, Regina. I'm in love, honestly and truly in love."

"Oh, my!" Regina breathed. "Did he say he loves you too?"

"Not yet." Maddalena flushed, then added quickly, "But he risks his life to come out here and meet me; that means something. Every time I see him I wonder if it could be the last time." She paused. Regina chewed on the end of her ponytail, her eyes shining. "So I'm going to let him—I mean, we're going to...you know."

"You mean...? Oh my heavens!" Regina said. "Aren't you scared?"

"I'm always scared. We could get caught. Akira could get shot."

"No, I mean aren't you scared of...doing it? I've heard girls at school say it hurts. Tons."

Maddalena shook her head. She hadn't thought about that, but it didn't matter. "So you'll help me?"

"Of course, silly! I'll ask my mom if you can stay over tomorrow. And after you and Akira...you know..." Regina blushed. "You have to promise to tell me what it's like. If it hurts, and everything!" She bounced off the bed and out of the room.

"I promise."

Maddalena opened the curtains. Manzanar was too far away to see, on the other side of the apple orchard she thought of as theirs now, hers and Akira's. No matter how far away she was, she liked to believe that if she looked toward Manzanar and thought about Akira hard enough, he'd feel it.

"I love you," she said, pressing her hands against the windowpane. Akira was out there, invisible, behind that fence, behind those dreary walls, living a life he didn't deserve. She hoped he was thinking about her. She was always thinking of him.

Tomorrow.

Twenty-Seven

April 7–8, 2011

Kira's phone rang. Dan, finally. "You won't believe what just happened," she said. "I know you're pissed at me, and I'm sorry, I really am, but I've got to tell you this."

It came out in a rush—the newspaper article, Akira, the murder, everything jumbled together. "Her father killed him, can you believe that? And that's not all. Akira is my grandfather. Maddalena loved him and she told my mom to name me for him, even before I was born, even though she didn't know Mom would have a baby, or that I'd be a girl. Isn't that crazy? I'm part Japanese. Here, let me read the article to you."

"Hang on," Dan said. "I came over there to help you, because you *asked* me to, and all you did was scream at me. And now I'm supposed to listen to some garbage about you being Japanese? This is ridiculous. You've got to come home and see another doctor. This guy is wasting your time—he's wasting our *lives*, Kira. All you do is talk about these dreams and you don't give a shit about us."

"Just listen, please, this is important! I can't ignore what's happening, and I'm finding things out about my family, important things, and I thought you'd be happy about that. Yes, Dr. Richardson encouraged me, and all you do is tell me to take the fucking meds and pretend everything is all right. Well, what if it's *not* all right and the meds would only cover up what's really going on? Not everything fits into your neat little world. All you want is a sane wife who can carry a baby to term. Did it ever occur to you that maybe I can't do that?"

"That's not fair. Besides, plenty of women lose a baby and have a normal pregnancy later."

"It was two." The words were out before Kira could stop herself.

"What?"

"I had a miscarriage a long time ago. Don't worry, it wasn't yours. It's not important now."

"Jesus, Kira, why didn't you tell me?"

"I just said it was a long time ago, and I didn't think you needed to know. I don't want to talk about that—what's important is that I found out about Akira, and if you loved me you'd understand that I need to make more of these fragments happen and figure out what's going on. Instead you want to make the whole thing go away."

"I'm trying to understand, but you're making it really hard."

"Prove it. Come over here and look at me, knowing what you know now, and then tell me I don't have a Japanese grandfather. I can *see* it, Dan."

"Give me an hour," he said, surprising her.

She waited on the porch, sitting one minute, pacing the next, swinging between excitement about Akira and worry that Dan would say no way she was Japanese and they'd end up arguing again. She thought about calling Dr. Richardson, but then the Audi's headlights swept around the corner. As she started down the stairs, the car cut to the curb, its headlights blinding her. She fell, a moment of suspension followed by a burst of heat, the bloom of salmon into green.

Soft light, no shadows. Kira can see everything. She is in the house, in the upstairs bedroom. Maddalena sits at a desk where today, this moment, there is no desk. She wears slacks and a white blouse, white tennis shoes. Her hair, dark brown shot with premature gray, is in that familiar low twist. She is young but long past girlhood, years of wind and sun and grief on her face. She has been writing.

Something is different this time, Kira realizes. She's observing Maddalena instead of *being* her, and Maddalena seems to know it. She's talking to herself but also to Kira.

After seventeen years, it is done. I have been thinking of this moment since Rosa was born. I can wait no longer. I owe my daughter the truth, owe Akira the honor of remembrance.

Outside, blue sky darkens at the edges, warning of rain. Poplars sway. Birds fall silent.

Rosa is seventeen, old enough to know that the man she believes is her father is not her father, old enough to know that her grandfather, a stranger to her, was a murderer. Old enough to make her own decisions about who to love. It has taken more strength than I'd imagined to withhold the truth all these years, an effort that left me trembling inside, my stomach and liver and lungs shrinking to nothing within the shell of my body. The years of lies, of silence, of enduring this marriage for Rosa's sake. The years of tucking her in bed, bathing and brushing my hair with shaking hands while he lay there, waiting. My skin would tighten, anticipating the touch of this man I never wanted, never loved.

Kira closes her eyes, opens them to tears. Maddalena slips the letter into an envelope and seals it.

What a relief to put on paper the letter I've written in my head a dozen, two dozen times, words I've wanted to say to Rosa since she was old enough to understand them. It's a relief to finally put things right, to give Akira his place in his daughter's world. Now Rosa will know everything—the love that began at Manzanar and survived the war but not hatred and prejudice, what Akira and I risked to be together, how we pledged ourselves to each other. How, when Akira died, I wanted to die too but couldn't let myself, because I was carrying his child. Now Rosa will know I had no choice but to marry the man my parents chose for me. To hide your shame, they said. But it wasn't my shame.

Knowing I carried Akira's child brought joy at first, then grief sharper than the barbed wire that had imprisoned him. Akira would never see his child, would never know he had one. It tore me open. Later, I was grateful that the baby looked like me, because life would be easier for her this way. An Italian girl with Italian parents, an Italian last name—no one would question the warm tones of her skin, her nearly black hair. Her eyes, green like mine, hid the truth. The planes of her face, that hint of the East—my husband had Slavic roots, I told the few who noticed. They had no reason not to believe me.

I will tell Rosa all of it, face to face. Then I will give her the letter as proof that she did not imagine our conversation.

Maddalena tucks the envelope into her pocket. Then, suddenly, the scene changes to the dining room. Kira recognizes the man she'd always thought was her grandfather. And her mother, a teenager, wearing a peasant blouse and long, beaded earrings, thick eyeshadow in '60s blue. Maddalena is clearing the table. Dishes rattle in her hands.

"You nervous, Lena? What for?"

My breath disappears. He sits back in his chair, one hand heavy on the tablecloth, his eyes on me. He has never trusted my silence. He is right not to.

"It's nothing. I worked in the garden for hours today, pulling weeds. My arms are tired."

"That so? I didn't notice nothin' different out there."

I meet his gaze without flinching, force a smile. "If you can't tell the difference, that proves how much weeding needs to be done. The oxalis and crabgrass went wild with all that rain."

"Can I be excused?" Rosa stands, ready to bolt. "I told Sarah I'd call her tonight. She's going to help me with my party invitations."

"Take a walk with me, Rosie. I've hardly seen you all week."

"It's going to rain, Mom. Please? I promised I'd call her."

"A short walk, that's all, before the light goes. It's so pretty before a storm. Then you can call Sarah."

"Let the kid go." My husband's eyes are searchlights. The toothpick he's chewing on jumps and waves. "Go on, Rosa." He jerks his head at the door, his eyes on me, and she bounds out of the room. "What's so important, Lena?"

"Nothing." I smooth my hair, smile again. "Can't a mother spend time with her only child?"

"You think I'm stupid? Something's not right with you."

I ignore him, pass behind him to the sink. Then he is on his feet, in my path quick as a lizard, his breath in my face, his fingers steel bands on my arm.

"I can see right through you, Lena. Right through you. Look me in the eye and tell me you're not gonna do nothin' I wouldn't like."

I twist away, make it to the front porch before his hand grasps my wrist.

"Let go."

"Get inside."

"Let go of me!"

He clamps a hand over my mouth and he must think I'd never do it, but he's wide open and I knee him with seventeen years of rage. I run down the steps and I see Akira falling, falling, and the blood, all the blood, and my mind floods crimson and I run, I keep running, and I see the headlights and I mean to stop but I cannot.

"What happened?" Kira said. She was on the couch, under her mother's handmade afghan.

"You tell me," Dan said. "I pulled up and saw you fall. By the time I got to you, you'd passed out. Scared me to death."

She half heard him, her mind still clouded with fear. That's what had driven her grandmother out of the house that night, fear and years of outrage and grief. The headlights, the helplessness, the desperation—Maddalena hadn't planned to kill herself; the letter was proof of that. If only Rosa had known. Kira brushed away tears. Why hadn't Maddalena stopped running? She meant to. Did the headlights draw her with the kind of self-destructive urge you get when you stand at the edge of an abyss, half wanting to fall? *Could she have stopped?* If Maddalena had lived, how different her daughter's life would have been. And Kira's.

Pain, bounding and clear, overrode her thoughts. "My ankle is killing me."

"I'll get an ice pack. We seem to specialize in those lately."

Dan went to the kitchen, then reappeared in the doorway. "But if you can complain, you must be okay. You *are* okay, right?"

"I guess so."

Dan anchored a bag of frozen corn to Kira's ankle with a dishtowel. Then he sat, looking at her as if he knew there was something she wasn't telling him.

"Ouch. Some nurse."

"You taught me everything I know," he said. "I'll get some ibuprofen." He came back with a glass of water, handed her three pills, and stood watching her.

"Don't worry, nurse," Kira said. "I'll take my meds."

"It's not that."

"What, then?"

"You're beautiful, and I fucking miss you."

They cried together then, Dan with his head on her chest like in the hospital, when neither of them knew how to go on living. Eventually they calmed, their breath synchronized, and Kira threaded her fingers into Dan's hair, soft and straight and black. Like Akira's, she thought.

What a strange thing to find out you're not exactly who you thought you were, or that you could be two people at once. If she could accept that, what else was possible? What other absolutes should she redefine? She would spend the rest of her life questioning everything, wondering what lay hidden beneath the known, or what she thought was known. There were no absolutes, no blacks or whites, no rules that couldn't be bent if enough heat were applied. The concepts of God, an afterlife, reincarnation seemed too rigid. Maybe it was simply that everything in the universe was connected, on every level—quantum entanglement taken to infinity, to the metaphysical, so that there was no such thing as a single entity, discrete in its skin, answering to nothing and no one. The whole universe was tangled, a snarl of consciousness and desire, fear and ignorance, wisdom and intuition, crossing every boundary of place and time. If this way of thinking was a kind of enlightenment, it had come in a straight line from Maddalena to Rosa to Kira. Except Rosa hadn't recognized it, or she'd let her husband's doubts keep her from the truth.

Dan was caressing her now. She would make love to him; she wanted to. For now, she would force Maddalena into the shadows, let her body overrule her brain, be Dan's wife. Later she would tell him about the fragment, how her grandmother died. Dan didn't believe in absolutes; he believed in possibilities, in the existence of things not yet given the stamp of proof by those who needed it. Surely, given enough time, he could take the next step and believe she had been given this knowledge. And that Akira was her grandfather.

They had come this far since Aimi. They'd survived. They had a bond, rich as blood in its fine moments, and Kira hoped it would hold. If it disintegrated, became something that existed only in her memory, it would be her fault. She accepted that. There was no turning back.

The next morning Kira woke before dawn and lay in bed while Dan slept.

Go there.

Maddalena could not be ignored. Kira started to get up and Dan rolled over. "Hey. Morning." He tried to pull her on top of him and pain blazed through her ankle.

"Owww, shit! That hurts like hell."

"Sorry," he said, nuzzling her breast.

"No, you're not." How tempting, the thought of their old life together.

Go there.

She let Dan make love to her again, her body going through the motions this time, her mind busy with images of mountains and horses. Afterward, while Dan cooked breakfast, Kira took a bath, listening to him bang around the kitchen and talk to himself. He sounded happy, as if their lovemaking let him think life as they used to know it waited in the near distance, its blanks and shadows already filling in with textures and colors.

"I got oatmeal in the works," he shouted. "Any raisins around here? How about brown sugar?" More banging, then a few growled bars of the Rolling Stones. "Brown sugar, how come you taste so good? Brown sugar, just like a young girl should."

"Your mind is in the gutter," Kira called.

Footsteps, then Dan's voice at the bottom of the stairs. "What'd you say, wifey-san?"

The nickname he'd given her on their honeymoon. He hadn't called her that since Aimi. She smiled and yelled louder. "I said you have a filthy mind."

"Yes, I do, you lucky girl. Hey, are you still naked?" A pan lid rattled and water hissed on the burner. "Uh-oh. Hold that thought."

Kira sank deeper into the tub. Robin's-egg-blue sky painted the bathroom window above motionless treetops. No whispering leaves today, no wind, no rain, only sunshine and the muted purr of mourning doves. She could almost believe the fragments had never happened.

Go there, go there.

Once out of the tub, Kira stood naked before the bedroom mirror with the housedress pressed against her. Then she set it aside and put on the white blouse again. It was dirty and grass-stained, but nothing else in her mother's closet looked right. She fixed her hair in Maddalena's low twist and crept downstairs, her ankle protesting.

"You look beautiful, wifey-san," Dan said. "I like the hair. But honey, that shirt is dirty."

"I know. It's fine."

Dan gave her a quizzical look. "Sit and eat."

Over breakfast he told her about his midcentury-inspired designs for a six-bedroom house in Palo Alto, with a budget he'd only dreamed of. Kira half listened, her mind back on the porch with Maddalena, running down the steps into the street.

"Let's head home after breakfast," Dan said. "I canceled my work stuff. We can pick up a pizza and spend the rest of the day in bed."

She shook her head. "I can't leave yet. Things are happening."

Dan went to the sink, made a big deal about scraping the pot and putting away the leftovers. "I see," he said finally, his back still turned.

"I don't think you do."

He swung around. "I thought after your big revelation you'd be ready to come home. You wanted some answers and you got them. Your grandmother had a lover and you think he was your grandfather. You think you're part Japanese. What else is there?"

"Don't ridicule me."

"I'm not. But just because they were lovers doesn't mean Akira is your grandfather."

"It makes sense, don't you see? Akira is the mysterious man Mom talked about, and Mom was the baby in my dream, the baby Maddalena rocked in the attic. I'm positive she was his daughter. And if Akira was her father, that makes me his granddaughter."

"You want to believe that."

"That's very supportive of you. Thanks very much." What had happened to her intuitive husband, the guy who believed in fate, serendipity, convergences?

"Do you have any idea how hard this is?" Dan leaned against the sink, rubbing his temples. "I don't know what to think, Kira. And on top of everything else, you tell me you were pregnant before Aimi. Give me a break here."

"You think this is hard for *you?* You're not the one whose brain is being hijacked. What about the fragments?"

"What about our life together? How many times do I have to prove myself to you? Now I'm asking you to do one thing for me. Come home. From what I've seen, the fragments can happen anywhere."

"I can't." Kira hobbled to the back door and into the yard. The pond slept, its glassy surface opaque. How long had it been here? Did Maddalena's husband build the pond for her? Did she enjoy feeding the fish, watching them snap at the surface, glitter in the shadows? What else did Maddalena like? What could she have possibly enjoyed, this woman who needed to see her lover's face in a photo in order to bear looking at her husband? Did she have any friends, a confidante? How did she manage to live, knowing Akira died because of her?

Go there.

If there were answers, they weren't here.

Dan maneuvered a kitchen chair through the back door, and the gesture brought tears to Kira's eyes. "Please sit down," he said. "Tell me what happened yesterday."

"You really want to know?" she said, and he nodded. "Okay. Remember that day when you sketched Maddalena in the wedding dress, and how weird it was that you made her sad even though I hadn't told you she was?"

"Of course."

"This is even weirder." She explained why this fragment was different, that she was watching Maddalena, not being her, and that her grandmother was telling her story in detail. "It's not just the newspaper article, Dan—I mean, the reason I think Akira is my grandfather. Maddalena put everything in a letter to my mom, but she died before she could give it to her. I know what she wanted to tell her. I believe it's true. If that makes me crazy, then I'm crazy. But I think I'm not. I just need more time."

"And you have to be here."

"Yes. Alone."

"You know, the premise behind quantum entanglement is kind of similar to the concept of karma, how what we do affects others and eventually ourselves. In that sense, we're all connected."

Maddalena, her daughter, her granddaughter. A bloodline.

"All right, here's the deal," Dan said. "We talk twice a day; I'll call you in the morning, and you call me before you go to bed. I just want to know you're not lying unconscious at the bottom of the stairs. Deal?"

"No calls, only texts."

Go there.

"God. Okay." Dan pulled her up, crushing her to him. "Do whatever you need to do so you can come back to me."

Kira nodded. The list she'd made—*Find Maddalena's house,* she'd written. That's what the voice in her head was saying. Go there, find her grandmother's home, see what was left of Manzanar, stand in the desert where Maddalena and Akira had been lovers. Kira had always envisioned Maddalena here, in Martinez, but her grandmother hadn't really lived in this house; she'd only existed here, died here. She had lived where Akira was. Owens Valley.

There. Yes, there. Find Maddalena.

When Dan left, Kira checked train and bus schedules, then packed a bag. She emailed Cam, promised they'd talk next week. The next morning she got to the station at four, half an hour before the first train to Bakersfield. Half dozing on the bench, she remembered the horse from her dream, all muscles and sweat beneath her, galloping through a wide ribbon of rocky land walled off by mountains. The sky opened above her, ahead of her, an infinity of promises.

Twenty-Eight

July 30, 1945

The desert lay in soft-edged shadows, lit by a half moon. Waiting for Maddalena, Akira spread the blanket he'd filched on top of the one he'd already stashed in the orchard. Six days since he'd seen her, six long days of wondering and doubt and hope, made tolerable once he knew she was safe. He pictured her silhouetted in her bedroom window, mentally filled in the details the shadows had hidden. Her hair had floated free, a backlit cloud, and he'd imagined burying his face in it.

Twenty minutes later Maddalena slid off Scout's back and kissed him with a wildness that surprised him. "I guess you missed me," Akira said. "I've sure missed you."

"Yes," Maddalena said, and kissed him again. He leaned into her and suddenly her plan, which had occupied her thoughts since yesterday, a plan she'd made with one hundred percent conviction, seemed reckless and foolish, as if her mother's disapproval had trailed her all the way to the orchard. The thought of their naked bodies entwined beneath these trees made her face burn.

She pulled away and settled on the blankets. "I'm terribly sorry about last time. We had houseguests and I didn't know they were coming until the last minute, and I couldn't get back to the camp to signal you."

"I went looking for you." Akira sat next to her.

"You did?"

"Of course! I was worried as all get out. At first I thought you'd gotten caught, then I was afraid Scout had thrown

206

you." He laughed. "Then I had this wild idea that I'd find your house and see you in an upstairs window."

"An upstairs window? Wait—you found my house? No, you couldn't have. You didn't!"

"I did. I knew it was you even though I couldn't see your face. I barely made it back to the camp before dawn."

"You did that for me? You're very brave." He must love her then. Did it matter if he didn't say so? His hand was on her ankle, sliding up her calf.

"I had to know you were safe." He kissed her, easing her back. *Go slow, don't scare her.* He'd never wanted a girl so much. Her lips opened and she softened beneath him. He touched her collarbone, her breast, and she stopped his hand.

Yes or no? She was thinking both, and Akira was waiting, as if he understood her doubts. He was sweet, kind, a gentleman. He'd stayed in the desert all night worrying about her safety, came back to see her even though she had disappointed him. He was watching her, stroking her hair. His hand moved to her ear, tracing its curves, and desire overwhelmed her doubts.

"Let me," she said, and unbuttoned her cardigan. They had no time for fears, hesitations, dreams. They had only this moment.

His hands and mouth were everywhere at once, his weight shifting. A rock dug into her hip and he silenced her cry with his mouth. Velvet and bristles and motion, cool air on thighs, the heat of breath. Her body drove into the ground, opened with the pain. It lasted forever and only a few minutes.

Maddalena pulled Akira down, his face against her neck, his hair in her mouth, a beautiful dead weight on her body, and she thought she would never be this happy again.

TWENTY-NINE

April 9–10, 2011

The bus pulled away, spewing orchid fumes into the desert air. Evening lazed over the town, wearing traces of the day's heat but none of its weight. The air was parchment thin, delicate and scented with earth. To the west, jagged peaks lined the valley, a tachycardic wall.

Kira set down her bag and got her bearings. Lone Pine, population two thousand. A small grocery on one corner, a hardware store and 7-Eleven opposite. Western-themed signs everywhere and, on a rooftop across the street, a life-size white horse, hooves forever raking the air. Beyond the town, thirsty remains of orchards yielded to sage-dotted slopes climbing toward the crenellated fortress of the Sierra to the west; to the east, the softer Inyo Range, with mineral-rich runoff that must taste of pink and blue, yellow and rust. So unlike each other, these mountain ranges, that they should belong to different continents. This was Owens Valley, land of water wars and Hollywood westerns, of farmers and ranchers. But that was years ago, when the soil was damp and rich, before the high desert valley became stripped and parched. Before its apple-fed town, Manzanar, became a prison. This valley was Maddalena's home. Akira's home too, though he wouldn't have called it that.

Kira headed for the motel a quarter mile up the road, her ankle aching after thirteen hours of trains and buses. The western sky shapeshifted in slow motion, red brushstrokes haloing over the Sierra. From an open lot, sharp scents of earth and rock. Distant yips floated and faded, the breeze bearing them east. The Sierra in silhouette, red sky headed toward indigo. The breeze carried dust and sage, a sense of familiarity, of homecoming.

The motel, booked at fifty dollars a night, was a white U-shaped building with a shouting neon sign. Two wooden chairs sat outside each door, and beneath the office window, on a shelf adorned with rocks and rodent skulls, a dried lizard lay twisted and brown like a fallen leaf. Kira touched its brittle head. A souvenir of a landscape doing its best to hang on.

The screen door to the motel office screeched as it opened, the sound reminiscent of campground cabins and mosquitoes. In a reception area where four people would constitute a crowd, two orange chairs flanked a dust-furred plastic ficus.

"Welcome to Lone Pine. I'm Mike." A man with gray-flecked hair rose from behind the countertop, a fishing magazine in his hands. Large brown eyes, a quick smile, a sun-toughened face; he could be forty or sixty. "You must be Kira." A fleeting frown as he took in the remnants of her black eyes.

"That's me." She pointed to her face. "Car accident. Airbags are brutal."

"Did its job, though. You were lucky—I've seen my share of the unlucky ones." Mike plucked a big plastic number 7 from a row of room keys dangling on a pegboard.

"Slow time of year?" Kira asked.

"A few fishermen, couple of hikers. It's early yet. You came at a good time, beat the cold *and* the heat." He handed her the key. "You need anything while you're here, you ask for me."

"Actually, there is something. I need to hire a driver for a few days. I want to explore the valley and I can't drive."

"Hey, Dustin, want to make some dough?" Mike yelled toward a back room. Then to Kira: "Don't worry, he's my nephew. Good kid."

A sleepy-looking young man in a Lakers shirt and ripped jeans appeared and nodded at Kira. "Hey."

"Lady here wants someone to drive her around the valley," Mike said. "Your outfit running okay?"

"Sure thing." Dustin scratched a wiry thatch of pumpkin-colored hair. "How's fifty dollars a day, ma'am? Plus gas. If you don't mind riding in a pickup truck."

"You're on. Tomorrow at eight," Kira said. "And no calling me 'ma'am.'"

Her room was classic cheap motel: two anemic chairs at a Formica table, coffeemaker on the mini-fridge, TV dominating the fake Colonial-style dresser, the toxic tang of bug spray, thick enough to taste. The bedspread, a quilted floral monstrosity, crackled when Kira flopped onto the bed.

Her phone chirped, a text from Dan. *You ok?* She'd forgotten about his message that morning.

Yes, ankle is better. Sorry about this morning. Sleep well. xx

She turned off the phone. No one knew she was here. She was alone in a way she hadn't been in years, completely free.

The next morning at eight Kira texted Dan an all-okay and stepped outside. Warm air caressed her arms, and the sky radiated promise. She stretched, breathing deeply. The day opened before her, a new path through the maze. At the thought, a current of nausea swept through her.

In the motel office Mike was sweeping dust from the tiny foyer while Dustin emptied a coffee pot into a thermos. "Morning. Where to?" Dustin said. "You want to go fishing? I know all the best spots."

"I got plenty of gear, you need anything," Mike said.

"No, I'm doing research." Kira handed Mike a printout of the newspaper article about Akira's murder. "Do you know anything about this? It was big news back in the '40s. The girl, Maddalena Moretti, was my grandmother."

"No kidding? I remember my dad talking about this," Mike said, tapping on the paper. "Biggest news around here besides all the movie folks who come to town. People want to shoot the Wild West, they come here; there's a movie museum down the street if you're interested. Anyway, there's never been many Italians here in the valley. Back then, just the Rossis up in Bishop and your folks. Everybody knew who they were."

"I'm looking for my family's ranch. Would that information be in the town records?"

"That's easy," Mike said, smiling. "It's the Marshall place now."

"You know it?"

"Pretty much everybody does; your grandma's family was downright famous—or infamous, I guess," Mike said. "Good luck. You change your mind about fishing, let me know. I got rods, reels, the works."

Kira followed Dustin to his truck and waited while he tossed McDonald's boxes, Subway wrappers, and Styrofoam cups behind the duct-taped seat. "Sorry about the mess," he said.

"No problem." Kira gazed at the mountains, so sharply etched in the thin air that they seemed steps away. She felt light, alive, but her nerves kept firing. She'd see Maddalena's house today. What else would she find?

As they drove north the Sierra kept pace, steely gray granite slopes and white-topped peaks that reined in the high country of Yosemite. To the east, the Inyos marched in waves, pixilated with rusts and piney greens. In between, a forlorn expanse of scrub brush, sandy earth, stunted trees, and a pencil-thin highway racing north and south.

Just past Lone Pine, Dustin swung west into a warren of skimpy dirt tracks. The truck hit a pothole and Kira yelped, grabbing the door handle.

"Sorry." Dustin glanced at her, his hair a brilliant pale orange in the sun. "You don't drive, huh?"

"What?"

"I was wondering why you didn't drive here if you wanted to explore the valley. Most of the people who come by bus are climbers. There's a Whitney shuttle from Vegas."

"I can drive, but I've got a bum ankle, and, well, kind of a medical condition. I was in an accident. Thus the black eyes."

Ten minutes later, at the end of a long, straight road that turned out to be a driveway, the truck stopped in front of a drab two-story house fronting the Sierra. A gravel track curved past the house to a barn, and flowers made a drought-defiant stand in lilacs and blues on either side of the porch.

"This is it?" Kira said. "My grandmother's house? We're here?" She fought back tears, a tightening in her throat. "I can't believe it."

She'd had no idea the place would be so isolated. She pictured Maddalena as a child, sitting on the front porch swing with a book or combing a ragdoll's hair. Jumping rope, playing tag. Who would she have played with? As far as she knew, Maddalena had never talked about her childhood, had never come back here. Not surprising, considering what had happened to her. Why would she want to return to the place where her father had murdered the boy she loved?

A lean woman wearing a plaid shirt and khaki pants answered the door, listening with narrowed eyes while Dustin explained the reason for their visit. Her hair was several shades past black, pulled back and knotted in a way that denied any hint of softness. She let them in with a look that said she was onto their plan to ransack the place, easing slightly when Dustin called her Mrs. Marshall. Kira introduced herself and the woman surveyed her as if Kira's eyes, hair, or clothes might prove she was kin to a murderer. Then she said they should call her Evie and opened the door.

In the living room, a 1970s nightmare remodel had ruined the house's Victorian bones. Avocado greens and mustard yellows adorned the walls and floors, and the couch wore an ugly brown-and-black plaid. A few antiques stood out among what looked like Ethan Allen furniture, but any evidence of the '40s had been obliterated. Placing Maddalena here was impossible.

"I really appreciate this," Kira said. "Do you mind if I take pictures?"

Evie hesitated. "I guess not."

Kira snapped a few shots and moved into the dining room. A slap of recognition—those windows, the western light. She *knew* this place. The birthday fragment had happened here, Hiroshima too. The table, the cake, Maddalena's legs stuck to her chair, the radio shouting news of the end of the war—all of it right here. She turned her back on Evie and Dustin, touched a windowsill, quelled another rise of tears. After a few moments she went into the kitchen. Cabinets and countertops in lime green, sunflowers on the tiled backsplash, a fake Tiffany light overhead. Unrecognizable.

"Can we go upstairs?" she said.

"I suppose so." Evie led the way, stopping at the top of the stairs where a hallway branched. On the right, two doors; on the left, one. "My granddaughter sleeps in that room when she comes to visit," Evie said, pointing to the single door on the left. "She's eight."

Kira ducked into the small bedroom. Instantly the floor buckled and her blood pooled in her feet. Maddalena's room, she was sure of it. Lightheaded, Kira braced herself on the dresser. Plain white walls, a plank floor worn down the middle, a lone window, a white iron bed dressed with a gaudy quilted coverlet. The wedding-dress fragment had happened here.

"Is something wrong?" Evie said.

"No, I—I'm just wondering if this could have been my grandmother's bedroom. It's lovely, perfect for a little girl. Your granddaughter, I mean." Kira touched the polished surface of the heavy dresser, the boards rippled and cupped with age.

"What a beautiful piece. Do you know how old it is?"

"No," Evie said. "Late 1800s, I'd guess. It was here when we moved in, the bed too, and a highboy downstairs. The man who lived here before us said the house was full of furniture when he moved in. I guess the previous owners couldn't be bothered to move it all. Your grandma's family." A stern look, as if Kira were to blame for her relatives' poor behavior.

Kira faced the mirror atop the dresser, set into a graceful arch of wood. Maddalena would have stood here like she was now, in a white nightgown perhaps, brushing her long hair. A teenager in love, glowing at the vision of her ripening body. An unwilling bride, miserable in a cheap, shapeless dress. The daughter of a murderer.

"Nice view," Dustin said, looking out the window.

Kira stood next to him. In the yard, a dozen chickens scratched at the pancaked earth. The massive barn, dwarfed by the mountain backdrop, looked weathered but eternal, its boards a velvety gray. Standing by the window on a summer evening, Maddalena would have looked out on that barn, those mountains. Kira crossed to the bed, lay down and closed her eyes. Maddalena had slept here, a young woman dreaming of her lover, skin damp, hair pulled off her neck. How quiet her world would have been. How lonely.

Evie cleared her throat. "You'll want to see the barn, I suppose?"

"Yes." Kira didn't move. The footboard was almost as high as the headboard, with onion-shaped finials. She touched the white paint, glossy but crackled over layers scarred with age. Maddalena's bed, where she'd dreamed of Akira. Mourned him.

"Come on, Kira." Dustin took her hand and pulled her upright.

"I need pictures," she said.

"I'll do it." He took the camera from her.

Kira followed Evie downstairs. The barn door yawned from across the yard and Kira's stomach lurched, an elevator in freefall. A speckled gray dog materialized beside her, cold nose nudging her fingers. When she stroked the dog's silky head, the elevator inside her gut slowed and steadied.

In the barn, the scent of hay-sweet manure thickened the air. Sunlight sliced through air vents, carrying whirls of dust, and the wooden floor, carpeted with spilled oats and hay, swallowed every footstep. Kira's body hummed. The dog leaned into her and she ruffled a feathery ear. A sense of churchlike peace, of belonging.

Kira turned to Evie, standing by the door with her arms crossed. "Would you mind if I stayed here alone? Just for a minute or two."

"I suppose not," Evie said. "I'll be in the kitchen."

Alone with the dog, Kira let the barn swallow her. Dizzy, drunk on animal smells, she leaned against an old feed bin, its boards soft and gapped with time. Men's voices drifted in from the fields. A hayloft loomed overhead; on her right, an open door led to dozens of cattle stalls. Kira followed the dog into another part of the barn, which held a wall of tack, two large wooden grain bins, and three stalls, one holding a swaybacked white horse. The dog looked at Kira expectantly.

"There's something about this place, huh, pooch?" Kira touched a bridle, the leather seasoned with oil and sweat, the silver bit scored with teeth marks. A Western saddle sat on a two-by-four rack, topped with a few smelly-looking pads. Kira sat in one of the empty stalls and breathed it all in, leather and sweat and horse and hay, the almost-taste of dung. She wanted to sleep cocooned in the thick air, wake with hay dust and the scent of horse embedded in her skin. The dog settled next to her, sighing. Nothing moved but the horse's tail, a restless swish and fall. Kira closed her eyes. Maddalena must have had a horse; that was why the barn seemed important. If any place would trigger a fragment, it was here.

215

She dozed off, then startled when the dog worried her hand. Evie would be waiting.

The dog padded to the door and looked back. Kira followed it around the barn to the paddock, where the dog sat and gazed at the open land. The emptiness was dizzying, vast beyond measure, the sky a sweeping infinity. Far ahead to the north, the gleam of a metal roof, what must be the remains of Manzanar. Not that far away. Give a girl a horse and she could get there. But in the 1940s, would a rancher's daughter have been allowed to ride alone in the desert, dangerous with heat and dust storms and rattlesnakes? During the war, the Japanese people at Manzanar were feared; surely Maddalena would have been told to stay away from them. But then, if she'd had a love affair at sixteen, and with a Japanese boy, she must not have been the type to let rules get in her way. How strong-willed she must have been, how fearless.

Kira ruffled the dog's ears. "I had a spunky grandma," she said. Brown eyes gazed up at her. Nothing moved except a hawk drifting overhead.

Find it. The ground tilted and Kira bent over, hands on her knees. Find what? She was *here.*

"Hello there, can I help you?"

Kira spun around. "Oh my God, you scared me!" she said to the man who approached.

"Are you lost?" he asked. His voice was kind, his face open and friendly, the opposite of Evie.

"No, Evie—your wife? She said I could look around." The dog's weight against her leg. "My grandmother lived here in the '40s."

"That right?" The man squinted, small, bright blue eyes, sharp as a bird's. "During the war, then." Kira nodded. "Hang on," the man said, and went to the barn.

The dog's nose again, insistent. Kira stroked the soft head, warm as a baby's, and thought of Baby Kendall for the first time since she'd left Martinez. How quickly the world had shrunk to the length and width of Owens Valley.

The rancher came back with a cigar box. "This was in the horse barn, under a floorboard that rotted out. Gave way right under me or I never would have found it. Couldn't bring myself to throw it out; figured it was important to someone. It's yours if you want it."

Kira took the box, her hands trembling. It was heavier than she expected. Inside, seven stones like flattened baseballs, one discolored tortoiseshell hair comb, and an envelope. Inside the envelope, a folded piece of paper and a photo, the same one as in the newspaper article. Kira turned it over. "For M, all my love. A." She couldn't move, couldn't take her eyes off that face. Her grandfather's face. The dog licked her hand and Kira started to cry.

"Hey now—oh, lordy." The rancher rubbed his stubbly beard. "I'll get Evie."

Kira wiped her eyes and put the photo back in the envelope. On the folded paper, written in pencil, was a song. "Girl on a Horse" was written at the top in neat lettering, and below it, "For Maddalena." A perfect G clef, staff lines carefully drawn, notes neatly blacked in.

The dog held up a paw. Kira took it, followed the animal's gaze into the desert again. "What are you looking at, pup? Is she out there?" The question ticked past, spoken before she could censor it. She didn't think that, did she? *Did* she? Jesus.

Shading her eyes, she imagined a small figure on a horse, headed across that wasteland toward Manzanar, toward the impossible. No, not impossible. Fuck the barbed wire and the guard towers, the men with guns—Maddalena and Akira had defied all of it, broken the rules. There, in that dismal prison, a teenage boy had written a song for her grandmother, loved her enough, apparently, to die for her. And she'd loved him back. As much as he did? Would Maddalena have died for him?

The voice again. *Find it.*

THIRTY

Maddalena sat up, shivering in her cardigan and socks. It was chilly for August, but that was the desert, changeable and unpredictable. They needed to find a more sheltered place before autumn set in, if the war went on that long. God forbid it lasted into the winter, a terrible thought made worse because snowfall would make it impossible to meet Akira. They would freeze, or worse, be caught, their tracks in the snow a dead giveaway.

She gave Akira a quick hug, then dressed, thinking how strange it was that she could do this thing that her mother would call ugly, a sin, and believe it was beautiful and right. But why should she believe making love was spiritually wrong when her mother had lied to her about the physical act itself? If her mother believed what she'd told her daughter—the man's pleasure, the woman's burden—Maddalena felt sorry for her. Who wouldn't want the glorious oblivion of desire, of being desired?

"Have you gone back to the Wilkins' shed?" Maddalena said. The empty shed Akira had found the night he went looking for her seemed the best alternative to the orchard. Besides lending shelter, it seemed safe enough, since Henry Wilkins would have no reason to go there at night.

"Yes, and it'll do fine, though the floor is hard. I'll swipe a couple more blankets from the hospital and make you a nest."

"At least we'll be out of the wind. I suppose I can't ride Scout there, though. The Wilkins' dogs might smell him and raise a ruckus."

"It's not too far a walk. It'll work out fine."

"Yes, but I like it here." This precious place. She would never be able to look at these trees without thinking of Akira, not if she lived to be a hundred.

"Me too. We'll go there when you're cold enough to want a roof over your head." Akira pulled her to her feet. "Come on, there's something we need to do."

"What is it?"

"Stake our claim on this place."

They found a tree with a broad trunk and a smooth, flat patch of bark. Akira pulled a Swiss Army knife from his pocket and began to carve an *A*. A romantic gesture, Maddalena thought, done by millions of lovers. But the way he did it, working the knife with solemnity and a sense of importance, touched her.

It was an odd feeling, this sense of loving and being loved. When Akira was nearby, close enough for her to touch, there was nothing wrong with the world. It was like being a child tucked into bed at night with the stars visible through the window and a quilt under her chin and music drifting up the stairs, only a thousand times better.

AS + MM

The lines and curves stood out against the dark wood, pale and moist. Maddalena touched the *A* and brought her finger to her tongue. It tasted sweet.

"I thought about carving 'loves' instead of a plus sign," Akira said, "but it seemed like it would be saying I love you but you don't love me."

"You love me?" she said, scarcely able to breathe.

"Of course. Don't you know that?"

"You've never said it."

"Well, I'm saying it now. I love you, Maddalena." Akira turned, arms outstretched, shouting, "Listen up, world! I love Maddalena Moretti!" Then he grabbed her hands. "*Do you love me?*"

"Yes! With all my heart, forever." She would live behind barbed wire with him now if she could, and she'd live through whatever they'd face when he got out. The thought brought as much fear as happiness. So much could go wrong.

"You have no idea how happy that makes me." Akira held her in silence for a moment. "Maddalena, I need to tell you something. When I met you, there was someone else."

"What?" That girl she'd seen, the pretty one. "But you said—"

"Don't worry." He held her tighter, kissed her hair. "It's over with her. For me, it's been over for a long time, but I've been a coward about breaking up with her. I know it sounds like an excuse, but I knew she'd be hurt, and at first I didn't know what was going to happen with us, if we'd even like each other."

"How can you say that?" He had doubted her, when she knew from the start that she loved him?

"Listen, I'm trying to explain. Something happened to me—to *us*, I mean. When I first saw you, I thought you were only another pretty girl. Then you came close to the fence that day like you didn't care about the guards and their guns, and I knew you were more than that. You were brave, with a mind of your own, and I liked that, but you were out here and I was in there, and it all seemed like a fantasy. Or an adventure. But that's not what it was. What it *is*. I can talk to you about anything, and you know what you believe in and you don't care if anyone else agrees or approves. And you're braver than any girl I know. I wouldn't have been surprised if you hadn't shown up that first night; most girls wouldn't have. The crazy thing is, I feel like we were destined to meet. When I'm inside that fence, I know you're out here waiting for me, and that's all that matters. That we exist for each other, that in some strange way you're with me wherever I am. I feel that every day."

"I do too," Maddalena said.

Akira kissed her as if he might never have the chance again. "*Shikata ga nai,*" he whispered.

"What?"

"It's Japanese. It means something can't be helped. That's how we think about being at Manzanar. I think *shikata ga nai* about you, but in a different way, a good way. Instead of feeling helpless, I feel like it's *us,* our being together, that can't be helped."

"Fate," Maddalena whispered.

He gathered her closer. "I will never let go of you."

Never. They would always be together. If she never saw him again after this night, he would be with her forever. It couldn't be helped, he said. Her blood slowed in her veins, her muscles softened. A slow unfolding of joy—he loved her!

THIRTY-ONE

August 14, 1945

On the day we heard the news we assembled in the streets. The war was over. Every voice in the camp repeated the same words: Hiroshima, Nagasaki, atomic bombs, surrender. The war was over, the war was over! It was all we talked about. Everyone cried—for Japan, for joy, from fear, in horror. Some of us could not speak. Others laughed and cried without knowing which was which. A young woman clasped her grandmother's hand in both of hers. A bent old man held up his cane. A woman wearing a flower-print hat sat down in the middle of the street.

The official end of the war would come soon, we were told. We would be freed with no restrictions, allowed to resume our lives. So we were told.

What we were not told was that there would be hatred beyond the fence. But we were not born yesterday. We would return home not as neighbors but as strangers, unwelcome invaders to people who had decided we would always be the enemy. Yet we could not contain our happiness. We repeated the news to everyone we met, at every corner and step, everywhere we waited or walked, and our voices woke the wind from its slumber. The air flung itself about with joy, leaped into gusts and tides and whirls, and we took off our hats, did not shield our eyes. We wanted the sting, the slap of it, wanted to be shocked into believing what we had come to think would never be true.

Truth: We would pack up our possessions and board the same buses and trains that brought us here.

Truth: We would watch the valley disappear and wonder how Manzanar could have happened. How it could have happened to anyone, what we had lived through. How it could happen to us. And how it could come to an end one day, the rules suddenly changed, the color of our skin, our Japaneseness, in an instant pronounced safe, friendly, American.

Truth: We were overjoyed. Disbelieving. Terrified. We would go home, live free in those communities that would not refuse us. We were the same people who had come to Manzanar three years before.

Truth: We were not.

Thirty-Two

April 10, 2011

All that was left of Manzanar was the gatehouse, a compact stone building with windows so pinched they insulted the view. The auditorium still stood, reborn as a visitors' center overflowing with photos and artifacts. On the way there Dustin had been quiet, giving Kira oddly gentle looks now and then.

"You okay?" he said when he cut the engine.

"Fine. Why?"

"Nothing. You just seemed a little, I don't know, shook up or something back at your grandma's place." He came around the truck and offered her a hand.

"I'm fine, really," Kira said.

At the entrance to the visitors' center Dustin blocked her path, his hand on the door. "It's just that the way you were lying there on the bed, it was like you were waiting for something to happen." Ignoring her surprised look, he opened the door and gestured her in.

For two hours they explored the exhibits. Crafts and games must have helped to pass the time in this place where days stretched long into evenings of ennui and where nights were tests of endurance. Display cases held bird pins of painted wood and wire, crude metal fishhooks, *goh* game pieces of smooth stone, bracelets made from melted-down toothbrushes. In one room, a guard tower mockup buried its searchlight in the ceiling. Photos showed daily life, work and school, mess hall lines that snaked around buildings, women making nets, men tending to machinery. Kira searched each photo for a face that might be Akira's. She wasn't sure which would be more disappointing, his absence from the photos or her inability to spot him.

Outside, three reconstructed buildings, two barracks and a mess hall, crouched together in the whitewashed desert, surrounded by broken concrete, rocks that had once adorned gardens, and the same unforgiving wind and dust Akira had endured. A fence replaced the barbed wire barrier that had once circled the camp, only this one contained nothing but lizards and birds and rodents. A guard tower, also reconstructed, dominated the land along the highway. There had been eight of these sinister lookouts, eight points of anchor for miles of barbed wire. Kira couldn't imagine living beneath their gaze; just the one was enough to put a stamp of violence on the place. But then, Manzanar was a concentration camp, after all. That's what Roosevelt had called it and the other nine camps where the Japanese were held, but people didn't like that. No one wanted to admit that Executive Order 9066 had stripped American citizens of their rights and thrown them into prison. Calling these manifestations of racism and injustice "relocation centers" and "internment camps" was far easier on the conscience.

Kira and Dustin wandered past markers pointing out where latrines, laundry rooms, churches, and gardens once stood. Heat lay on Kira's skin like plastic wrap; breathing was like swallowing smoke. And Mike had said it wasn't hot yet. Kira twisted her wind-whipped ponytail into a knot, wondering how the women of Manzanar had managed to maintain their waved bobs and smooth upsweeps. How had they managed *anything* in this hellhole?

Not far from the camp's western edge, a marker announced the hospital site. Kira tried to imagine a sprawl of wards and operating rooms and offices, hallways with gurneys and wheelchairs and linen carts. Strange to think of Manzanar as a real city with a hospital, a city where people came into the

225

world or left it, gave birth or gave up hope. An instant city built with haste and apathy, it overpowered the valley's nearby towns, depositing ten thousand Japanese in a place where only white people had lived since the Native Americans were displaced. With the government yelling about traitors and spies, who could blame the valley residents for being terrified by their new neighbors? Yet there was no excuse for intolerance, for hating and distrusting people because of their appearance. What damage had Manzanar done to Akira, a vulnerable teenager? Kira kicked at a stone, sending up a small duststorm. What damage? It killed him, this place. It fucking killed him.

A small cemetery lay beyond the fence, anchored by a pointed stone tower adorned with kanji, a memorial to all those who died at Manzanar. "Soul Consoling Tower," it was called. Chains of paper cranes blanketed the base, neon confetti against the bleached stone. Kira wondered how quickly the desert would erase them.

"You know what I can't get used to?" she said to Dustin. "How short the fence is. I pictured it ten or twelve feet high."

"I guess the guns were enough to keep people inside," Dustin said. "Besides, where would they go? There's nothing around for miles, and even if they got as far as Lone Pine or Independence, what good would it do? They couldn't exactly show their faces."

"Imagine living in a prison next door to a town called Independence."

"No kidding. My grandpop said the searchlights lit up the valley. He and his buddies used to joke that Lone Pine didn't need streetlights after Manzanar was built." Dustin wiped his face with the hem of his shirt. "You ready to go?"

"Not yet. I want to walk the perimeter."

"I'll drive back to town and pick up some lunch. Meet you in the parking lot."

"Deal. I'll buy," Kira said. Beneath her sweat, her skin felt tight.

At the hospital site, she climbed five concrete steps that led to nothing. If Akira had used this staircase to go to work, where might it have taken him? Nowhere but another place in a prison three layers thick—flimsy walls, flesh-rending metal, and in the mountains that hemmed the valley, impenetrable rock. A terrible place, yet she felt at home here, like Manzanar was hers now because of Akira. She knotted her toes, digging into this mournful place. What would he have done with his life, her grandfather, if he'd had a chance to live it? What stories would he have told her about his childhood in Berkeley, about life in a desert prison? She imagined him laughing, his voice deep and rich, imagined walking with him, her small hand in his, or lying tucked in bed while he read to her. Scenes straight out of a Hallmark Hall of Fame movie, shallow and sentimental, but she could do no better. She couldn't trade soft-focus, imagined family memories for real ones because this place had taken that possibility from her. Taken everything from her family.

The wind clawed at her hair and she looked south across the stunning, brutal terrain toward Lone Pine. Two kids in love. They must have felt that a continent stood between them.

Kira walked. At the southeast corner of the camp, the strangled trickle of Bairs Creek cut through what had been a picnic area. Some playground that must have been, with a guard tower looming overhead. The wind grabbed handfuls of dust, tossed them joyfully. In their wake, only loneliness and the feeling that the wind could abrade a person, scrape away skin and muscle and bone until nothing was left.

She'd had enough. Limping, Kira hurried to the parking lot, ignoring the signs and markers and their impossible task of re-creating the past. Nothing could reveal the truth about life in this horrific place. Barracks, churches, hospital—little but wood and tarpaper, cheap imitations of life outside the fence, desperate attempts at refuge. They said nothing about the spirit of the people who lived here. People who suffered,

227

like Akira. He lived here by force, loved someone forbidden to him because of who he was.

The desert filled Kira's mouth, coated her skin. Manzanar was too barren to trigger any fragments, too stripped of meaning and memory by wind and blowing sand. The remnants of life here lay long buried in dust. When people left this place at last, they took everything with them. Manzanar was a ghost town without the town, without the ghosts.

Back at the motel Kira showered, then flopped down on the bed, her wet hair wrapped in a towel. A crack in the ceiling ran from corner to corner, pointing to an abandoned spider web.

Her phone chirped. *Hey. Want some company?* A wave of guilt because Dan didn't know where she was, then irritation that he wasn't keeping his end of the bargain. Not that she had been either. She texted back—*Not yet. Soon. xx*—and turned off the phone. Dan could wait. Dan had to wait.

She toweled her hair and combed it, wet and heavy and sleek. Looking in the mirror, she searched for evidence of Akira. One minute she was sure he was her grandfather; the next, afraid Dan was right, that her link to Akira was wishful thinking. She'd never thought of herself as a romantic, but apparently she was an expert at romanticizing. The only proof she had about Akira, if she could call it that, was Maddalena's letter to Rosa, and that didn't exist anywhere except inside her own head. All she knew for sure was that her grandmother had a Japanese boy for a lover, and he'd written her a song, and he'd been murdered. Just because Maddalena named Kira after Akira didn't prove she was his granddaughter.

And yet...

She got the cigar box and sat on the bed. Strange keepsakes, the seven rocks. She took one, rolled it between her palms to feel its smoothness. It grew warm, and warmer. Cupping it in both hands, she willed the heat to intensify, the color shift to begin. Nothing. She waited. There—a glimmer of pale pink. It cooled, deepened to an evening blue, and joy flooded through her, the headiness of falling in love. Blue became black velvet wrapped around her body, and the room disappeared. She floated, suspended, separate from time and place, where nothing existed but this joyful nothingness. Then, gradually, the blackness thinned and the room reappeared.

Shaken, Kira dropped the rock. She flicked on the bedside light, then the overhead, ran to the door and checked the deadbolt, downed half a beer left over from lunch, took the photo out of the box, touched Akira's face with a shaky fingertip. Whatever it was that she'd just experienced, it wasn't a fragment—it was more intense, pure, a glorious sense of being held, of being loved. Yet in its wake, all Kira felt was fear. Why? Wasn't this what she wanted? There was risk in any discovery, she knew that. And maybe joy and fear had to coexist here, in this place that both welcomed and threatened her.

She went back to the box and took out Akira's song. There must be a piano or guitar around, someone who could play the song for her. Dustin would know. She'd call him; they could go get a beer.

Dustin picked up her call, said that a bar on Main Street had a piano and he played a little; he was happy to help her out. Not a question in his tone, not a hint of curiosity, as if he knew patience would lead to revelation.

Kira put the song in her bag, everything else back in the box, and the box in the bottom drawer of the dresser underneath a sweatshirt. Outside, shivering with the breeze on her damp hair, she gazed at the dark sky. Akira's sky, a tapestry of points of light.

That feeling—floating, joyful. She wanted it back.

THIRTY-THREE

August 15, 1945

On a day that had seemed like it would never come, Maddalena rode to meet Akira. The war was finally over. Akira would be free. The thought carried joy and sadness with it. How would they find a way to be together?

Maddalena tipped her head back, gazing at the night sky that opened like a blue-black umbrella with no handle piercing its middle, a vast sweep of darkest blue that seemed to end at the mountains to the east and west, and at the valley floor to the north and south, but didn't actually end at all. Because the truth was that the universe was endless and that space stretched out so far into forever that time became elastic, something you couldn't measure no matter how many times you tried. That's what scientists insisted on, what schoolbooks stated in solemn black and white. Maddalena had accepted it as truth, but she'd never been able to think that big. The universe was like a soap bubble, there to admire but nothing you could grasp. And so its endlessness had never seemed true to her, fact or no fact. Not endless the way the war had seemed. The sky, to her, had always ended at the clouds, or at the canopy of stars, or in the fringes of pink and lavender where the sun rose, or where the full moon hung over the Sierra like a gigantic Ping-Pong ball. But on this night, she could believe the universe had no end. If she held her breath and let her mind float free, her thoughts whirling around her like the desert dust—which she knew was real because she saw it and felt it, smelled it and tasted it every morning, noon, and night—then she could accept that the miraculous stuff of science was true. She could do this now because she had learned that the impossible could be true—that Akira and she would both be in Owens Valley, that they would see each other and not look the other way, that they would fall in love. Impossible that the war was over at last and the people of Manzanar would be free. Yet now suddenly possible, and Akira would be free. It was only a matter of time.

On this night, the stars were thick as sifted flour, silver smiles that outshone the quarter moon. Maddalena was part of the night, part of the desert, the valley, the world, part of a universe that never ended. Akira too. They were alone together in their universe, where no one else was riding through the silent desert, no one else was risking as much as they did for love, for the wild impossibility of love. The stars were watching as she made her way to Akira, counting Scout's steps as if they were the minutes, the seconds until she would see him there in the silvery, silent shelter of the apple trees. And the stars approved.

Sensing Akira before she saw him, she slipped off the horse and into his arms. "It's over," she said.

"Yes," he replied, the word filled with disbelief.

"When will you leave?"

"I don't know."

She kissed his neck, then his mouth, her body erasing the space between them. As they moved into the trees, Akira told her what Manzanar was like that day, how the people had filled the streets, looked at one another as if they'd only then, at that moment, realized there would be goodbyes to say, friends to write to and remember and miss. The moment passed quickly, tossed aside by the swift confluence of emotions, of bodies restless in the streets. Over and over again, the words, "The war is over," said calmly, dully at first, because the news couldn't be real. Then, as the day lengthened, the words gained strength and joy. The war was over. They would go home.

"My father cried," Akira said. "My mother couldn't talk. She covered her mouth like she was going to get sick and stared at my dad and me like she'd never seen us in her life."

"What about you?"

"I felt numb, to tell you the truth; it's still hard to believe. I stayed with my parents until they got over the shock, then I went to the canteen. There was a party there, but I didn't want that, so I left with my friend Paul and we walked the camp, street after street. We talked about visiting each other—he lives in Huntington Beach—and all the things we're going to do when we get out."

"Like what?"

"Like eat swordfish and daikon and seaweed, and drink beer, and sleep in a decent bed. And go wherever we damn well please." He laughed.

"Is that *all* you want?" Maddalena said, sliding her arms around his neck.

"No, beautiful girl. Come to Berkeley with me," Akira said. "Will you?"

"You know I will." No more stolen hours, no more hiding. They would make a home together, in a place that would let them love, grow old together.

The war was over.

THIRTY-FOUR

April 10–11, 2011

The bar was called The Wild West, and inside the front door was a set of swinging half doors, the kind seen in every saloon in every Western movie. The rest was standard-issue dive bar: deer heads decked out in Christmas lights, wadded-up dollar bills peppering the ceiling, beer signs, and a muted widescreen TV set to ESPN. A row of broad-backed men flanked the bar, their bulging waistlines pushing beer-logo tees or plaid flannel shirts to their limits. Skirting the empty dance floor, scuffed from years of stomping and sliding, a few young couples wrapped themselves around small tables. An upright piano, veneer curling like old wallpaper, stood in one corner next to a jukebox. Waylon Jennings was belting "I've Always Been Crazy."

Kira nudged Dustin. "Listen. They're playing my song."

"Funny." Dustin surveyed the room. "Somehow I don't think you're kidding."

They found seats at one end of the bar, a massive oak slab slathered with wax that failed to smooth decades of dings and scratches. Kira ordered two Anchor Steams from a muscular guy with a gray buzz cut and a beard that rivaled ZZ Top's.

Jennings hit his last chord and the jukebox went silent. "Let's do it," Dustin said.

They crossed to the piano, where he made a show of warming up his hands. Kira nudged him. "Just play it already." He picked out the melody, then added a few chords.

"Think I got it," he said, and started from the top.

233

The tune was sweet and yearning without being sentimental, with a happy little allegro run, like wind-tossed leaves, that intersected the ardent melody. It didn't sound at all like something a teenage boy would write.

"The man who—" Kira tried to talk around the lump in her throat. Even without words, the song seemed like Akira's voice. "The man I think is my grandfather wrote this."

Dustin glanced up, still playing. "Nice tune. Tweaks the ol' heartstrings." He finished the song and the couple nearest the piano clapped. Dustin took a dramatic bow, and the jukebox started up again. Johnny Cash, "I Walk the Line."

Back at the bar, a heavyset man leered at Kira, legs splayed around a belly sized for quintuplets. Feeling benevolent, she smiled at him, then chugged her beer. What a sweetheart Akira was to write that song for Maddalena. A romantic kid in love with the wrong girl. Dan flickered into Kira's thoughts. She could be having dinner with him right now, going home to make love, doing it on the living room floor because they couldn't wait the thirty seconds it would take to get to the bedroom. But Dan was on another planet and the thought of being with him had all the clarity and vividness of a faded Polaroid.

"Another round," she told the bartender. "And two shots of Jack." Getting drunk seemed like a fine idea.

"Your grandpa wrote that song, huh?" Dustin said, still working on his first beer. "Where'd you get it?"

"It was in the cigar box," she said. "The one with the mementos." The bartender slid the beers across the bar, then poured the shots. She gave him a flirty thank-you and crossed her legs, an elbow on the bar. Hearing the song had freed her, left her flush with success. There was still no proof of her bloodline, but she was making progress. That joyful floating in her motel room had pushed the malignancy of Manzanar into the background, given her hope.

"Very cool," Dustin said. "So, boss, when are you going to

tell me why you're really here? Nope"—he held up a hand, shaking his head—"forget I said that. None of my business."

Sleepy-looking Dustin was full of surprises, and damn sharp. Maybe she'd tell him the whole story, but not tonight. Tonight she would do her best to forget everything.

"Cheers." Kira downed the shot and ordered another, swinging her leg to the jukebox beat. "So, Owens Valley native son, entertain me. Tell me a story. Tell me about the famous water wars. I loved *Chinatown*."

"You really want to know about that?" Dustin shrugged. "Okay."

He explained how L.A. had bought out the ranchers and built an aqueduct, let the valley go nearly dry so the city's farmers could water their own orchards. That was why there were so few ranches in the valley now; the only ones left were diehards. Kira kept up with him at first, but with no dinner, two beers plus the leftover one in her room and the bourbon, her edges were blurring. She watched Dustin talk, nodding to show she was listening, distracted by the whiteness of his teeth, the length of his fingers, the russet hair on his forearms. When he laughed, his eyes darkened from pale blue to violet.

"Wanna dance?" the quintuplets guy asked, his belly pressing against Kira's thigh.

"No, thanks," she said. "Maybe later." She turned back to Dustin's eyes, the adorable fan of freckles across his cheekbones.

"Say the word, sweetheart. Name's Mitch." Mitch wandered off.

Another shot of Jack appeared, the glass thin and cool on her lips, the liquor a tepid dose of comfort. Damn Dustin for smiling at her. He was young, too young. At least ten years younger, in fact, even if she was interested, which she absolutely was not. On the periphery, Mitch leaned into view and smiled. She smiled back. It felt good to be wanted. Of course, Dan wanted her, but he wanted too much from her, in ways she couldn't deliver. Was that even legitimate, or did she think that because she was drunk and paranoid and hundreds of miles of mountains and valleys separated them? What seemed all too clear right now, though, was that losing Aimi and finding Maddalena had put parentheses around their marriage.

The jukebox took a breath, then Emmylou Harris began to croon "Beneath Still Waters." Kira grabbed Dustin's hand. "Come on, I love this song," she said, and dragged him to the dance floor.

"This isn't a good idea," he said, holding her at arm's length.

"Dancing is always a good idea." She moved in, forced him to put his arms around her, sang along with Emmylou. "Beneath still waters, there's a strong undertow, the surface won't tell you what the deep water knows."

"You're drunk."

"So what? Can't a girl have some fun?" Kira stumbled, fire darts shooting through her bum ankle, and the next thing she knew she was kissing him.

Dustin ducked out of her arms. "If you're trying to tempt me, it's working. But I'm not super eager to piss off your husband."

"What makes you think I'm married?"

"The wedding ring is a pretty big tipoff."

"Oh, right."

"I think it's time to get you out of here." Dustin headed to the bar.

"I'm having fun," Kira called after him. She stood on the dance floor, swinging her hips and singing. Mitch hovered nearby and she held out her hands, giggling at how fast he moved. She slung her arms around his neck, undeterred by his aroma of garlic and beer. He wanted her. He wanted her even if Dustin didn't, even if she was married, and she needed that. Needed someone's arms around her.

"Party's over," Dustin said, holding out Kira's backpack and jacket. "Let's go."

"Leave the lady alone." Mitch swung Kira across the floor, and she leaned back in his embrace, one arm flung out.

"Come on, Dustin, dance with us."

"Like hell," Mitch said. Kira tripped again and he caught her, grinning.

Dustin trailed them across the floor. "Kira, let's go."

"Fuck off," Mitch said.

"Cool it over there," the bartender called.

"You fuck off. I'm taking her home." Dustin planted a hand on Mitch's shoulder. "Get your hands off her."

"Get your fucking pansy-ass hands off *me*."

Mitch spun out from under Dustin's hand and Dustin shoved him; then Mitch threw a punch. Kira screamed as Dustin hit the floor, blood spurting. Mitch grabbed her, pinning her back to his chest, and she struggled to free herself until she realized he was enjoying it. Twisting in his arms to face him, she said, "You're a good dancer, you know that?" and when he smiled she kneed him. He bellowed and crumpled and the bartender came running.

"Fuck man, you all right?"

Dustin was on his feet, his face dripping blood. Kira grabbed their things and pushed him toward the door. "Hurry! Can you drive?"

"*You're* sure as hell not going to."

Dustin drove with one hand over his nose while Kira stuffed Kleenexes into his cupped hand and mopped up the blood that ran down his arm. She apologized the entire five minutes it took to get to the motel, was still apologizing when he drove away.

In bed, she watched the shadowed ceiling spin above her. She'd never once thought about cheating on Dan. She'd forgotten what it felt like to be in love, but Dan hadn't. He was home, in *their* home, waiting for her with no idea how many lies she'd told him, the things she'd hidden. He trusted her. She had to remember that, here in this strange place where he seemed like a memory. Cheating was a transgression Dan would never forgive, if he ever found out. And it wasn't a secret she could live with.

❧

The next morning Kira woke to a text message from Dan and a head that felt like a stuffed mushroom. The remorse she'd felt the night before was gone, sucked into the desert sand and silenced. She texted a quick *All ok here* and got in the shower. At nine, Dustin's truck was waiting outside her door. She collected her things and went to the office, where Dustin lounged with his feet on the counter.

"About time," he said.

"I can't believe you showed up," she said. "I'm so sorry. And embarrassed."

"Don't hold your liquor too well, do you?" Dustin pointed at his bruised nose and gave her a wounded-puppy look. "I hope you know you've ruined my social standing. No way I can hang at The Wild West anymore."

"Oh God, I'm so sorry."

"Kidding. Not exactly my crowd."

Kira groaned. "No fair teasing anyone who has a hangover this bad."

"Apology accepted. And it's only fair that you should suffer with me."

Mike came in as they were leaving. "Sounds like a hell of a night," he said, smiling.

"I'm never drinking again," Kira said.

"Right," Mike said.

In the truck, Dustin handed Kira a cup of coffee and revved the engine.

"Thanks." Sipping the coffee, she wished she could ignore the kiss and the thought of whatever else she would have done if Dustin hadn't said no. He seemed chill enough, but her shame ballooned by the second. "Hey, I'm sorry about, you know, kissing you and everything. I've never cheated on my husband, honest. I was really drunk."

"Understatement. Actually, I was flattered, or I was until you threw me over for the potbelly guy." He glanced at her, his eyes a softer blue. "No worries. I know you don't go around doing that kind of thing all the time."

"I wouldn't have blamed you if you'd ditched me today," Kira said.

"Nah, we're a team. And you're kinda fun when you're drunk. Are you in the habit of starting bar brawls?"

"Stop it. Anyway, I owe you. I'll buy lunch." Her stomach contracted at the thought.

"It's a start." Dustin accelerated onto the highway. "What's his name, anyway? Your husband."

"Dan. Dan Kaneko."

"Japanese. Huh. Okay, boss, where to?"

"Independence. The Eastern California Museum."

As he drove, Dustin drummed on the steering wheel, whistling Akira's song.

"It's a good song, isn't it?" Kira said.

"All love songs are good songs."

"I can't believe I have it. Something of his, I mean." Akira seemed real now, more real than Dan.

Twenty minutes later Dustin dropped her off at the museum, on the western fringe of town. It was empty except for two librarians, and so quiet that they could probably hear Kira's head pounding. She told one of them she was looking for information about her grandmother's family, and the librarian directed her to a bank of filing cabinets.

Kira riffled through the folders filed under *M*, hardly breathing. Then, there it was: Moretti, the folder distressingly thin, the sole document in it the article about Akira's murder. Apparently no one in this valley remembered anything about her family but a scandal. There had to be more—someone who'd been close to Maddalena, a friend who would remember something besides the love affair that ended in tragedy. Kira went to find a librarian.

When Dustin picked her up two hours later, she handed him a list. "The librarians here are kickass. You know any of these names?"

He nodded. "A couple. What is this?"

"Families who had ranches near Manzanar during the war. Maybe someone who knew my grandmother is still alive."

"The public records office is up north, in Bishop," Dustin said. "We can look up these folks there. Most of the ranches are gone, but I'll bet some of these people still live in the valley."

Forty minutes later they were in Bishop, standing in front of a records clerk who looked blank when asked if she knew the Moretti family. "The name doesn't ring a bell," she said. "Maybe Kathleen knows. Her family's been here since the dawn of time." She turned to a birdlike woman perched at a nearby desk. "Kathleen, did you know some Italians down at Lone Pine named Moretti? Lived there during the war?"

Kathleen thought for so long that Kira wondered if she'd dozed off. Finally she said, "Wasn't that the family involved in that terrible murder?"

"Yes, we know about that," Kira said. "I'm trying to find someone in the valley who might have known my grandmother. Could you look up the people on this list?"

An hour later Kira and Dustin left the office with four names and addresses written in Kathleen's spidery hand—two in Bishop, one in Independence, one in Lone Pine. Four chances that someone would remember Maddalena.

At a sandwich shop where they stopped for lunch, Kira asked a wraithlike old man sitting outside if he'd known the Morettis. "Sure did," he said. "Knew 'em before all the trouble." He eyed Kira. "Why?"

"They're my relatives. I'm trying to get some information about them."

"Huh. Well, let's see. Al Moretti sold me some cattle once. That was years ago, during the war. I was just a kid, but he cut me no slack. Drove a hard bargain, but his stock was good quality. Tough customer, Al Moretti. His boy too; can't remember his name. He was my age. Not a whit of good in him."

"Did you know the daughter? Maddalena?"

"Afraid not." The man shook open his newspaper. "Good luck to you."

They struck out in Bishop; neither person who answered the door knew the Morettis. "Next up, Regina Cooper," Kira said. "On North Clay Street in Independence."

Thirty minutes later, Dustin pulled in front of a plain yellow house with a "Home Sweet Home" sign hanging on the front porch. Two plastic deer stood next to a mailbox in a circle of white bricks and pink geraniums.

The woman who answered the door, Florence Cooper, hadn't ever heard her mother, Regina, mention anyone named Maddalena, and these days she didn't always make a whole lot of sense—she was eighty-four, after all. But they were welcome to talk to her. Florence led the way to a shuttered bedroom where an old woman was dozing.

"Ma? Someone's here to see you," Florence said.

Regina nodded, her eyes shut. Her white hair, in a wispy pixie cut, framed a spider's web of wrinkles. Soft jowls blurred what was once a heart-shaped face, crowned by delicate, pale brows.

"Ma, they're asking if you knew someone named Madeleine."

Regina pursed her lips, then shook her head.

"Actually, it's Maddalena," Kira said. "Maddalena Moretti. Her family lived on a ranch near Lone Pine during World War II."

Regina's eyes opened. "Lena? My Lena?"

"You knew her?" Kira and Dustin exchanged triumphant looks.

"Lena was my best friend." Regina sat up and peered at Kira, then reached for her glasses on the bedside table. Her eyes were a faint blue, cloudy with cataracts. "Who are you?"

"I'm her granddaughter, Kira. This is my friend Dustin. I'm very glad to meet you."

"A granddaughter! How wonderful! Sit down, dear." Regina pointed to a straight chair next to the bed. "Flo, dear, get us some iced tea, will you? Is this young man your husband?"

"No, he—"

"You have pretty hair, dark like Lena's. Not as curly, though." Regina patted her white wisps. "I had blonde hair, straight as rain. Lena always said how much she envied it. I wanted her curls, of course. You know us girls, never happy with how we look."

"What was she like?" Kira said. "She died before I was born."

"Yes, such a terrible, terrible thing, how young she was. I went out of my mind when I heard she was gone. I simply couldn't believe it. She was full of life, that one, and smart as a whip, got *A*s in everything. She used to help me with my homework, especially arithmetic. Long division! Heavens to Betsy, I couldn't make heads or tails of all those numbers. I would have flunked without Lena's help. She had the patience of Job, going over and over those numbers with me. I was better at hairstyles and such. I worked as a beautician before I got married." Regina patted Kira's hand. "You're Lena's granddaughter, are you? Bless my stars. She was such a dear, and very pretty. She had the prettiest big green eyes, like you."

"Did she have a horse? What kinds of things did you do together?"

"Oh yes, of course, a big bay. A beautiful horse, his name was—oh, I don't remember," Regina said, her voice rising in frustration. "My memory isn't what it used to be. Old age is no picnic, let me tell you! But let's see. We did the usual girl things, I suppose. We had sleepovers and baked cookies and talked about boys and clothes. Lena liked to try on my clothes because I had fancier things than she did. I had this one dress she was crazy for, white with a red belt. It fit her, but she didn't have much of a waist. She was small like me, but sturdier. The war changed everything, of course. Then she met that boy from the camp. Have some tea, dear." She gestured to a tray table where Florence had put iced tea and cookies.

"Akira. Did you ever meet him?"

"No, I never did," Regina said. "I wanted to, Lord knows, to see what all the fuss was about, but I never so much as laid eyes on him. I helped Lena write a letter to him once. She asked me for advice because she didn't know much about boys. I never would have had the nerve to do such a thing myself, but that was Lena for you. She took that letter and threw it right over the barbed wire, right under the guards' noses." A wavery smile. "And then there she was, sneaking out at night and going off to meet him. It was all so exciting, but it scared me to death! She said she was in love, and I suppose she was, but heavens! I wish I'd talked her out of that whole affair. Of course, there was no telling Lena anything—once she made up her mind, that was it. She had a wild streak in her." Regina sank back against the pillow, tears in her eyes. "We were young then, of course. So very young."

"Do you remember what happened?" Kira said. "How did Maddalena's father and brother find out about her and Akira? Where were they when he was killed?"

"Didn't the article say where?" Dustin said.

"No, only that my grandmother's brother found them. Do you know, Mrs. Cooper?"

Regina's eyes were closed. "Is she asleep?" Dustin mouthed to Kira.

"She does that," Flo said. "Just fades out. Give her a minute."

Regina's eyes fluttered open and she clutched Kira's hands. "Lena! Oh, my dearest, dearest friend, I've missed you so much. That man they made you marry, I hated him for taking you away. And then your letters stopped coming and they told me you were dead." Her voice shook and she pulled Kira against her thick, soft body. "I'm so glad you came back."

"I'm glad too," Kira said. She was kneeling next to the bed, her head on Regina's belly. The old woman smelled familiar. And that voice, she knew it. She could see Regina at fifteen, sixteen, in the birthday party fragment, her blonde hair swinging as she pirouetted in that polka-dot dress with the red belt.

"Ma, this isn't Lena," Florence said loudly. "It's her granddaughter."

"I missed you so much. So terrible, all those years, so terrible what they did to you and that boy." Regina wept a little, then her eyes closed again. In seconds she was snoring softly.

"I missed you too," Kira said, and began to cry.

"Missed her? What kind of nonsense is that?" Florence said. "I think you'd better leave."

"Kira, come on." Dustin's hand on her shoulder, insistent. She felt half asleep, trapped in the smell of Regina's powdery skin, the pillow of her body. Dustin pulled her up and steered her out of the room.

"The nerve, making an old woman cry like that. I don't know why people have to go around digging up the past." Florence glared at Kira on the word "people."

"She didn't mean anything by it," Dustin said. "Just playing along, right, Kira?"

"Yes, I'm sorry." The room was in sharp focus now. "She thought I was Lena, so I thought she'd want to hear that

244

Lena missed her too. By the way, does your mother still have those letters from Maddalena?"

"Can't say I've seen anything like that," Florence said, crossing her arms.

"Would you ask her? Please?" Kira scribbled her phone number on a piece of paper from her purse and held it out. "Please call if you find anything. It would mean a lot to me." When Florence didn't take the paper, Kira left it on the hallway table.

She wept quietly all the way back to Lone Pine. For a moment, kneeling beside Regina, she'd felt like Maddalena. The old woman's scent and warmth felt familiar, and everything she said felt right, as if Kira had known all along that Maddalena was good at math, had a horse, wrote a letter to a boy at Manzanar and got it to him somehow. Plainly, she was fearless. Sixteen years old and she knew what she wanted. And when she couldn't have it, she wanted to die with Akira but had chosen instead to save her unborn child. Rosa. Until the day she ran in front of those headlights, Maddalena had protected Rosa as best she could.

Kira dug Kleenex out of her bag and wiped her face. She shared DNA with a woman like Maddalena, and yet here she was, wandering around in the desert trying to figure out what a bunch of dreams meant and ruining her marriage in the process. Her old fear stirred, reinvigorated. What if she lacked the capacity for motherhood, for loving anyone in that self-sacrificing way? She'd tried to will her first pregnancy out of existence—what if she'd fooled herself into thinking she'd wanted Aimi but she really didn't, and that was why Aimi died? And she seemed hell-bent on sending her marriage into a death spiral. What if she couldn't really love *anyone?*

Manzanar appeared, then receded in a scrim of dust. The desert, in all its supreme cruelty, was toying with her, making her think she was Maddalena. If she stayed long enough, she might disappear completely.

Kira let her head fall back on the scorching headrest. She wanted a bubble bath in a bug-free bathroom and a glass of good wine. She wanted to curl up in Dr. Richardson's big chair and take his meds and be fine, absolutely fine. No more fragments, no more questions without answers, no more fighting whatever it was that ruled her.

"I'm done, Dustin. Take me back to the motel, please."

"Sure," he said. "We'll hit the last place tomorrow."

"No, I'm going home. We found Regina, and I've got the box. That's enough." She pretended she didn't see Dustin's questioning gaze.

At the motel, Dustin let the engine idle. "I'm going to miss you, boss. Let me know if you're ever in town again."

"I will. Thanks for everything." Kira hugged him. The truck trundled off, a toy superimposed on the twilit Sierra. Mountain guardians of this desperate valley, but not of Maddalena. The Sierra had failed her. When she left the valley in mourning, the mountains watched her go, witnesses to devastation, to injustice, to the murder of a teenage boy. That's what love got you, at least in Owens Valley in the 1940s. Maybe anywhere, even now.

Kira stepped into the dead quiet of her motel room. It would be a relief to get home.

THIRTY-FIVE

August 20, 1945

We should make a plan," Akira said. "I'll be leaving soon."

Maddalena snuggled closer, twining her naked legs around his. She missed the orchard, the apple trees standing guard along with Scout. He would have stamped his hooves and snorted if anyone came near. If the night winds hadn't grown so violent, they'd be there still. The shed was cozier, even though the door didn't close properly and the floor was hard, but she didn't like not being able to see outside. It gave her a jittery feeling, which she supposed would pass with time.

"What sort of plan did you have in mind?" she asked. It didn't matter what it was as long as they'd be together.

"I'll need to go back to Berkeley with my parents," Akira said. "I'll wait to tell them about you until they're home and settled; it'll be easier on them. I'll find some work and save up money for train fare for both of us, and to rent a room for a while. Then I'll come back to get you. You'll have to be ready to go anytime, so have a suitcase packed and keep it at Regina's. I'll write to you to let you know when I'm coming."

"Send it to Regina. I never get letters, so if you wrote to me my parents would ask questions."

"I'll meet you at the train station in Lone Pine, and we'll take the train to San Francisco, lay low for a while. You won't be able to say goodbye to your family, but you can write and let them know you're safe."

Leave without saying goodbye? She hadn't thought of that, but of course it was necessary. She'd come back once her parents had gotten used to the idea that she was in love,

247

that her life was going to be different from the one they'd imagined for her. Maybe Akira would never be welcome in their home, but they would be happy to see her. They would realize how happy she was, and maybe they would forgive her.

"Can I meet your parents?" she said.

"Someday. They'll need time to get used to the idea that you're not Japanese. But when they see how much I love you, I think they'll accept you. Especially once we're married and they get to know you."

Akira stood and pulled her up with him, then knelt in front of her. She stood there naked, disbelieving, her skin alive in the cool air.

"Maddalena, I love you." He kissed one of her hands, then the other. "Will you marry me?"

"Yes, yes! I love you, Akira." She threw her arms around him, happier than she'd ever been. A proposal in the desert, in an empty shed, hospital blankets under her bare feet—it was theirs. It was perfect.

They made love again, and afterward Maddalena lay next to Akira wondering what it would be like to be his wife. *Mrs. Akira Shimizu*, she thought. *Maddalena Moretti Shimizu*. What an elegant name.

"I should go," she murmured, then drifted off.

A rattling sound woke her. "Akira, wake up!" The shed door bounced and shuddered against the frame.

Akira went to the door and listened while Maddalena half whispered a Hail Mary. A minute went by, then two. The door quieted. No sounds but the wind, a distant howl. "Coyotes," Akira whispered. He pushed the door and it swung open, fell back against his hand. "It was the wind," he said. "Let's get out of here. I'll walk you home."

"That's dangerous," Maddalena said.

"I don't care. If anything's going to happen, it's going to happen to both of us."

They dressed quickly and hid the rolled-up blankets under an old seed bag. Then Akira took her hand and they set out across the desert. Maddalena shivered. It was too dangerous, what they were doing, yet there was no going back, no undoing what they had started. She would say goodbye to Scout, to her home, leave her family, make a new family with Akira. They would be together. That was all that mattered.

When they were fifty yards out from the paddock, Akira took Maddalena's face in his hands and kissed her. "Wherever you are, wherever I am, you're in my heart," he said. "I'll never let go of you. Remember that." A coyote answered, its howl sharp on the wind.

"I will."

"Go now," he said. "Sweet dreams."

THIRTY-SIX

April 12, 2011

The next day Kira got as far as the door, then parked her bag and hurried to the motel office to tell Mike she wasn't leaving after all.

"What'd I tell you?" Dustin said to Mike. "Pay up, dude." Mike handed him a folded bill, muttering something about knowing better than to make bets with Dustin.

"You bet that I wouldn't leave?" Kira said to Dustin. "Then you know me better than I know myself, which is pretty scary after only two days."

"Yep. My mom says when I was a kid I knew things, like who was on the phone before she answered it or what someone was going to say before they said it. It creeped her out. So, you ready to check out the other name on that list?"

"Not today," Kira said. "Tell me, if you were a teenage boy at Manzanar and you wanted to hook up with a girl outside the camp, where would you go?"

Find it.

"Oh, shit." Kira sank into one of the tiny lobby's orange chairs, her bones crumbling. That first fragment—men's voices, boots crunching on rock, immobilizing fear—she hadn't connected the dots. That was Akira's murder. That was what she was supposed to find, not the house where Maddalena had lived but the place where Akira died. It was why she'd come here. If she wanted to find a connection to Maddalena and Akira, she had to go to the place where they'd been together. Where Maddalena might have died with Akira, but for Rosa. Cold sweat soaked Kira's T-shirt.

"Here, drink this." Dustin gave her a cup of water. "You don't look so good."

The screen door stood between Kira and the Inyos, fine wire hashtagging the mountains, blurring their hues. It still surprised her to see such beauty in this desolate place. It was a changeling, this valley. Had Maddalena thought that too? Did the valley become more beautiful when she fell in love, uglier when Akira died?

"Better?" Dustin's face was inches from Kira's, his hands on his knees.

"Yes, thanks. It's that medical condition I mentioned," Kira said. "I get dizzy sometimes." At this moment, not a lie. "I'll bet wherever they used to go to be together was where he died."

"You want to try asking Regina again? She probably knows."

"No, I don't think we'd get past Florence. Not this soon anyway."

"Okay. So where would they go, where would they go?" Dustin hummed, pouring coffee into his thermos. "There was an old fishing shack up Shepherd Creek, couple of miles into the foothills. That could be it. Kids used to go there to get high. I bet it's still there."

"Meet you at the truck," Kira said.

Back in her room, she turned off her phone and left it on the bedside table. The newspaper article and the cigar box went into her backpack; for whatever reason, she wanted them with her. Maddalena's presence? That made no sense, but what did anymore?

The truck was idling in the same spot where she'd said goodbye the night before, where Dustin hadn't believed her goodbye. She swung her backpack onto the seat and climbed in.

"Let's go."

251

❧

The fishing shack stood by the banks of the listless creek, little more than a lean-to furnished with rusted cans and the stink of fish. "Nope," Dustin said, peering inside. "Not here. This wasn't the place."

"Why do you say that?" But Kira knew it too. The place was cold, damp in a way that leached every bit of warmth from your flesh, hostile enough to bar lovers at the door.

Dustin shrugged. "Some things you just know. Okay, plan B. You got that article on you?"

"In the truck."

Leaning against the pickup's hood, Dustin scanned the story, talking as much to himself as to Kira. "Let's see. Odd that they don't say where it happened, but maybe they wanted to keep people from snooping around. From what this fellow Marco says, it sounds like he and his dad were on foot. That means wherever your grandma and her honey were, it was probably someplace close to your grandma's ranch. I can't think of anything around there, but I'll drive down that way and you put your antennae up."

They headed east out of the foothills, toward a dark blot on the landscape northwest of Manzanar. Kira pointed to it. "What's that straight ahead?"

"Used to be an apple orchard, not much left of it now."

"It looks like it's close to Manzanar. Let's go there."

"Sure thing. It wouldn't have been the greatest place to hang out, but it's not like they had a lot of choices. And there would've been more trees back then."

Up close, the orchard looked like a relic of another time, before the water wars, when the desert was ripe and the trees exploded in springtime, white blossoms jettisoned by hard green fruit. Now, their dull leaves edge-curled, thin bark mottled with thirst, the trees stood farther apart than they should have, half of their contingent missing. Twisted limbs spiraled, reaching for neighboring branches that were no longer there. Kira could walk between the trees, arms out to her sides, and not touch a leaf.

Dustin leaned against the truck, face to the sun, while Kira wandered through the orchard. Near the center, an overpowering scent of fruitwood lingered. Parting the low branches of a gnarled tree, she stepped under its scant canopy and touched its trunk, a riverbed of furrowed bark. Within seconds she fell to the ground, lay there as if weighted, fingers grasping the earth. She was whirling, airborne, caught on a wave, spinning into the speeding sun. Faces, fleeting and transparent, there and not there: Aimi, Dan, Rosa. A searing joyful pain, an endless alabaster shimmer, warm as a mother's breath, sweet as her milk.

Aimi, Mom, I love you. Dan, I love you.

The whiteness dimmed, took on color, brilliant greens and rich earth hues. The ground held her, a tranquil bed of rocks and roots, a nest of trees, the quiet, the warmth, the quiet.

I love you.

Don't lose it.

I will never let go of you.

Kira closed her eyes. *I will never let go.*

She could sleep forever.

"Kira, wake up. What happened?"

Kira opened her eyes. She felt drained, as if she'd been walking for days without food or water. "What time is it? How long was I out of it?"

"I don't know, not long. I looked over and you were lying here, scared me out of a life or two." Dustin helped her sit up.

They had been here, Maddalena and Akira, loved each other here. This unforgiving earth beneath twisted trees, within sight of searchlights scanning the sky, it was a place of peace and joy. Akira hadn't died here.

"Was that a seizure?" Dustin said. "You have epilepsy?"

"No."

"I didn't think so. What happened?"

"I don't actually know." It was the truth. She'd felt suspended in pure emotion, like she had in the motel room, except this time her emotions and Maddalena's were threaded together. A loss of self and at the same time a perpetuation of it. It reminded her of being pregnant with Aimi in the early months, when her body's swelling was more emotional than physical, when her skin bloomed and the ember inside her felt like immortality.

"Tell me," Dustin said.

Dustin, who seemed to know things he couldn't—he would believe her. She told him everything, and he listened without asking a single question, shadows of analysis or delight crossing his face.

When she finished he said, "That is the coolest fucking thing I ever heard. I knew there was something different about you. But this is unreal."

"That's a good word for it." Of all the people in Owens Valley, Dustin had to be the only one who could have listened to her story and believed it.

"This isn't random, hell no. This is happening for a reason. Holy moly." Dustin stood and held out a hand. "Your little detour paid off. Let's go back to Foothill Road and head south like we planned. We're on a roll!"

In the truck, Kira opened the cigar box. "Look. Seven rocks, all alike. Why would Maddalena keep them?"

"No idea," Dustin said. He picked up the hair comb, scratched at it with a fingernail. Dark flecks fell onto his jeans. "Oh jeez."

"What?"

"Your grandma was there when Akira got killed. Shotgun, right? Very messy."

Kira was still processing that when Dustin held the photo at arm's length, squinting at her. "Yup, there's a resemblance."

Kira began to cry. He saw it. Dustin, the guy who knew things he couldn't, saw the connection. It wasn't wishful thinking like Dan said—she *was* Akira's granddaughter, and she wasn't crazy. The fragments were real.

Thirty-Seven

August 22, 1945

Akira found Annabelle at Bairs Creek. She jumped up when she saw him, said yes when he suggested a walk even though he'd avoided her for weeks. He was a damn coward for not owning up to her sooner, but now there was no point in hurting her with the truth. She was going home to Bainbridge Island in a couple of days, a forced separation. It was easier this way.

They walked nowhere in particular, the silence heavy. A couple of blocks ahead, a family hauled suitcases to the street. "Look, that'll be you soon," Akira said. "You'll get your life back."

"Yes," Annabelle said, sounding anything but happy.

"I'll miss you, but maybe we'll see each other again someday."

Annabelle stopped. "What do you mean, *maybe?* Are you breaking up with me?"

"It's not like that, Annabelle. We'll be hundreds of miles apart."

"That has nothing to do with it. You're dumping me because of that girl."

"It's not like we could see each other."

"Yes, we could."

Damn it, what did she want him to do, marry her on the spot? He froze at the thought. She probably did.

"Annabelle, be reasonable. We'll write, and maybe we can figure out a way to see each other. But you know how things are. You're a pretty girl, and you'll find a nice guy at home

256

and before you know it you'll forget about me."

"You'd like that, wouldn't you? Wouldn't you! I was in love with you; did you even *know* that?" Annabelle's voice caught. "In *love*. I would have married you like *that*." She snapped her fingers. "But now I wouldn't marry you if you were the last man on earth. You're so selfish you wouldn't recognize love if it slapped you in the face."

She was trembling, her hands balled up like she might hit him. He wished she would.

"I'm sorry, I mean it. You've got to believe that." Akira tried to take her hand but she backed away. "You've meant a whole lot to me, you know that? We had some good times."

"Good times? Is *that* what we had? Oh, what a fool I was to fall for you! Hiroki and Jackie were right; I should have dumped you months ago."

"I'm sorry, Annabelle. I wish you knew how much. I never wanted to hurt you. And I won't forget you."

She looked at him coldly and stalked off, and he stood there feeling about as sick as anyone could when he'd wronged a girl. If he could, he'd go back in time, figure out a way to say goodbye without breaking her heart. What a mess. Instead of being happy that the war was over, he felt terrible about hurting Annabelle. The price he paid for loving Maddalena. And soon enough, he'd hurt his parents too.

He headed home. After more than three years in one small room with his parents, he was about to put distance between himself and them, more than he'd ever imagined. But as long as they were at Manzanar, they were a family. He was a decent son; he would help them through the weeks ahead. At least he could give them that.

No need to worry, Maddalena told herself. Her time of the month had come and gone without a drop of blood, but the bleeding could start any day, any minute. And if it didn't—

that was a terrifying thought, but not nearly as terrifying as what would happen if her parents found out. Her mother knew that Maddalena's cycle was like clockwork, and she'd notice if there were no sanitary cloths hanging on the clothesline behind the outhouse. Maddalena would have to fake it, stain the cloths with wine or animal blood. Another lie. She was tired of lying, avoiding the truth. Once she and Akira were together, there would be no more lies, only love, and telling each other everything.

Not tonight, though. She would meet Akira tonight and say nothing about the baby. A lie of omission, and necessity, even though it would seem wrong to make love when Akira didn't know what her body held. Still, she had to do it. He would be leaving soon, and if he knew she was pregnant he would worry, maybe even refuse to go. She couldn't let him do that. He needed to leave Manzanar behind and help his parents. He would learn the truth soon enough. They had time. Besides, it was bad luck to talk about a pregnancy too soon.

She rode to Manzanar to signal Akira, then stabled Scout and went into the cattle barn to see if one of the cows had a scrape or cut. She didn't need much blood, just enough to dab onto one of her cloths. The barn was empty except for a few cows and calves not sent to pasture. Not a cut or scrape in sight.

Maddalena sat on the edge of a water trough and watched the calves nuzzle their mothers. Poor little things would be sold before long. Would the mothers mourn? They seemed so devoted. And they knew what to do with their babies, while she didn't know the first thing. She would have to learn, and Akira would too. They'd make a good home for the baby. They would be happy, a family.

But honestly, she didn't know any of that. All she knew was that she was pregnant. For now, no one could know, not even Regina. There was plenty of time. What was inside her wasn't a baby yet, only a speck of new life. She would wear loose clothes and eat more, so that if anyone noticed her body changing they'd think she was getting fat.

She could fool anyone but her mother.

Maddalena put her head on her knees and let the tears come. How could anyone be so happy and so sad at the same time? And frightened. She and Akira had the future ahead of them, a future together. That was all she hoped for, all she should think about. They would leave Owens Valley together, raise their child together, with love. Sitting on the train to San Francisco, they would plan and dream. The train would rock back and forth, back and forth, and so would they, their bodies touching. They would fall asleep listening to the chug of the train engine, the singing of the rails. A lullaby.

"Crying in a cow barn—that's a new one." Marco stood in the doorway. "Don't tell me you're sorry those darling calves are going to die. Mmm, mmm, mmm, veal parmigiana." He rubbed his belly.

"Oh, shut up," Maddalena said, rising to leave. Marco blocked her path. "Let me by."

"What have you got to cry about, anyway?"

"None of your business."

The look of pleasure on Marco's face made her sick; suddenly everything made her sick. A whiff of manure, familiar as rain, and her stomach turned. She made it to the outhouse before she threw up, as quietly as possible in case Marco had followed her.

She wanted to sleep for hours in a cool bed in a safe place, Akira beside her. There was so little time left.

Thirty-Eight

April 12–13, 2011

Heading south, Dustin cruised along Foothill Road, detouring now and then on one of the dirt tracks that webbed the desert. "Shit," he said, swerving away from a pothole. "This is like driving through a minefield."

"Everything out here blends into everything else," Kira said. "I feel like I'm going blind."

When they were halfway to Lone Pine, she pointed toward a clump of small trees and woody shrubs about a hundred yards off the road. "Over there. See that bright spot in the green? I bet that's metal. Let's go look."

Dustin got them as close as possible, then they set off on foot. When they rounded the trees to the west, there it was—a small shed, no more than seven feet high and about that many square, with windowless walls of corrugated rust and a hole where a door should be. The roof sagged, pierced by sunlight.

"This is it," Kira said, and stopped. She couldn't say why she knew, only that she did. Her body seemed light, fragile, free of pain. She glanced south. What were those kids thinking? Maddalena's home wasn't far off, probably half an hour's walk. They had to have known they'd be seen, betrayed, caught. But of course they were young, in love, invincible. Willing to risk their lives for love.

She turned to Dustin. "I'm afraid."

"Go on," Dustin said. "Go inside. You have to. And I'm right here."

She stepped inside the shed, into a tiny inferno where a

crazy-edged trapezoid of sunlight illuminated the wooden floor. *A wooden floor.* She stood for a moment, her body sparking, then knelt and flattened her palms against the knotted wood. Then she curled on her side and closed her eyes.

This was it.

Her grandparents had lain here together, had made love here, made plans, told each other secrets. Just like in the orchard, except Akira had died here. This wooden floor might hold his blood, now dried to dust. Tears ran down her face and neck and she made no move to wipe them. Let them run into the wood, find Akira's blood, regenerate it, mix her cells with his.

Her mind skittered, snatching at memories, the fragments, trying to knit together what she knew. Her great-grandfather, a murderer. Her grandmother, forced to marry someone she didn't love. She'd hidden the truth from her child all those years, waited patiently, painfully, to write the letter that would tell Rosa the truth about her family. What had happened to the letter? Surely someone had found the envelope with Rosa's name on it. Did it end up in Joe Brivio's hands instead of Rosa's? Had he destroyed it? It didn't matter. All that mattered was that Rosa died without knowing the truth.

But Kira knew. She curled tighter, convulsed in tears, remembering her mother's death, the bizarre heat that had melded Rosa's hand to hers. Rosa had held Maddalena's memories without knowing it, had been tormented by them. And she'd passed them on to Kira.

The shed grew hotter, the sun brighter. Kira's breathing slowed, her mind subdued. Her grandmother had loved here, had seen her love, her life, destroyed here. She'd risked everything for the boy she loved, would have died with him. But she chose to live for the sake of her child. Kira asked herself if she could say that about Dan, about the children she'd failed to bear. Would she risk everything for him, endure an existence she hated for the sake of her child? Dan was home, waiting for her, hoping for her. He believed in the kind of love that blurred boundaries, offered that love to her, would have offered it to Aimi or to any other child.

Dan and Maddalena, separated by time and bloodlines, believed in the same thing. They loved fearlessly, defiantly. And Kira couldn't. She cried again. Finally, exhausted, she wiped her eyes and went outside, where Dustin sat with a forearm draped over one knee, gazing at the mountains like a man who wouldn't mind sitting there forever. Kira sat next to him, and together they watched the sun tip the Sierra with crimson and rust. A hawk traversed the horizon, dodging the flames.

"I want you to go," Kira said. "I'm staying here. My phone is in the motel room—please get it and call Dan for me. Dan Kaneko. The password is 2464. He'll be worried, so tell him I'm okay and that I love him and I'll call as soon as I can."

She expected an argument, but Dustin nodded. "I've got a blanket in the truck," he said. "I'll come by in the morning, bring you some food and water." She protested and he cut her off. "Yes or no? You say no and I don't call Dan."

"Yes."

"Good choice." Dustin went to the truck, came back with the blanket, a hooded sweatshirt, his thermos, her backpack. "Be safe," he said, hugging her.

He started to leave and Kira pulled him back, kissed him quickly. "Thank you."

Inside the shed, Kira spread the blanket on the floor. There was a reason she'd come to Owens Valley, to this tiny shelter in the desert. There was more to come. She would wait.

She woke hours later, consumed by darkness, and moistened her parched lips and throat with cold coffee from Dustin's thermos. Pulling the blanket tighter, she dozed again, a half sleep dotted with images, random and overlapping—the attic stairs, Maddalena in her wedding dress, the high wail of a baby, Maddalena kneeling before the cabinet, a milk-soaked blouse, hay and horse sweat, shifting muscles beneath her legs. Moonlight through tree branches. The sweep of searchlights. Men's voices in the darkness. A flooding fear that emptied her mind.

She surfaced again, the shed's wrinkled metal walls shuddering. Groping for the doorway, she stepped outside and the wind caught her. Kira trembled, shielding her eyes from the spit of sand. Then moonlight stepped from behind the clouds, revealing the desert in silvery shades of charcoal. Small tornados of sand and dust spun past the shed, a black-on-blacker silhouette, then clouds swallowed the moon again and everything disappeared.

They had lain there helpless, heard the men coming, the terrifying tread of boots on rocky soil. Even with warning they could have done nothing. There was nowhere to run, nowhere to hide. Their shelter was a trap.

They were so young.

Kira held a hand in front of her face, saw blackness dark as old blood. The wind again, pummeling her, and her body surged with energy, a rushing sensation. Maddalena running into the street, the sweep of the headlights. Blood, secrets, grief. The love child Akira never saw. Arms out to her sides, Kira inched around, one small circle, then another, another. She opened her mouth, let sand coat her tongue, crunched it like glass between her teeth. The desert rose around her, sandblasting her face, her ears, her neck. She welcomed it. Let it whip and scour her; she could do nothing to stop it. The desert had its rules, its private violence. It had brought Akira there, given him to Maddalena, sheltered the two of them, betrayed them to the men with guns.

Kira shook her head and almost fell. Why did it matter? It was so long ago, lost to everyone but her. None of it mattered.

She kept turning, dizzy now, each step a vertical correction. No, everything mattered. Maddalena, Rosa, Kira, Aimi, a shared history, a bloodline. An inevitable transmission of self, a revelation of truth. Kira understood—if she had died without knowing the truth, and if Aimi had lived, she would have passed the dreams on to her daughter, leaving her to discover what must be known. It had been there all along, her family's terrible truth. Her mother had carried it with her, dormant because she failed to understand. But Kira knew. She understood. She was meant to pass what had happened here down to her children.

Not Aimi. Kira cried out, the loss lacerating. She doubled over and fell backward, the rocky earth biting into her hands, her skull, her back. Crying in dry, gasping breaths, she pressed her arms and legs into the desert floor, willed it to hold her, absorb her. It had swallowed the remains of Manzanar; let it consume her too. She belonged here, the desert part of her now, alive in her spit and blood and cells. Lifting her raw palms to her mouth, she tasted blood and dirt. Akira's blood, here in this soil, and now hers. This bloodstained earth, tying generations together. The wind leaped up, found her on the ground, slapped her. Shivering, she cried for Maddalena, for everything her grandmother had wanted, everything she'd lost. For her mother, for what she never knew.

Rosa never knew. And so Maddalena gave her memories to her granddaughter, made her live them, burdened her with the past. No, enlightened her. A gift.

Kira opened her eyes wide, summoned the shadowed sky, the invisible mountains, the fast-running wind, the deep silence of the desert. How much there was to see. Digging handfuls of the sandy dirt, she rubbed it into her flesh, welcomed the sting of it. She was here, in this place that belonged to Maddalena and Akira. She understood everything—what love could be, what it took from you. But what did it matter? Knowing changed nothing.

Longing seeped through Kira's bloodstream. She cried until she choked and retched, until the wind died and she lay still, eyes open, muscles soft, mind at rest. Knowing changed everything. Dan was part of her, as much as Aimi was, as her mother was, as Maddalena. His love made it so. She wanted their bed, his head dark on the pillow, the long line of his body beside her.

&

She dreamed that Dan was nested behind her, his face in her hair, his leg over hers. Half awake, she tried to move and couldn't, screamed and broke free, saw a figure in the half-darkness and screamed again.

"Kira, Kira, it's okay, it's me." Dan sat up, reaching for her. "Honey, it's me. I'm sorry, I didn't mean to scare you."

"Oh my God, you gave me heart failure. When did you get here?" Kira shivered, her muscles rigid.

"I don't know, maybe a couple of hours ago. I tried to wake you but you were out cold."

"How did you find me?"

"Dustin called and I took off right away. He met me at the motel and drove me out here. Hell of a nice guy to do that in the middle of the night."

"He was supposed to tell you I'd be out of touch for a while."

"Like you'd *been* in touch? Right. When I said I was coming, he told me he figured as much and that I should call him when I got here."

"I'm not done here. You need to leave." Kira could feel his eyes on her, his face indistinct in the darkness. "I'll come home soon, I promise."

"No way I'm leaving you out here alone. If you're staying, I'm staying. End of discussion."

She was dead tired, incapable of arguing. She lay down and Dan settled next to her.

"I should have gone to Martinez; then I would have known you were gone," he said, his voice drifting toward sleep. "I was trying to give you privacy, but I shouldn't have left you alone no matter what you said. Stupid of me, with everything you've gone through. I love you so much. I promise I'll never let go of you again."

Never let go. The words reverberated and Kira's hands flared, wildfire hot. Sparks of orange and green lit up the shed, blinding her, and she cried out.

Silence. Stillness.

She can see again. Maddalena is curled on the floor beside her, her breath coming fast. Kira touches her, and Maddalena slides toward her and dissolves, leaving a sense of warmth, of weighted air beneath Kira's skin. She shifts under the arm draped across her. Not Dan's anymore. Akira's.

It should be impossible to see much in the seeping morning light, but she can see everything, hear everything. Akira's breathing, his heartbeat. Wind shuddering the metal door. A coyote. Footsteps. She shakes with every breath.

I have heard it all day, that alarm inside me, and I ignored it, gave in to desire and came here when I knew I shouldn't, refused to leave him hours ago when I knew I should. I fell asleep. A mistake, a mistake.

This is what I heard in the silence: boots striking the desert floor, voices loud with anger and righteousness. They don't come quietly because they know we cannot run. There is nowhere to go. I know what is coming. Akira does too, and his arms tighten around me. I clasp his hands, and in the seconds that remain of his body pressed to mine, I tell him I love him, over and over. I am still saying it when the door swings open and my father and Marco stand against the pink sky. The mouth of a shotgun stops my heart.

"See? Like I told you." Marco is speaking. "I followed her here two days ago, figured she was having some fun with one of the boys from town. Goddamn Jap bastard."

Marco drags me out of the shed and I spit at him. I am already screaming.

266

"Don't hurt him! I promise not to see him again, I promise, Papa, please! Let him go!"

My father's fingers move, restless on the gun, dark hairs sprouting ugly on his knuckles.

Akira lunges for my father, shoves the shotgun up, and they fall outside the door. I scream and Marco throws me against the wall. My hand rakes the rough metal and I feel nothing. Marco pulls Akira to his feet, pins his arms behind his back.

The gun barrel rises. I scream again, turn to Akira, start to run to him. But the baby, think of the baby. Akira never knew, oh God, he never knew.

Marco shoves Akira toward the open desert and the gunshot echoes off the mountains. I scream, voiceless, run through raining blood and fall on him, the taste of him on my tongue.

My life is over.

Thirty-Nine

We heard the shot in the hours before dawn. Startled awake, or waiting for night to fade, or working the night shift, we flinched and went on with our lives. It wasn't the first time a Manzanar sentry had hit the trigger—of course we assumed that was what had happened. The war had ended, but hatred has no expiration date. Men could be shot, and if they had a drop of Japanese blood in them, no questions need be asked.

It wasn't the kind of thing a person ever got used to.

The day Akira died, the bells on the mess halls rang all day. We learned of the killing when the white girl's father appeared in the near dawn outside the western fence, screaming obscenities. We cannot repeat what he said, though it will take us the rest of our lives to forget. A policeman rode close to the fence to try to calm him, to make sense of what at first was unintelligible. As the man's meaning became clear, the policeman spat from his horse, his eyes telling the man the spitting was meant for him.

Unable to work or sleep or eat, we crowded around the barracks and mess halls. Some of us stayed with Annabelle, prostrate on her bed, her body shriveled and empty of tears, the sheets full of vomit. Those of us who knew Akira best retrieved the body, Paul and a few other boys, walking past the guardhouse looking straight ahead, eyes carrying disbelief, jaws set in fury. "Put your fucking guns down," Paul said as they passed the sentries. "We're bringing him back."

Akira's father tried to go with them, but we held him back

268

because no man should see his son like that. Akira's mother collapsed in the garden, crushing the plants she had tended with love. Some of us carried her home. She would need more care than we could offer. Who can survive the loss of an only son?

Once the news was out, many of us claimed to have heard the gunshot, the white girl's screams. Some of us said the man, her father, hit the girl, threatened to kill her too. It wouldn't surprise us if it were true.

Perhaps all of it was true. Perhaps we said what was needed to make the unbelievable real.

Akira's friends brought him back, cradled in twelve hands, shrouded in blankets so that no one could see his wounds, his face, his loss of dignity. Beneath our sadness we struggled with pity, anger, blame. He was in love, some of us said. Others argued that love shouldn't take precedence over honor, respect for one's parents, our traditions. How do such things happen? Perhaps Akira was weak. Perhaps he forgot the Buddha's Second Noble Truth and yearned for attachment, the indulgence of the self, which can lead only to suffering.

We merely observed.

Akira was young, fueled by desire and impatience. We understood why he acted recklessly, tempted fate in the face of hatred and prejudice. But he was not to blame. Manzanar killed Akira.

We suffered, all of us, Akira's friends and relatives, Annabelle, his parents most of all. All of us grieved together, prayed together.

The white girl, we knew, would suffer alone.

Forty

Kira finished giving shift-change report and went down the hall to say goodbye to Baby Kendall. She found him in his nurse's arms, sleepy-eyed on her shoulder.

"Hey, little guy, I hear you're ditching this joint," Kira said, taking the baby and jogging him gently. She wondered if his nurse had heard what had happened, knew why she had come to say goodbye. "I'm going to miss you. Promise to be nice to your parents, okay? No waking them up twelve times a night." The baby felt good in her arms, warm and solid, scented with clean blankets and sweet formula.

Since she'd come back to work, it was as if she had never left. New micro-preemies arrived almost daily and the chronic babies were still there, the ones whose lungs and eyes and brains would never recover from the treatment that had saved their lives. Kira didn't like taking the meds that Dr. Richardson had given her—they made her feel dull and rigid—but it was the price she had to pay to return to work. And to reassure Dan.

She'd scared him half to death in Owens Valley. Dustin had arrived with food and water just after sunrise, and the men couldn't wake her up. They took her to the hospital in Bishop and she was unconscious for eleven hours after that, and when she woke, she couldn't speak. There was nothing wrong with her voice; she simply couldn't make herself talk. The scene in the shed had silenced her, and it wasn't because of the violence she'd witnessed. It was because lying on that wooden floor she had *become* Maddalena. Not like in the fragments, limited to thoughts without context, excerpts of Maddalena's memories. That night in the desert, she *was* Maddalena, flesh and soul.

In the hospital she'd clung to Dan, shook her head at the doctors' questions, let the nurses draw blood, check her eyes. Dan told the doctors she had passed out but he didn't know why. When Kira could speak again, she made a big deal of being dehydrated and hungry, growing cold and disoriented in the desert. Of course she didn't mention the fragments, and apparently Dan and Dustin hadn't either, because instead of ending up in a psych ward she'd gotten discharged. See your doctor when you get home, the docs said, get another EEG and some neuro tests. She promised, Dan promised, and Dustin sped them out of there as if a posse were on their heels.

They'd gone from the hospital to a restaurant, where the men ate and Kira drank cup after cup of herbal tea, trying to soothe her stomach and nerves and wondering what to tell them. Nothing, she decided. She'd come here alone and did what she needed to do alone, and now she needed to make sense of it alone. She knew Dustin had a dozen questions lined up, but she could give him no answers. Dan, she knew, would listen if she chose to talk and respect her silence if she didn't. For now, she chose silence.

Back at home, she and Dan had resumed their lives, Kira quiet but nervous, something unsettled inside her. Waiting for it to resolve, she read, walked, and made peace with Camille, who'd been hurt by Kira's neglect. Kira told her enough to soothe her, and then with Camille's help she cleaned out her mother's house. She brought home Maddalena's portrait, all the photos, the opera CDs, the housedress and necklace and earrings. She slept long and deeply, without dreaming. The fragments were gone. Either they had run their course or the meds were working, but there had been none since that night in the desert.

Gradually the unsettled feeling faded, as if some tangible thing inside her had dissipated into every cell, bringing with it a sense of peace. The images and emotions of the dreams and fragments remained vivid, their residue like a scarf loosely woven with bits of satin and silk. Now and then a piece broke free and drifted off and Kira would be with Maddalena again, remembering everything. It was all there, crystalline and somehow pure. But she hadn't disappeared again. She was herself, here in Berkeley, here with Dan. Life seemed normal, if there was such a thing.

Forty-One

January 1, 1946

Manzanar became a ghost town on November 21,
1945. For months, free to go, we had been drifting away,
the young among us eager, the oldest afraid. We had grown
accustomed to life there, a life measured by wind and heat
and cold. Strange that the loss of privacy and dignity that
had distressed us could have become normal. Granted our
freedom, we clung to the familiar, feared the unknown.

We knew, returning home, that we would not find what we
had left. Those who had property had lost it. Everywhere,
signs told us we weren't welcome: Go Home, they said.
Go Back to Japan. But Japan was not home. Home was
America—California, Oregon, Washington. But our country
didn't want us.

Some of us went back to Berkeley, found a tenement on
Parker Street with rooms for rent and a sign that announced:
Japs Welcome. A rarity. Akira's parents took a room, trying,
like the rest of us, to remember what it was like to live
beyond the reach of barbed wire and searchlights. We visited
one another, shared our worries, our food, our cigarettes
on those days when we had them. Like many of us, Akira's
father failed to find work. He spent most days in a chair,
staring at the wall where, he pointed out, there should have
been the radio and phonograph they'd been forced to leave
behind. And there, on the other side of the room, over there
should be the Steinway they had bought for Akira. While
Akira's father sat, Akira's mother cooked rice, took in sewing,

bargained with fishermen, talked to herself. She had no garden, no interest in knitting.

Some of us made a habit of pulling down signs that said No Japs Allowed or Go Home, Yellow Bastards. Those few of us who had homes to return to boarded up the broken windows until there might be money to repair them, pruned overgrown rosemary and rhododendrons, filled buckets with uprooted oxalis. We told ourselves the war was over, our ordeal behind us. We told ourselves we would go on. We men, trying to comfort our wives, turned our heads when they cried.

We had not been prepared to go to Manzanar, and we were not prepared to leave it. Stripped of our surroundings, we had one another and not much else. At Manzanar, we had watched our families divide, leaving our ways and traditions scattered in the dust.

Freed from Manzanar, we lost everything again.

Akira's parents lost the unthinkable. They buried their child in Oakland, in a place of beauty, where they visited him often and failed to understand anything.

Forty-Two

When Kira got to work, the bed for the transport was already prepped—a ventilator, three IV pumps, two arterial lines, the works. A micro-preemie, a twenty-six weeker, placenta previa. They'd gotten him out fast, but he was dusky, and it was hard to say how long he'd been compromised. Still, there was hope. For now, there was hope.

The transport team rolled in. Baby Lopez was a fighter, the transport nurse said; no way he should be on settings this low. He'd gotten blood, was on the usual fluids, diuretics, morphine. But surprisingly, he didn't need to be paralyzed. Instead of fighting the ventilator, he lay there as if he knew it was keeping him alive, his translucent little chest chugging. Kira placed a pinkie in his palm, and his tiny fingers, ridiculously long, closed around it. He gave a froggy kick.

"Well, hello to you too," Kira said. Younger in gestational age than Aimi by two months, he was a miniature piece of perfection. She felt a flash of ovarian yearning.

Room C was Grand Central Station that day, with transport teams overlapping amid a constant stream of doctors, X-ray techs, respiratory therapists. But at Bed 7 things were quiet. Baby Lopez had two good blood gases in a row. Baby Lopez was defying the odds.

"Let's wean," the attending said. He turned down the ventilator's rate and watched the baby for two full minutes. "Gas in an hour," he said when he left.

"You're doing great," Kira told the baby. Even his blood pressure was good. "You're a miracle boy."

275

That's what it was, all of it—a miracle. Conception, gestation, birth. A too-complex-to-be-believed fact of nature. An improbability. At the hospital it was hard to remember that most pregnancies went well, most babies were born healthy. Prenatal care aside, so much of it was plain luck, what with all the genetic variables, the potential for disaster. And then there were babies like this one, determined to beat odds that were astronomically not in his favor.

So much could interrupt a life. If only Akira had known he would have a child, that generations would live on after him.

The next blood gas was good. Baby Lopez lay quietly under his eye mask, a miniature sunbather in the phototherapy light, legs splayed below nonexistent hips. Kira wanted to trace every part of his body, feel his perfection. Wispy black hair. Toenails the size of pinheads, a delicate network of blood vessels beneath wet-parchment skin. She wanted to pick him up, tuck his tiny head under her chin, warm him with her breath and body. But he wasn't that strong yet, and an hour later he proved it when his jaundiced skin went blue. Kira turned up the oxygen and suctioned him, got another blood gas.

The gas wasn't bad. He was holding his own. *Come on, miracle boy.*

Baby Lopez was still holding his own when Kira left work. He had months of ups and downs ahead of him, if he was lucky, and if he wasn't lucky... Well, she wasn't going to think about that.

She went to the store, bought what she needed to make four pans of lasagna for the big party the next day. Mariko and Kenji were celebrating forty years of marriage at their house, and a hundred people were expected to show up. Forty years. Kira had trouble conceiving of that kind of longevity since she had none in her DNA, marital or otherwise. But she'd married into it, so there was hope.

❧

276

The next day, the party that had started at noon was still going strong at five p.m. A glowing Mariko greeted guest after guest, talking nonstop; Kira had never seen her drink so much wine. Twice she'd watched Kenji thread through the crowd to interrupt a conversation and kiss his unsuspecting wife. When it was time for cake—a long table was filled with them, Emma's carrot cake and a dozen more brought by guests—Kenji raised his voice above the clamor and said he wanted to say a few words.

"Speech, speech!" Emma called, and everyone took up the chant, the rhythm of their voices accented by applause. Kenji chimed a spoon on his wineglass and the room went quiet.

"Forty years is a long time, and I'm lucky to have spent them with my soul mate, the best wife and mother of his children a man could ask for. I've had an exceptional life, and in large part it's due to her." Mariko tucked herself into his arm and Kenji kissed her. "And I'm lucky to have my children close by and my son as my business partner. What is a life without family?" Everyone cheered and whooped and clapped. Kenji turned to Kira. "I hope you know how much we miss your mother."

"I know. She would have loved to be here today," Kira said. "And *she* could have made all that lasagna instead of me."

Kenji laughed and lifted his glass. "To Rosa. And to Aimi." A murmur rose, cloudlike and emphatic. "And to my family and friends—I love each and every one of you. And most of all, to my beautiful wife. I love you more than life."

More cheers and whistling. Kira squeezed Dan's hand.

"Here's to another forty years with you, my love." Kenji swung Mariko into a dip and kissed her while everyone applauded.

Dan whispered in Kira's ear. "I'm shooting for forty years too. Fifty."

"Is that all?" Kira said, laughing. "Hey, listen, this party's gonna go all night. Let's go visit Aimi and Akira and watch the sunset."

In the three months since Kira and Dan had learned that Akira was buried at Mountain View Cemetery, they'd visited his grave a dozen times. Call it serendipity or fate, but they'd buried Aimi in the same cemetery as her then-unknown great-grandfather. It hadn't been hard to find Akira once Dan pointed out that his parents probably would have taken his ashes home. Mountain View Cemetery in Oakland, with its peaceful acres of flowering trees and shrubs and a ridgetop overlooking San Francisco Bay, was the first place they'd thought of. All three Shimizus were there, mother and father and son, marked by a single monument near a plum tree whose falling blossoms adorned the grave. Kira cried the day they found the grave, for Akira and his family, and for Maddalena, who should have been buried with Akira instead of next to the husband she despised.

Ten minutes after leaving the party, they drove through the cemetery gate, past the first fountain, the second, the third, winding upward past tulip trees whose thick white blooms perched on glossy roosts, where the roads were empty and the hills waited in silence. They went to Aimi's grave first, pink marble on a sunlit slope. An origami crane Dan had made lay on the marker's base, the white-and-gold paper wilted from sun and dew.

"I'll make a new one," Dan said. "One for Akira too."

After they'd pulled the weeds invading the tufts of lavender around the grave, Dan took two small white stones from his pocket and handed one to Kira. It had been his idea to adopt the Jewish tradition of marking each visit with a pebble, and Kira liked its documentary aspect, the mounting evidence of remembrance, proof to passersby that the person buried here was loved and remembered. They placed their stones, kissed their fingers and touched them to the angel atop Aimi's headstone, then walked up to Akira's grave.

The Shimizu marker, made of rough-faceted granite, faced west, toward the bay. A handful of pebbles surrounded seven rocks lined up along its base, rocks they'd taken from the desert near Manzanar to serve as body doubles for Maddalena's rocks, safe at home in their cigar box. Dan cleared the crumpled leaves scattered around the marker and Kira plucked dead blooms from a vase of flowers that Mariko had left the week before, rearranging the survivors. Freesia, irises, and roses—yellow for freedom, blue for faith, white for hope, Mariko said. They added their pebbles to the cluster of stones, then hiked to the ridgetop.

The fogless bay sparkled with amber light, stirred by a light breeze. San Francisco looked like a miniature kingdom surrounded by sapphire blue, its tallest buildings reaching for a streak of sun-laced clouds. They stood gazing at the distant city, Dan behind Kira, arms folded across her chest.

The wind picked up, raising the hair on Kira's arms.

Manzanar. Wind would always remind her of that beautiful, desolate place. A strange setting for a love story, but that's what it was. Her grandparents, young and unknowing, risk-takers. Not survivors, but givers of life, of indelible memories, kids who believed in the kind of love that would persist through generations. Kira lifted her face to the soft air, so different from Manzanar's. This place had a gentler sort of beauty, kinder, more forgiving.

"Hey," Dan said, nuzzling her hair. "What do you say we make a baby?"

"Yes," Kira said. The word held promise, peace. "Yes, soon."

The wind rose again, and she saw mountains in the distance where water should be, the open desert where tall buildings rose from the bay. Thin air and open sky, struggling trees. Sagebrush. Snow on mountaintops. Akira had never left the desert and Maddalena had never gone back. But Kira and Dan would go. They would take their baby to Manzanar and he would crawl in the dust.

ACKNOWLEDGEMENTS

This novel would not have existed if I hadn't had the great fortune to study with Joshua Mohr, Lewis Buzbee, Nina Schuyler, and Karl Soehnlein in the MFA in writing program at the University of San Francisco. I'm grateful for their guidance and wisdom, which I recall every time I put words on paper. Thanks also go to my grad-school-and-beyond lifelines, Charlie Kennedy and Emily Vajda, readers of early drafts and lovely writers both, for their sharp critiques and gentle friendships.

The San Francisco Writers' Grotto has provided community, inspiration, and support in many forms. Thanks to everyone there, particularly Lindsey Crittenden, Laurie Doyle, Thaisa Frank, Anisse Gross, Yukari Kane, Jason Roberts, Ethel Rohan, Julia Scott, and Maury Zeff.

The Eastern California Museum and Manzanar National Historical Site were tremendous resources, as were many books and photographs documenting Manzanar. In the interest of storytelling, I deviated from the facts at times, in minor ways (for example, most Japanese Americans from the San Francisco Bay Area were sent to camps other than Manzanar, unlike in my story), but I depicted the place and the experiences of its 10,000 prisoners as honestly as possible.

Heaps of gratitude go to Molly Cameron, Lisa Okuhn, and Lee Nachtrieb for listening, believing, and making me feel the love; to Shinji Eshima for music, inspiration, entanglement, and very dry vodka martinis; and to my sons, Christopher and Lukas Mondoux, without whom I would never have experienced the surreal bond of motherhood.

Finally, mega-thanks to Jaynie Royal, the dynamo behind Regal House Publishing, for believing in this story and thus giving my characters the chance to jump off the page and into people's lives, and for offering damn good advice.

CPSIA information can be obtained
at www.ICGtesting.com
Printed in the USA
BVHW082241070519
547697BV00001B/102/P